ANOINTED

RISE OF THE ANOINTED

BOOK THREE

JASON C. JOYNER

Anointed
Copyright © 2024 Jason C. Joyner
ISBN: 979-8-9896909-5-4 (paperback)
ISBN: 979-8-9896909-6-1 (ebook)

Published by Legend Bound Books
Blackfoot, Idaho

The characters and events in this book are fictional, and any resemblance to actual persons, living or dead, or events is coincidental.

Edited by Lindsay Schlegel, lindsayschlegel.com
Cover design by Kirk DouPonce, DogEaredDesign.com
Interior design by TLC Book Design, TLCBookDesign.com

Library of Congress Control Number: 2024910524

TO NATHAN, MATTHEW, CALEB, AND MICAIAH

I don't need a superhero adventure
when I get to be your dad.
You all inspire me to greater heights
and bigger feats.

CHARACTER KEY

Demarcus Bartlett: Demarcus is a 16-year-old African American with the gift of super speed and reflexes. He is the son of a single mother working hard to provide a better life. A natural leader, sometimes Demarcus can be overconfident.

Lily Beausoleil: A 16-year-old only child, due to the death of her mother and brother, Lily can manipulate light. Her depression is improving after she joined the Anointed. Her light can turn to heat if her temper flares.

Harry Wales: Fun-loving Harry is sixteen and has the gift of teleportation. Initially he was nervous and jumpy, but practice has given him control and confidence. His mum is from England, so he has some interesting habits.

Sarah Jane Langely: A quiet red-head who has great compassion and the ability to heal. At seventeen, she's shy and finding her voice slowly. She is the conscience of the group.

Simon Mazor: The youngest billionaire and founder of the Alturas Collective, until it collapsed at the failure of the Launch Conference. He can supernaturally influence people, but an injury to his eyes diminished the ability. Now he's trying to find his way back into favor with the Archai, an ancient group that wants to control world events.

John Presbus: The elderly mentor to the Anointed youth, he watches out for them and counsels them in using their gifts. His mysterious past is overlooked due to his immense wisdom and spiritual guidance.

Kashvi: A girl of Indian descent who opposes the Anointed. Her special ability is to manipulate water, which makes her a dangerous opponent to anyone she goes against.

Aasif: An Afghan American teen boy, his fiery demeanor is backed by a sonic attack that can create great force or stop his foes with pain and vertigo.

Pastor Julio Sanchez: The pastor of Living Water Christian Center, his church provides cover for the Anointed youth. He knows their secret and trusts John to guide these youth out of his building.

Roberto Pearce: A researcher of antiquities, especially those with paranormal possibilities, he is recruited by the Archai to go on a special expedition. He is unprepared for the consequences of what he'll find in the ancient chambers of Babylon.

Ji-young Kim: An investigative journalist for the alternate news source the Bay Area Underground, she stumbles across the Anointed early on and tracks their activities throughout the story.

Dr. Franklin "Ratchet" Lowry: A friend of Pastor Sanchez, Ratchet is a scientist and research at Applied Sciences. His expertise in practical applications in physics and electronics makes him a new ally for the Anointed.

Rosa Gonzalez: An 18-year-old woman who was at the Launch Conference, she has super strength. Her traumatic life leaves her vulnerable to being influenced by Simon Mazor, who keeps her under his control as his unwilling assistant.

PART ONE

CHAPTER 1

THE LATE-NIGHT HIGHWAY STAYED QUIET, PERFECT for Demarcus walking along the side of the road. His mama was surely freaking out at this point, since she always watched the evening news. But his phone wouldn't turn on from all the water thrown at him. Anyway, he needed time to figure out how things had gone horribly wrong.

He pounded his fist into his hand yet again. Nothing helped the overwhelming guilt that threatened to strangle his conscience. It was his idea. He had pushed trying to confront the other superpowered teens his friends had dubbed the Corrupted, by setting a snare for them. Except the tables turned when the Corrupted lured them into a trap at Hyde Pier. Then when they had the chance to retreat, he jumped back into the fray.

It was Demarcus being an idiot that had caused Sarah Jane to go missing. Lily to get hurt...John to be killed...

Oh God, please forgive me!

He'd prayed that over and over since he and his best friend, Harry, had dropped Lily off at her house. Harry had offered to teleport Demarcus as well, but he couldn't face going home. Not yet. He didn't know if he'd explode or crumble under Mama's questions. Walking might give him time to corral his runaway feelings.

Then there was the gnawing in his chest. He'd tried pushing his palm into his sternum, but had gotten no relief. Something had changed when the disheveled man touched him. Demarcus couldn't figure out why the man had attacked all of the gifted people tonight, no matter what side of the fight they were on. Whatever the reason, that attack left a sucking wound from what felt like inside his soul.

Cars whizzed by intermittently. There wasn't a lot of traffic at 1 a.m. Still, he couldn't help but wonder what passing drivers thought about a black kid in a torn-up suit walking down the road at this hour.

A flash of blue and red lit up the night. Ah, well there was one person who'd taken an interest in him. A cop.

Demarcus fought down a rising panic. It was always a worry before, but after the confrontation at Hyde Pier, he couldn't handle another conflict. Either he was going to be in trouble for what happened in San Francisco or for being as a kid out where he shouldn't be. Or with his luck tonight, both.

He stopped and faced the bright lights of the police cruiser, keeping his hands in the open. No sudden moves—even though he could race away before anything happened.

The officer got out of the car, a man with a trimmed salt-and-pepper beard and a pale complexion. He looked Demarcus over cautiously, with his hand staying close to his belt. If the man got spooked, would he reach for a Taser or a gun first? Demarcus had to proceed with care, not letting his frayed emotions affect how he reacted.

"What are you doing out on the road this late?" the officer asked.

"I'm heading home, sir."

The officer cocked his head to the side. "Walking on the 101? Did your car break down?"

"No, sir. My...ride fell through, and I didn't have money to get a ride share."

"Let me see your ID."

Demarcus told the officer where his wallet was and reached slowly to get it out. He didn't have a driver's license yet, but his school ID would reveal his identity. He wondered if his name was already all over the police reports.

"Why are your clothes torn up and wet?" The officer eyed him with suspicion.

"I—I was at a party and things went south. I'm honestly just trying to get home." Demarcus wondered about the cuts on his face and the multitude of bruises on his body. He probably looked like a wreck.

"I'll be right back after I run these." The officer returned to his cruiser. Demarcus stepped to the edge of the lights so he wouldn't be blinded. He pulled at threads of his ragged sleeve. Sand trickled out. How was he going to tell this story to his mama? He'd either cause her to have a heart attack or end up dead himself.

He reached for his phone, forgetting he couldn't text his friends to see how they were doing. Lily had been beaten up worse than the boys. He knew she'd given as much as she could both fighting the Corrupted kids, then chasing off that smoke creature that appeared at the end and overwhelmed them. When he'd left Harry, he was going crazy worrying about Sarah Jane. Demarcus finally convinced him to get some rest before searching for her again.

Tomorrow they would tear the city apart to find their friend.

The officer climbed out of his car again. Handing the ID back, he said, "So, Demarcus, there are some interesting reports coming out of San Francisco. I'd like you to come with me to talk about things."

Demarcus's shoulders slumped. Of course, this night would end with being questioned by police. Time for a personal appeal. The officer's badge read "Riley."

"Officer Riley, sir, it's been a crazy night. I'd rather rest tonight, if it is possible, and I would be willing to talk tomorrow."

"A male matching your description is wanted for questioning. Let's do this the easy way, okay?" A hand lowered toward his belt. What would he reach for first?

The sound of squealing tires cut through Demarcus's thoughts. An out-of-control silver sedan skidded across the asphalt, careening right towards them, headlights bearing down.

CHAPTER 2

THE WILD CAR SLAMMED INTO RILEY'S POLICE CRUISER as Demarcus caught the officer up in his arms and sprinted fifty yards away. Metal tore and screeched when the two vehicles compacted each other, and the runaway car rolled through the spot where the two of them had just been standing.

Demarcus skidded to a stop, groaning as he set Riley down. His muscles ached more and more as the night wore on. Riley stood stunned for a moment.

"Wow. That...that was a close call." He looked Demarcus up and down. "I guess you are one of those people from Hyde Pier incident earlier. Thank you."

"Should we check on the driver?"

"Yes. Right. Are you okay from that run? That was something." Riley's eyes were still large. The run must have shaken him. Maybe the officer would forget about questioning him, or saving the man would earn him a break.

They started jogging back towards the accident scene. The front end of Riley's cruiser was mangled. That was a freaky close call.

A new flicker of light erupted under the other wrecked car. Flames!

"Is that guy on fire?" Demarcus asked.

"It looks like it." Riley started to run. Demarcus took that as his cue and blitzed down the road.

"Be careful! You don't know if the scene is safe!" Riley called with a huff.

All night Demarcus had been warned about things. Enough trouble had come from him racing in and disregarding people's advice. This time he'd better listen. He scanned the wreckage, looking for any immediate trouble besides the flames under the car. Nothing appeared ready to explode or otherwise cause issues—as far as a sixteen-year-old could tell.

Demarcus came up to the driver's side door. A man drooped against the side window, the airbag from the steering wheel propping him up. Blood dribbled down the side of his bald head. Demarcus pulled on the door handle, but it didn't budge.

"How do I get in? The door's stuck."

Riley came up to the car. "Those flames are dangerous. If they hit any leaking gasoline, it's going to get worse."

"We need to get this guy out first. Any ideas?"

He pulled his baton from his belt. "Stand back." Riley hit the back-door window a couple of times until the glass shattered. He reached in, unlocked the door, and slipped in behind the man.

A crackling sound drew Demarcus's attention. Fire began to wrap around the hood near the passenger side of the car. "Officer Riley, we've got a problem. Can you get the door open?" He kept tugging on the handle.

"He's leaning that way. We have to be careful with his neck."

"Yeah, but if we don't get him out, the neck won't be a big deal either way." Demarcus could start to feel heat radiate over the hood. The smoke floated into the night air, the acrid smell of burning rubber stinging his nose.

The door clicked, and it opened. The driver's left hand flopped to the side. Demarcus took a piece of glass and punctured the air bag, letting the air out so he could reach across and unbuckle the man. He carefully pulled the man out as Officer Riley stood ready to take him.

"I'll take him. I have a feeling you've done enough heroics tonight."

They moved away as fast as they could with Riley carrying another man, even if he was a beanpole of a guy. Demarcus kept an eye over his shoulder. "When do you think it will explode?"

Riley chuckled. "That's a Hollywood trick. They plant explosives to make a car fire more dramatic with explosions. Unless there's something to explode, they will just burn. Sorry to disappoint."

The man groaned as he was laid on the pavement. His tattered basketball jersey had blood smeared down it. Riley pulled out his radio and called for an ambulance, along with back-up.

The officer regarded Demarcus for a minute after the call. "You saved me and helped save this man tonight. I think you're not the one who started the chaos at the pier." His eyes searched Demarcus's face. Hopefully he saw sincerity.

"Yes, sir. I mean, no sir, I didn't start it. My friends and I were trying to stop a kidnapping, and things got a little crazy. I'm willing to talk about it anytime." He let out a deflated breath.

Riley put his hand on Demarcus's shoulder. "You've done well, and it's been a hard night. I've got my hands full with this guy. When he comes to, he'll explain why he totaled my cruiser. You'll need to talk at some point, but you go home and get some rest tonight. I'll cover for now."

Demarcus couldn't help his jaw dropping. Something had gone his way tonight. After the disastrous evening, he had a tough time believing it. Scenarios of running from a police officer faded. He didn't realize how many sketchy outcomes his mind could come up with in such a short time. "I appreciate it. My name is Demarcus Bartlett, and I live in San Jose. If you need me, I'll come talk to you."

The man stirred. Riley turned his attention to him. "Go on, Demarcus. I appreciate your help. Let's hope that others will see things the same way."

Demarcus was ready to take his shot to get home. He wasn't out of the woods when it came to his mother, but at least he didn't have to worry about the police tonight. He started with a jog, then engaged his speed and flew down the highway.

CHAPTER 3

LILY THRASHED AGAINST NEBULOUS ENEMIES. ROPES entangled her, only to melt away. Her head swam and flipped. She tried to cry for help, but the words wouldn't come. Every time she wiped her brow, a mixture of blood and sweat made her hands sticky. Her right hand didn't even want to work.

An angel, bright as the sun, flew from the sky, dive-bombing a demon. It missed the black, fiery creature and fled, the demon leaping into the air after it.

One more image. An old man falling to the ground. Haunting words echoed in her soul: Failed. Failure.

Lily kicked against her blankets and pummeled her pillow. "Ahhhhh!"

The throbbing in her right hand woke her from her fitful sleep. The nightmares wouldn't stop.

Where was she? The last thing she remembered was fighting for her life in downtown San Francisco. Glass shattering. Water pouring everywhere, breaking things in elemental fury. A trolley flying in the air towards her.

She glanced at her hand. The wrist was swollen, the area around her thumb black and blue. How did this happen? It hurt to move her hand or thumb.

Her door flew open, and her father and stepmother dashed in. "Lily, are you okay?"

Lily shook her head and stared numbly at them. Her mind couldn't filter between reality and fiction. Surely the horrible images that replayed in her head couldn't be true.

Her father, Jack Beausoleil, sat on her mattress and pulled her into his arms, stroking her hair and trying to soothe her. Kelly stood back, her hands clasped in front of her. Dad smelled of a muscle rub. He must have been tense from something. And the scent of fresh dough wafted in the room. Kelly baked when she was upset.

They weren't nightmares after all?

"Daddy, my head's confused. I was having dreams of being attacked, of people getting hurt. I even saw John die in front of me. But I'm really worried that some of them are true."

Dad and Kelly shared a look. Uh oh, something was up. A shiver rippled across her skin. The sheets over her legs became heavy, weighing her down. "What is it? I need to know the truth."

"You don't remember?" Dad asked. The lines on his face crinkled even more.

She tried to crawl back through her memories. What stood out? A blue dress with heels. Laughs and warmth with friends. Her handsome friend Demarcus in his bow-tie. Pain. Suffering. Hate.

What was going on in her head?

Lily burst into tears. Why was it so hard to remember? "Dad, I'm having a hard time getting my thoughts straight. Things are so strange, they can't be real, right?"

The look of anguish and pain on his face broke her heart. If her dad looked like that, what could be going on? "You still remember that you have…special gifts, right?"

Lily nodded. How could she forget her gift from God? She went to point with her right hand, but the pain zinged in her arm again, causing her to wince. Okay, she'd have to try this left-handed. Flaring her fingers out, she sent little sparks of light dancing through the air.

Her dad stared, then a smile widened across his face. "Good, you didn't lose that."

"Daddy, what's going on? What aren't you telling me?"

"Something bad happened last night. We don't know all the details, but your friends Demarcus and Harry brought you home unconscious. They said you did something that zapped your brain? I can't stay on top of this power stuff. They hoped with rest you'd be okay, so we got you in bed and have been watching the news half the night."

"What did the news show?" Her voice trembled.

"Kitten, we don't want to traumatize you more," Dad said softly.

Lily tried to take his word, but the images jumbled in her brain too much to separate reality from her imagination.

"I need to see for myself," she whispered. Kelly nodded, then slipped out and returned with her laptop. She sat on the other side of Lily's bed and scooted close to her.

"I'm so sorry, sweetheart. I wish this weren't true." With that, she clicked on the play button of the video paused on the screen.

The scenery looked like San Francisco, near Fisherman's Wharf, but it resembled a war zone more than a tourist destination. An overturned trolley lay in the road, broken in half. Shattered glass, broken-up pieces of asphalt, knocked-over signs, and other debris littered a couple of blocks. And in the park, a sheet covered a body on the ground.

A news voice-over described the images. "Eyewitnesses describe a scene of chaos and horror. Somehow people were able to manipulate water, sound, and light to sow destruction in the area around Hyde Street Pier. Several injuries were reported, but only one fatality. The other victims are in local hospitals being treated for their wounds.

"Authorities are not ready to speculate whether this was a terrorist attack or if it was some new kind of weaponry. They said the investigation is ongoing."

It was true. All of it.

The video triggered a cascade of thoughts that abruptly lined up, ordering themselves like a puzzle falling into place. Her breath came in short gulps as she saw the glass shatter on the streets of San Francisco. Water roared in a great wave towards the shore. She remembered hanging on for dear life in the Alcatraz lighthouse as it shook around her. Her hands trembled with the memories.

A throbbing pain gripped her chest, causing her to gasp. Her dad leaned in, asking if she was all right. No, she wasn't, because another piece of the puzzle fell into place with a grim image.

"John's dead, isn't he?"

Dad dropped his eyes, then nodded. She saw a tear drop down his cheek, matching her own.

He locked his gaze with hers. "What happened to you, Kitten? Why are you so confused?"

A hazy memory flitted around the edge of her memory like a hummingbird dancing through the air. "I can make holograms with the special gloves that Ratchet gave me. But the side effect is that it somehow shorts out my brain temporarily. It makes me all goofy. I think I had to use that power to help our group. But I can't fully recall what triggered it."

Dad's eyes grew large. "You continually amaze me. I am proud of you; I want you to know. I was going to take you to the emergency room, but Demarcus suggested that wouldn't be the best place right now. They gave us a run-down about the night. Your mentor dying. Sarah Jane missing."

Wait, what? "She's missing? Why didn't I remember that?"

Kelly put a hand on her knee. "Look, maybe we should take a break and not stress you too much."

Lily pushed away the bedspread. "If my best friend is missing, I need to get out there and help find her."

She rolled and put weight on her right hand to stand, but the pain made her buckle. "Oh, my wrist!" She fell back against her bed and slumped to the floor, ushering in a new bout of crying.

Dad rushed over and picked her up. "Look, baby. You're not going to find her this minute. I've talked to her parents and offered our support. You've been through a lot of trauma. You need to rest and gather yourself so you can properly help your friend. We need to get that wrist checked out. It doesn't look good."

A feeble protest didn't get her anywhere. Lily wasn't in any shape to rush out searching just yet. They led her downstairs to get some food into her. Kelly must have changed her into sweats and a t-shirt, because it was a matching outfit. Her dress from the dance had been ruined by sea water and debris. Somewhere near the pier her stupid heels had been left behind. Her feet ached, a cut on her head throbbed, but nothing overshadowed the pain in her wrist.

She couldn't believe when the clock said three in the afternoon. How long did their battle go last night? And what did that hologram thing do to her to knock her out so long?

As she ate a grilled cheese made from fresh bread, her mind started to sharpen. Her memory was returning slowly. She could picture different things with clarity from the night before: The confrontation with the mean girl Missy Austin at the dance. Battling the Corrupted kids and running into Rosa and Simon—both thought to be dead. Then there was the man who put his hand on her and caused the terrible chest pain. It felt like he had sucked out a part of her soul. No matter how she swallowed or moved, it felt like something sat in her chest, pulling at her insides.

Lily dropped the unfinished half of sandwich and stared blankly out the window, because a police car pulled into their driveway. Two officers came up to their front door and the doorbell rang, the chimes echoing off the tile in the entryway.

Dad opened the door. "Can I help you?"

One flashed her badge. "We'd like to talk to your daughter, Lily, about a complaint."

CHAPTER 4

LILY WANTED TO DRAW ALL THE LIGHT OUT OF THE house and sneak away. Police at the door wanted to question her? There had been a ton of witnesses at the pier—surely her friends would be seen as the good guys in this. Right?

Wait, that was probably the case. They had to get evidence either way, and just needed to talk to all the parties involved. Maybe they needed help identifying Kashvi and Aasif, or Rosa and Simon Mazor. Wait until the world found out that he was alive.

Her dad held his ground in the doorway. "She's had a very hard day. In fact, we were about to take her to the clinic for an injury. Can this wait?"

"We've just got a few questions for her. It would be best to do it as soon as possible."

He looked back at her. Lily nodded. She'd do her duty and help the police find the ones who caused the damage at the pier. Even though her friends, trying to set a trap, triggered things in the first place.

Dad led the officers to the living room, and Lily followed. The woman had dark hair bobbed just above her shoulders. The man's head was shaved, and he had a soul patch, which intimidated her. They both sat on the couch, while Lily sat in the loveseat across from them, joined by her father.

Her brain still felt scrambled—she wasn't fully sure why. Hopefully she could give them the details they needed.

The woman took the lead. "I'm Officer Lopez, and this is Officer Olowe. We're going to record this conversation for accuracy." She held up a digital recorder. "We wanted to ask you about the incident at the dance at Everett Academy last night."

Oh, snap.

This wasn't about the pier! They were here to ask about the altercation she'd had with Missy Austin last night. After everything that had happened in the battle, their tussle at the dance seemed trivial at best. But the sight of blisters rising from Missy's cheek after Lily had returned a slap flared in her mind.

"W-what do you want to know?"

"Tell us about the incident." Lopez sat straight, her eyes boring into Lily.

"I was at the dance with my date. Missy grabbed my shoulder and started yelling at me. Then she slapped me and insulted—" She fought to hold back tears. "My mother who died last year. So I slapped her back."

Lily could tell her dad was giving her the look. That was less important than convincing this officer that she was telling the truth. Would they believe her when her palms were sweating and her heart was thumping? She even felt a little dizzy. She'd make a terrible criminal.

"Is that everything?" Lopez tapped her leg and waited for a response.

"Pretty much. She picked the fight and hit me first. I have witnesses."

"Did you do anything to provoke her?"

They must have talked to Missy. There was no way people at the dance would know something had happened during the week, unless Missy had told them.

"Not at the dance."

"What about at school?"

Lily flicked a stray strand of blonde hair out of her face. Shoot, her hand trembled when she did it. "Missy has been bullying me since last year. I finally stood up for myself."

"How exactly did you do that?" Lopez stayed cool, not betraying anything on her face. Lily would hate to play her in poker.

"I told her to leave me alone. I think I pushed her against a wall to make my point." The ache in Lily's chest intensified. She was trying to avoid telling about the other thing she had done. But the more she tried to hide it, the worse the pain thrummed inside.

Before Lopez could reply, Lily raised her hand. "There was one other thing. I pulled a prank on her. That may have been why she confronted me at the dance."

Lopez and Olowe nodded. "What was the prank?"

Her stomach flipped inside her. Was her meal going to come up? They were going to make her do this in front of her father. Well, Lily had done something that had snowballed into a worse problem. Time to own it now.

"I...I cut her skirt so that the back part fell off." Her cheeks flushed as she said it out loud.

"Lily! I can't believe you'd do that." Her father couldn't hold back a response.

"We have one more question," Lopez said, interrupting her father. "What did you hit her with at the dance?"

"My hand." That was the truth.

Lopez looked puzzled. "Only your hand?"

"Yes, ma'am."

"Then how did this happen?" Lopez held up a photograph. Missy's cheek was covered with red-tinged blisters. The angry bumps glistened with the reflection of the camera's flash. Lily flinched at the sight. She hadn't realized her hand had lit up when she swung at Missy. The light must have caused the burn on her cheek.

"I'm…not sure. I didn't mean to do it. If she hadn't hit me, nothing would have happened." Her voice wavered. What more could she say? She wasn't ready to admit her power to random cops.

She tried to keep eye contact with Lopez, but she couldn't help but see the anger in her father's eyes out of her peripheral vision.

Lopez clicked a button on the recorder and stood up with Olowe. "I think we have everything we need. You'll be hearing from our office soon."

Dad stood as well. "Are you saying we should get a lawyer?"

The officer tilted her head to the side, thinking. "It might be a good idea."

Her dad led them to the front door, and they thanked Lily for her time. All she wanted to do was run and hide at this point. She thought of using her phone to reach out to Demarcus, Harry, and SJ, but didn't know where it was.

Even if Lily knew what had happened to her phone last night, she wouldn't be able to reach SJ. Somehow Lily would have to connect with the guys and they could begin figuring out how to find their missing friend.

If her father didn't kill her first.

CHAPTER 5

THE LIGHTS WERE ALL ON AS DEMARCUS APPROACHED the house. This was not going to end well. He slipped into the garage and opened the kitchen door.

"Is that my son who is coming home waaaay past curfew? You'd better have a good reason for being this late." Mary Bartlett stood in the doorway to the living room, a thin robe over her nightgown. She was so mad steam almost rose from her.

"Mama, I am so sorry."

"You'd better be sorry. Do you know what time it is? I hope you at least got that young lady home at a decent time, or you're going to be grounded so long your kids will have to sit in the corner."

He realized he was standing on the step to the garage and was shrouded in darkness. She couldn't see the condition he was in. That might buy him some grace. Not much, but a little.

Demarcus stepped across the threshold and into the full light. Mama gasped and switched into mother hen mode. "My boy! What on earth happened to you? Did you get in a fight?"

That was one way to put it.

She grabbed a dishcloth, ran it under warm water, sat him in a chair, and started dabbing at the dried blood across his forehead. He winced at times, but he wouldn't make a noise for cuts. Not when someone had lost his life.

"You'd best get talking, son. I want to know what happened. Don't you leave anything out."

How would he begin? *It began with my superpowers, then there was a supervillain, and well, you've seen enough comic book movies with me to know what happened next.*

"Mama, I'll tell it all, just promise me you'll let me finish," he pleaded.

"I will do my best."

Demarcus thought for a moment. "You know all those shoes I've been buying this summer? It's because I have super speed. I can outrun cars on the highway. That's why I started working, to pay for the shoes I wear out."

She cocked her head. "Interesting, but I don't see—"

"Mama, no interrupting. Please. When I went to the Launch Conference this summer, it was because the guy leading it was looking for youth with special gifts. He found out about me...and my friends. We all have powers. That's why we started hanging out together. John, the older guy I always talk about, is our mentor, and he says they're from God. He's been trying to help us use them wisely.

"But we had other kids with powers battle us recently. That strange attack on Applied Sciences? That was them, and we fought them there."

He noticed Mama was rubbing the same spot on his head over and over. There couldn't possibly be any dried blood left. She might end up causing a new sore if she continued.

"We devised a plan to ambush them, except they turned the tables on us. Did you hear about the damage in San Francisco tonight?"

She nodded. "I had plenty of time to watch the news, waiting for you." She lowered her hand and squinted at him. "Are you saying that was you?"

"Yes, ma'am. We tried to stop them, but some other dude with a weird ability attacked us. We managed to scare them off..." His voice faltered as he thought of the next part. "But John was killed in the fight. Sarah Jane is missing, and Lily got hurt. I got her home safely, but I took some time to get back so I could think."

The room grew silent. He glanced up, then wished he hadn't, as Mama's withering glare loomed above him.

"I am not in the mood for such crazy stories, young man."

Demarcus stood up, his body stiffening from just a few minutes of sitting down, the beating he took catching up with him. "I'll show you." With a whoosh, he took off up to his room, changed into pajamas, and darted back to his seat. "Ta-da," he said, his voice flat.

Mama slowly pulled out another chair, the leg squeaking against the linoleum floor, and sat down. She fanned herself with the soiled dishcloth. "I cannot believe my eyes."

He felt tears welling up, with no way to stop them. "I'm sorry I didn't tell you, Mama. Life has been so crazy since finding out, and I never knew how to say it. I didn't want you to worry, and things over the summer hadn't been near as bad."

She slid her chair over until she was close enough to hug him. It felt good to be in her arms. He held her tight, and it comforted him as his thoughts turned to his friends. And John.

"Do you need something to eat?"

Did he ever *not* need something to eat? Especially with his speed, his metabolism required fuel all the time. He nodded, and she hopped up to pull together a ham sandwich in her own record time. A glass of lemonade was next, and he greedily guzzled down the whole thing, disregarding the tartness.

After a minute of eating, he pulled out his phone. "I didn't call because my phone got waterlogged. One of the kids we fought could control water, so that didn't help my electronics at all. Do you have some rice?"

She clucked at him. "Do I have rice? Whose house do you think this is, anyway?" In a minute she had his phone and battery in separate plastic bags, surrounded by rice grains.

"Oh, that's right. There's something else that's important I need to tell you," Demarcus said through bites of his sandwich.

"I don't know if I can take much more tonight." Mama took a long drink of water.

"I met my father. He's in the area."

He ducked as she sprayed water out in shock. Coughing, she picked up a napkin and wiped liquid from the table. "You are trying to give me a heart attack tonight, aren't you?"

Demarcus shrugged sheepishly. "I'm not trying to. Honest."

"Well, you're doing a pretty good job of it, I'd say." She shook her head and rested her head on the table for a moment. Peeking out, she asked, "So how did this happen?"

"Somehow this got tied in with the bad guy we fought. The weird one that hurt us the worst. I got a message from Tony Carter last week, saying he wanted to meet. We did, and it didn't go well. I wasn't planning on seeing him again. But he was at the pier tonight and tried to warn me about the weird dude. He had been given money to come up here and contact me. For some reason, the guy wanted my father to mess me up some way.

"And, it worked. But Tony did help us a bit tonight. He said Sarah Jane healed him of something."

"Oh, my boy. Such little drama for so long, and now it comes all at once. What did I do to deserve this?"

The energy was draining quickly from Demarcus. Now that he'd gotten home safe and had some food, exhaustion raced to overtake him.

Mama must have noticed. "You are going to pass out right here, and you are way too big for me to tuck into bed anymore. Get yourself upstairs and into bed. We'll figure things out tomorrow."

Demarcus started to trudge upstairs, but he was caught into another big hug by Mama. She whispered in his ear. "I was worried sick about you, but I knew the Lord had you in his hands. I've always believed he had a purpose for you. As hard as it is for a mama to see her boy hurt, I already have a feeling that I will have to rely on him even more to take care of things I can't. The same goes for you—trust him to take care of things."

The words sounded appropriate, but his heart felt empty. *Lord, help me to see the path you have for me.*

His chest continued to throb and ache, and no peace settled on him from his prayer. He collapsed on his bed, nightmarish thoughts chasing him into a fitful sleep.

CHAPTER 6

SLIDING INTO THE PASSENGER SEAT, LILY WORRIED that her time had come. Sure, Dad had said he was taking her to get evaluated at the urgent care clinic. But she wasn't completely convinced she would survive the trip. Maybe that was a little dramatic, but his cold demeanor and hard glare during the end of the police interview suggested she had crossed one too many lines. Between the dread of the car ride and the throbbing pain under her ribcage, her world was crumbling again.

Her hand, the reason for the visit, barely registered on her list of concerns.

She hadn't mentioned the chest pain. There was something different about it. A sixteen-year-old shouldn't have to worry about a heart attack, and it started after the guy attacked her. Demarcus mentioned having it as well, which made her think it must be supernatural. It would stay a secret for now, even as she caught her breath on occasion when it gave her a piercing jolt.

Dad gave Kelly a kiss and entered the driver's side of the car. He pulled out of the driveway and headed toward the clinic. The silence between them was suffocating. At the moment, Lily would have preferred to shrink and hide from the confrontation, but in her exhaustion, she couldn't take the quiet, angry treatment.

"Daddy, I can explain—"

His chest rose and he slowly let out a breath. Jack Beausoleil was not a quick-tempered man, but the events of the last few weeks had cut his fuse short. She sealed her lips, waiting for him to take the next step.

"Lily, I'm trying hard to be understanding. I let you off from being grounded with John supervising you on youth group events. I've been trying to cope with learning about your powers the last few days. But I can't have you running around, helping to tear apart a city, and using your abilities for such harmful actions. What exactly did you do to Missy?"

"Daddy, you know how awful she's been to me over the last year," she blurted out.

"Yes, and it upsets me as a father. But you were raised differently, and we're talking about you right now, not some spoiled brat who is mean at school."

Okay, at least he acknowledges she's nasty. That's something. "She was the one who sent the email to you with the picture of me in my pajamas helping Demarcus in San Francisco. Then she's been dogging me at school."

Lily had to stifle tears for the next part. "Last week she made comments about Mom, and I lost it. I zapped her skirt to make the back fall off. After that I didn't see her until the dance. She slapped me and called Mom a pill-popper. So, I hit her back. The problem was, my hand lit up from my anger, and it must have burned her cheek. She got blisters from it.

"That's when Demarcus took me out of the dance, and before any administrators could deal with it, we left to deal with the attack at the piwer." She stifled a slight grin as she recalled the face of the official who had approached her when Harry teleported in and took her away.

Their car pulled into the parking lot of the clinic. Thankfully it looked quiet on this Sunday morning. Her dad cut the engine but didn't take off his seat belt. Lily sat quietly, waiting for a response.

"You're telling me that you didn't mean to hit Missy with your power activated?" He spoke softly, carefully.

"Yes, Daddy. I promise it was not my intent to use my gift. It leaks out at times with my emotions." She gulped, wondering where his mind was going.

He popped his belt and opened the door, not looking her in the eye. "Let's get you looked at before they get busy. We'll continue this discussion after."

Great. She had something to look forward to.

———

The physician assistant pressed on different areas of Lily's wrist after reviewing the x-rays. *Ouch.* Her wrist did hurt after all. It was hard to move her hand around, but she didn't have any tingling in the fingers, which seemed like a good thing.

"You fell on the road with your arm outstretched, is that right? That's how you caught your hand and then hit your head?" The woman put her hands in the pockets of her white lab coat. The name badge read, "Keri."

That was the story Lily and her dad had agreed on in the waiting room. Technically, it was true—she had landed in the road awkwardly, which bent her wrist back. She left out the part about falling because of Rosa's super-strong punch throwing her into the air to begin with.

"That's right."

Keri examined the cut and bruising on her forehead. "Looks like a pretty good tumble." After doing some tests to rule out a concussion, she sat down on a stool. "There's a buckle fracture at the end of the radius. I'm also worried about a bone in your wrist called the scaphoid. Sometimes it can be broken without showing on the first x-ray, but it's important to make sure we don't miss it.

Thankfully, the treatment of the first fracture will protect your scaphoid. I'll get you a splint that you'll have to keep on for a few days. When the swelling goes down, we'll have you follow up for a cast."

The PA left for the splint. Lily let a few sparkles out of her fingers, but the exertion aggravated her pain. She grimaced and turned off her lights.

"That's probably not a good idea," Dad said, glancing up from a tattered magazine. Lily noticed the magazine rack only had worn copies of old issues, one of which was a tech mag with a headline about "Simon Mazor, tech billionaire." Her chest discomfort increased as she felt the blood drain from her face. Why did he have to be ever present?

Keri returned, fitting Lily with a splint that limited her movement. She was supposed to ice and elevate the wrist, use Tylenol for pain, and come back in a few days. They checked out and headed to the car. What was her dad going to say after thinking about everything?

They pulled out of the parking lot in silence. Lily worried that he was still really mad, but then he pulled into her favorite coffee drive-thru. They waited in a short line before she got her quad shot with mint mocha flavoring. She blew at the steam coming from the lid while eyeing her dad, who gave a tip and pulled away.

A truce offering?

"Kitten, I thought hard about what you told me regarding Missy. She's been a bully ever since she turned on you. I am very disappointed in what you did to her at school. That's not how we do things, and we'll have to figure out how to reach out to her family." His voice stayed quiet and even, a good sign. Still, heat rose to her cheeks, not from her hot caffeine elixir, but from the shame of what she had done.

"I also don't condone you hitting her, but it sounds like you were provoked. Your powers are a new thing, so I hope this is an issue with learning control. There's no manual for having supernatural powers, despite the comic books. But there's also no guide for having a child who can zap people who annoy her."

The shard of pain in her chest tore at her heart as they pulled into the driveway. Lily could barely stand the lancing fire that throbbed as her guilt from hurting Missy ate at her. Her dad focused on pulling the car into the garage, so he missed the peak of the attack.

He killed the engine, but neither moved to get out. "I know how much it hurts about your mom and Luke. That's way out of bounds for Missy. But we're going to talk about your power and lay down some serious boundaries. It's beyond me how to help guide you through this, but we'll get there."

Lily sipped from her coffee, letting the warmth slide down her throat as she thought about the costs of her foolish action. There was no avoiding consequences, but after a minute she worked up the nerve to bring up the thought now coming into focus. "I understand. Just one thing I need to ask. Can I help rescue SJ?"

Dad stared into her eyes for a full minute before responding. "I guess heroes can't avoid their calling, can they?"

CHAPTER 7

THE SMALL APARTMENT SHUDDERED AS THE DOOR closed. Simon Mazor plopped onto the couch while Rosa took care of their guest. The ache deep in his chest felt like acid burning a hole through him. The adrenaline of the night had worn off, and he wanted to drop into a deep sleep. But his excitement reminded him of being a kid on Christmas Eve.

After waiting months to fully regain his sight, it would be a matter of minutes before it would be restored. As long as Rosa didn't give his guest a concussion.

She came out of the bedroom and dropped onto the floor cross-legged. Strange, as she normally paced with a feral energy. Mouthy comments were her norm, but today there was no snark. Rosa must not be feeling well either for her tongue to be so quiet.

"What was that...thing at the pier?" she asked, her voice hushed. Rosa had pulled out a rosary and was fingering the beads. Simon had never seen her do that before.

"I don't fully know. The people I used to work with had hands in many activities—scientific research, supernatural studies, and mystical forces. They searched for ways to end the chaos in this world and were open to different ways as long as it accomplished their goals." Goals that didn't include him once he'd lost his ability to influence people.

His control over Rosa continued even though he'd lost most of his vision to the incident at the Launch Conference over the summer. Her level of brokenness left her vulnerable to even his diminished strength. Usually he kept her in that submissive role. Not now. This conversation was the most genuine thing they had shared in their time together.

"If you're trying to help this group, why would they let that thing attack us?" Rosa ran her fingers through her shoulder-length hair, letting the wild strands fall loose.

The thought had chased him all the way back from San Francisco. Why would the Archai let this other agent strike at them as well? He had thought the secretive group of four would have explained Simon was working for them. Perhaps it was the heat of battle.

"I think it sensed power and came after the sources, and in the confusion of everything got us as well. Next time we'll wear name tags." He offered a wink to make it light-hearted, even as doubts nagged at him.

Rosa shivered. "I don't know if I want there to be a next time if we have to face that. It brought back things I just want to keep buried."

Simon knew the emotions tied to the abuse Rosa had suffered, but she had walled off specific memories, so he didn't know the details. Still, the wounds were deep enough to give him fertile ground to keep his tentacles wrapped around her mind. Here she was, such a fragile woman underneath the bravado she normally projected. His control took advantage of the emotional pain to hold her mentally hostage.

A spasm tightened inside him, making his breath catch. The thought of manipulating someone triggered a rush of regret he'd never had before. He'd noticed occasional twinges of guilt in the past, but nothing like this. He shook the feeling off.

The Archai had some explaining to do. He'd get his eyes healed. He'd once again be able to focus on reading expressions and using the subtle signals to steer people the way he wanted them to go. Then he would prove his worth and take his place in their plans.

A startled cry came from the bedroom. Rosa began to get up, her brows furrowed in anger. Simon waved her back. "I'll welcome our guest. I don't want you to upset her."

"Either way, she will be very upset."

Simon made his way to the bedroom, his hand trailing the wall. Even though his latest tech glasses had improved his vision somewhat, the world was still blurry and unsettled. He had learned to trust other senses.

When he felt the doorway, he slowed and leaned into the room. A girl with reddish-blonde hair sat on the edge of the bed, her fingers clawing at a restraint holding her other hand to the bed post. Frantic breaths escaped her lips, along with a smattering of words. Prayers?

"Hello, Sarah Jane. I'd like to talk to you about something."

The girl jumped back onto the bed. "Simon Mazor. I should have known it was you who used your freak to carry me off. What do you want?" Her voice began with fear but morphed into anger as she spoke.

Huh. The meek girl he'd discovered at the conference had a little fire in her after all. He'd expected her to cower in fear. She sat on the bed in a tank top and skirt, her shoulders up in a pose of defiance.

Simon moved closer to Sarah Jane and slipped his glasses off. The scarring from his burned eyes would be apparent to her, but he couldn't read her reaction. "Your friend Lily did something to me. I need you to heal me."

CHAPTER 8

THE SUN BROKE THROUGH THE GREY CLOUDS AND into Roberto Pearce's stupor. He had to think about where he was. The last couple of months were foggy, like his consciousness had been lost in a smoky haze.

His mind! He could think clearly. There was no...creature overriding his brain. Groaning, Roberto flexed his hands and rolled to his side. He could control his movements again. His body felt like he'd been a speed bump on the highway, and a sharp pain pierced his chest, but he was no longer a puppet on a string.

"What happened?" His voice was hoarse from a lack of water. He licked his lips, listening to the sound of birds chirping and traffic rolling by.

Dizziness enveloped him, so he rolled to his back. His eyes didn't want to open. Inhaling deeply several times, he finally felt the vertigo pass. He blinked to force his eyelids open. A teary haze blurred his vision. He sat up and found himself surrounded by trees. Must be in a park somewhere. Laughter danced through the air and hit his ears. How long had it been since he'd heard that sound?

Roberto sat up and massaged his temples. Faint images came back to him: crawling into a cave in Iraq. Working with two kids with special abilities. A confrontation near the ocean, with screams, glass shards, and water flying everywhere.

The Hoshek.

He felt his chest. Was he truly free? There was a tether deep inside him, a cord of darkness holding on to some anchor within. When he thought of it, the ache increased, a hearty stab of pain.

The sunlight ebbed and Roberto looked up. His eyes widened and his heart jumped like a rabbit. Staring down at him was a dark cloud of malevolence—a thick, pulsating body of smoke with electrical impulses coursing around its form. The Hoshek perched at the top of a tree, partially blending in with the foliage.

But Roberto had nowhere to hide.

A rumble inside his head spoke to him. *Your form is still required to continue the work of the Archai. The followers of the elder escaped us last night, but not before we were empowered by their corruption. This city will be the vanguard of a spiritual Black Plague that will spread east and west. You will provide camouflage until your body is no longer needed and is discarded.*

That's right. The Hoshek had been cast out of his body when the elder spoke the ancient words. But it had picked him up and chased some angelic being of light before it faded. Instead of being free, he was prey to this primordial evil. Why wouldn't it leave him alone?

Roberto tried to scramble up and run, but his body fell to the ground, paralyzed. His breath came in gasps as the smoky tether retracted, pulling the Hoshek's thick form down. Just like in the temple ruins in Iraq, the Hoshek smothered Roberto. He coughed and choked, his body spasming, until the smoke infiltrated his cells again. Instead of hovering outside, the Hoshek had resumed residence within him.

Cornered in the recesses of his mind, Roberto mentally wept. For a few minutes, he'd had a taste of freedom from this...possession. To fall back under the total domination of this creature from hell pushed him to despair. It seemed impossible to escape this torment.

Maybe his only release would be when the Hoshek's mission was complete, and Roberto was discarded, as the beast had said.

Commotion sounded from nearby. The Hoshek used Roberto's mouth to grin as he walked toward the source of the dispute. Roberto tried to pull any kind of string for control, but he was beaten back.

At the edge of the park was a parking lot with cars starting to file in for the day. Two men argued over a fender bender. Curse words flew as they pointed at the damage and each other. The Hoshek walked right up to the men, who stopped their argument when he pushed into their space.

The one with a beard shot him a look. "What's your problem? We'll handle this."

The other guy with a clean-shaven head nodded. "Back off, weirdo."

The Hoshek drew in a deep breath and exhaled. Smoke escaped Roberto's lips and wisped around the heads of the two men. A film passed over their eyes, darkening the irises for a moment. Their confused expressions transformed into angry snarls.

"Go and share with all those harboring anger, those causing contention and discord. Spread hate and darkness to those around you, and we will be an army of rage, ready to tear down the teetering structures of society, so a new one can be rebuilt," the Hoshek said, using Roberto as his mouthpiece.

Both men shuddered, then marched off toward people in the lot and those walking along the street, looking for victims to infect.

Roberto turned to see the dome of the Palace of Fine Arts nearby. Any gathering of people would suit them just fine. As he huddled in his mental corner, the Hoshek stepped out into the street to spread the new message of darkness to more servants.

— INTERMISSION —

THE GLORY! THE UNMITIGATED MAJESTY!

Even with the things he had seen in the past, nothing compared to the blaze of light and love that he now experienced. The weight of so many years melted away. Every concern that had weighed him down lifted off him. How trivial it all seemed now that he was in the presence of his Lord.

His heart lifted in worship. There was no other response possible. His lips moved in silent speech, pouring out adoration.

All the trials. Serving so many days, waiting so long, trying to be faithful to his mission. And now, every tear and pain had been worth it.

"My beloved."

A voice he hadn't heard in ages. He cried freely, joyous and overwhelmed at the warmth flooding him. "My Lord! How I've longed for this day."

"Oh, my faithful friend. I eagerly wait until the day you enter into your rest in my Kingdom. But I need you to tarry a little longer. There is darkness that is trying to overwhelm my children, your recent charges. The enemy comes in like a flood, and you will help establish my standard to resist."

His emotions swirled. There was no disappointment in this glory, but he longed to stay. Yet if his Lord had need of him, he would sacrifice once more to see this through.

"Here I am, Lord. Send me."

PART TWO

CHAPTER 9

LILY FLOPPED ON HER BED, THE PAIN STILL THROB-bing in her wrist. She caught sight of her reflection in the mirror. Her eyes were puffy from crying all morning. A messy blonde ponytail hung behind her with strands flying everywhere. Scratches dotted her face, and a couple of bruises had developed.

If Sarah Jane had been around, all Lily's injuries would be healed. But she was more than a healing tonic. SJ had become a soul sister—one who needed Lily and their friends in Anointed. Her adrenaline kicked in as she considered where SJ might be and what it was going to take to find her.

Lily's phone was on her dresser, where she guessed it had been since she was brought upstairs. The screen had cracked in the battle, but thankfully that was the only damage. Now she finally had time to check in on Demarcus and Harry. She couldn't remember if they had been hurt.

Her splint kept her thumb from moving, and it was awkward to type and swipe with only her left hand. She tried tapping out a message to the boys. Man, not having a thumb available cramped her style.

Before she could finish her message, a notification pinged. A message from Ji-young Kim, the journalist they saved from the Corrupted last night? Lily didn't expect that. She tapped on the notification to open it up.

"Thank you for saving me last night. That was the scariest thing I have ever experienced. I hope my investigation

did not bring trouble upon you. I realize now your group are heroes.

"I think you may be needed again. One of my contacts said there's been strange activity at Mount Sutro Park. Strange noises and an increase of fog (although it's a foggy place already). Sounds like it may be the two people who captured me yesterday.

"If you could contact me, I'd like to help you find these people and bring them to justice."

Lily stared her phone for a minute. She massaged her neck with her good hand and tried to fight the rising frustration. Light seeped out from under her brace, warming her fingers. Those two teens with powers had caused them enough trouble. And now she needed to figure out where in the world Mount Sutro was. It better not be far. She hadn't heard of it before, having been in the Bay Area for just over a year. It was going to be hard enough to get out of the house, never mind being away for who knew how long.

A map app showed it was a recreation area farther north, near San Francisco. She didn't have transportation that could get her there from the South Bay area. But Harry and Demarcus could do it.

This was crazy. Shouldn't they be looking for SJ?

Pacing her room, Lily's thoughts ricocheted around in her head. Of course SJ was more important. Somehow, she had disappeared at the end of the confrontation at Hyde Pier. But who would know what had happened to her?

Lily's chest tightened as her irritation grew, the dull burning inside her flaring up. The creature! The smoke monster...or whatever it was. It had attacked everyone with gifts during the battle. The man that was associated with it seemed to be connected to the Corrupted teens as well. And the one person the creature didn't reach was SJ.

There must be a connection.

Blackness spread behind her eyes. She clutched her rib cage and knelt on the floor, biting her lip to keep from crying out. The creature's attack had sucked something out of her, but it left a raw wound behind. It was like a black hole pulling at her from inside. *Oh Lord, help me, please.* Drawing in ragged breaths, she rocked forward and backward for several minutes. Finally, the sharp pain leveled off to a dull throb. Okay, it confirmed a link if thoughts like that caused such a reaction in her.

That was it then. She'd contact her friends and talk them into checking out the mystery at Mount Sutro. They would start there to track down SJ.

She fumbled with her phone to pull up Demarcus's contact info. If she was feeling so terrible, maybe he was dealing with a similar pain. She needed to hear something encouraging from her friend right now. She needed to know she wasn't alone.

CHAPTER 10

THE PHONE TRILLED WITH A MUTED RING UNDER HIS pillow. Demarcus's eyes opened with a start, the sunlight filtering through his blinds and landing on his face. He'd crashed for a couple of hours at least. He felt around groggily for his device. Wait a second, there was something plastic under there instead. He was a little old for the tooth fairy.

Oh, yeah. If there was a chime, his phone must be working again! He pulled the phone out of a baggie, rice spilling out over his sheets. The shattered screen was rough as his fingertips passed over it. Part of him wished he could still catch a bit more sleep. But the ringtone was the one set for Lily, so it couldn't wait.

How are you? We need to find SJ. May have a lead.

Demarcus tapped out a reply. *I'm okay. You? What lead?*

Our friend Ji-young Kim thinks she knows where they are. You good to go?

Mama's not happy and wants me to lay low...but we need to find SJ. What next?

She posted a thumbs-up emoji. *Let's get Harry. Check things out.*

Demarcus wasn't so sure that was the best idea. The situation with Mama could be classified as tenuous. She hadn't killed him—yet. He struggled to imagine how she would she react if he ran off searching for Sarah Jane.

But the other reality was that a friend had disappeared, and that fact compelled him to do something about it. Mama would have to understand. He whipped a message out to his buddy, then dug out some training joggers and a quick-dry athletic shirt. If they ran into the water girl, he'd be a little more prepared to handle her. His special shoes from Ratchet still felt damp, but they would work.

Demarcus zoomed downstairs and wolfed down a couple of waffles and hard-boiled eggs. They couldn't be outmaneuvered again. This time he had to give it all to come out on top. The last two weeks had been one set back after another: The retreat from Santa Cruz. The attack on Applied Sciences. The ambush at the pier.

No more.

God, we've messed up and given our enemies ground. Help us to do what is right, and to stand against evil. We need you.

He hoped the prayer would bring a measure of peace to his mind, but his chest ached with the words. Something residual from the man who attacked them seemed to linger within him. He wondered if Harry and Lily were dealing with the same thing.

Demarcus finished guzzling some water as Harry ported in front of him. Dark undereye circles paired with Harry's pale complexion made him look like a zombie. His red hair was disheveled, his clothes wrinkled.

"Dude, did you get any sleep last night?"

Harry shook his head. "How could I, knowing Sarah Jane is missing? She's out there somewhere. I've been searching everything I can online to find any kind of information. Please tell me you and Lily have an idea where to find her."

Sarah Jane and Harry had gone on their first date last night, before being rudely interrupted by a superpowered attack. Demarcus understood how hard Harry was taking things, because he would feel the same way about Lily.

"Let's go get Lily and see what kind of lead she has. We'll find Sarah Jane. She's special to all of us, but I get it, man."

Harry whispered his thanks, then took Demarcus's hand so they could port to Lily's house for a pick-up.

———

Lily met the boys outside, and they vanished before her parents could ask any questions. Demarcus wanted to assure them he'd watch out for her, but his insistence on being overprotective last night may have led to John's death. Lily was strong enough to fight her own battles. He smiled at the thought of the ways she used her powers, from stopping a tsunami wave to creating the hologram that led the smoke monster away.

Harry used his GPS to find a couple of waypoints to get them to the Mount Sutro recreation area. The nature area was just west of San Francisco. "So, is Ji-young going to meet us there? And does she know if this relates to Sarah Jane's disappearance?" he asked.

Lily checked her phone. "No, but she sent a few messages about how the fog over the area has been pronounced today, and that strange sounds have been reported as well. Her best guess is that Kashvi and Aasif are hiding out there. She didn't say anything specific about SJ, but she's got a good network of informants all around the region."

"She must have a lot of connections. Think how fast she's caught on to us the last couple of weeks," Demarcus said. He hoped she was truly an ally now and this wasn't another trap. But if it could bring answers about Sarah Jane, he'd tackle whatever came their way.

After a couple of hops, they ended up in a parking lot facing a dirt trail that led up into the mist. A sign described areas for hikes and mountain biking—so there were plenty of places to hide out. A chill hung in the air from the fog blanketing the area, while the damp smell of earth and leaves wafted by. Demarcus looked back toward the city and saw the Transamerica Tower and other San Francisco landmarks, meaning the fog was localized over Mount Sutro. With this eerie mist, it probably was quiet today, even for a Sunday afternoon.

Lily wrapped her arms across her torso and shivered. She had braided her blonde hair, and it hung over her shoulder and her long sleeve T-shirt. She wore shorts and had basic tennis shoes on. More practical than her dress for homecoming from last night. The one new accessory was the splint on her right forearm.

"How are you going to do with one hand?" Demarcus said, concern slipping into his voice.

She twisted her arm with a grimace. "It affects me a bit. I'll have to make it work."

Harry made gun fingers and mimicked Lily's twisting motion. "Yeah, that might mess up your aim. I hope your left-hand shoots as straight as the right." Harry's usually fun-loving humor landed like a lead brick. He stuffed his hands in his pockets.

Thoughts of Mama's disappointment if she knew where he was right now weighed on Demarcus. They needed to get this job done and get out. Time for a plan. "Okay guys, I think we spread out a bit so the sound guy can't hit us all at once with a blast. What if I lead the way, Lily lights things up in the middle, and Harry, you watch our rear and be ready to port us back here if needed?"

Lily shook out her left hand, flexing her fingers. "I'll leave the strategy to you guys here. But keep in mind, I'm not sure what I can do in the fog."

A week ago, Demarcus and Harry had argued over tactics in battling the Corrupted. They didn't have time for it today. Would Harry push back on who was taking the lead?

Harry rolled his eyes but agreed. "I think that works—if you don't rush ahead."

"Don't worry, this isn't the day for that. Let's go find some bad guys, hopefully." Demarcus stepped forward to be swallowed by the clouds.

CHAPTER 11

THE WAY THE FOG ENVELOPED THEM SO QUICKLY freaked Lily out. She'd heard of fog as thick as soup before, but this was ridiculous. The temperature dropped several degrees and she fought to stop shivering. She lit her skin up and tried to shoot a beam forward to help them see, but all it did was bounce off the fog and make things worse.

A tap on her shoulder made her jump.

"Whoa," Harry said. "It's just me. I think this is like driving in the fog. You can't use brights or it just reflects back on the driver. Maybe bring the level down a few notches."

She dialed the brightness down and it helped somewhat. The path directly in front of her was mostly visible. Demarcus had to stay closer than his plan intended, and Harry crept along just behind her. It was the perfect set-up for a horror movie: three teens purposely wander into the mists, never to be heard from again. The thought didn't help, and her pulse thumped as she tried to quash its cycling through her mind.

They made their way slowly up the switchback track. Demarcus tripped over an exposed root and barely avoided planting himself in the mud. A branch whipped back and caught Lily in the face, making her yelp in pain.

Demarcus caught her arm and pulled her away from the rogue branch. "Are you okay?"

"I'm fine. I just need to be quiet." Her cheek stung where it had smacked her, but she wouldn't confess that.

"How do we know we're going the right direction? What if they're not even here?" Harry's eyes darted back and forth.

"We saw how clear the city was." Lily spun her finger in a circle in the air. "I don't think this is an accident."

"She's right. We'll follow the trail and if nothing happens on the way, you can port us down instead of trying to make it back," Demarcus said.

"Let's get going then. If this isn't going to help us find Sarah Jane, we need to be doing something else," Harry grumbled.

They set out again, huddled more closely together this time. It was tedious hiking. Some areas were muddy enough to suck their shoes down, making the trek a slog. Lily found the right amount of light to illuminate their path without blinding their view, but her arm throbbed from the effort. The thought of dealing with her dad swirled in her mind, and the more she dwelled on it, the more she noticed the ache in her chest.

"Do you guys...have any pain from the dude who grabbed us?"

Demarcus stopped and they ran into him. Harry landed on his butt from the impact. "Warning next time, eh?"

"You've got that too?" Demarcus replied, rubbing his chest.

She nodded.

Harry tried to brush dirt off his rear end. "I've got it too. It's a shared thing then. I figured he must have hit me harder than I realized."

The pain throbbed in Lily's chest, and it made her suck in a shallow breath. "I think it's a side effect of what he did to us. Did you notice that the creature that came out of him seemed to mimic our powers? Or did the opposite?

It sucked the light away at one point and then dashed around like Demarcus."

Demarcus shook his head. "I was too busy trying to get to you to protect you, and it left John open for...the attack."

Lily put a hand on his shoulder. "I appreciate the thought, but we've all got some pretty cool abilities. I can take care of myself. And John..." She choked back a cry.

Harry crouched down low and pulled on her shirt for her to do the same. "We can talk about John later. I think we might have company. Listen."

Lily strained to listen. Besides her pounding pulse, she couldn't hear a sound. "I don't hear anything."

"Exactly. We could hear the wind rustle the leaves a minute ago. It could be What's-His-Name is dampening the sound."

Lily dropped her light and darkness enveloped them. No afternoon sun penetrated the thick air. They looked around, to no avail. Their eyes weren't used to the dark, and Kashvi had blotted out the sunlight.

With a blink, Lily switched her vision to infrared, but all she saw was an amorphous cool blue mass floating around her. Snap, the fog blocked this trick as well.

Until the water coalesced into a thick stream and lashed out at them.

CHAPTER 12

DEMARCUS FELT LILY'S BODY TENSE BESIDE HIM and he braced for impact. Sure enough, a wall of water plowed into him and knocked him backwards. He landed sprawled in a bush and fought to get out of the branches. He could only see a couple feet in front of him.

Where were his friends?

He tried to climb back to where he'd just been standing, but more water thudded into his gut and made him double over. "Lily, Harry! Where are you?" he gasped.

A brilliant light exploded to his left. Demarcus quickly pulled out his special glasses from Rachet and put them on. His vision wasn't darkened, but it protected him from Lily's power. The air cleared enough that he could see Lily's form in the center of what appeared to be a spinning halo, vaporizing snaking strands of water away each time they contacted her light.

If she was okay, could he figure out where Kashvi and Aasif were hiding?

The water looked to be coming from right in front of him. But his speed was neutralized because he couldn't dash through the underbrush. He tried to run ahead on the trail, but there was no traction in the mud, and once he got a few yards away from Lily he couldn't see where he was going.

Not cool. He was not used to being, well, useless.

He tried whipping his arms in circles, and it cleared some of the fog. A form ahead barely peeked through the shadows: Kashvi. Now at least he had a target.

A sound pierced the air and dropped Demarcus to his knees. His head swirled and it felt like someone drove a spike straight through his head. He tried to cup his ears, but the sound reverberated all around him. He managed to look up and see Lily thrashing on the ground as well, light streaming around her haphazardly.

So hard to think. These two were so powerful. How would they stop them?

The sound broke. Demarcus shook his head repeatedly to try and clear the ringing in his ears and the blanket over his thoughts. Lily groaned ahead of him.

Water lashed around his body like ropes. They pinned him to the muddy ground and started to squeeze. In his peripheral vision he could see Lily in a similar predicament.

A female voice cried out from uphill. "Let him go! I've got your friends."

Harry's voice rang out from far away. "Let him go? Bad choice of words, but all right."

The fog began to drop. Water sloshed from the air and drenched Demarcus, as if he weren't wet enough with the liquid restraints. He heard a scream from high in the air. A body plunged towards the ground, arms flailing. Aasif's cry pierced the air again. What was Harry doing? Killing the dude?

Then Harry ported alongside Aasif for a moment before they both disappeared again. A water whip just missed where Aasif was about to land.

There, high in the trees. Harry and Aasif dangled precariously off of a branch. Demarcus couldn't see the look on Aasif's face, but his angry curses suggested he wasn't happy. Harry held on to the trunk with one hand and kept Aasif angled toward the ground.

"You can take me out, but there's nothing to stop your friend here from dropping. And I bet I can get to my friends faster than you can possibly hurt them. If you want your buddy to make it, let my friends go," Harry yelled.

The water tightened around Demarcus. He wasn't sure playing chicken was the best plan. A small cry came from Lily. He had to do something to help take control of the situation.

Demarcus started vibrating as fast as he could. His body sank into the mud a bit, but the water couldn't keep its hold on him, and it quickly sloshed away. He pushed himself out of the mud and clambered up the hill to catch Kashvi's arms and pull them behind her. The girl tried to fight her way out of his grip, but he wouldn't release her.

Before Kashvi could do anything, Lily approached with hands glowing. Mud dripped from her tangled braid. Even with her looking like a mess, she was a beautiful sight to behold.

"This ends today. You two won't torment any other people," Lily said, her voice as solid as steel.

A strange sound came from Demarcus's captive—the quiet sound of weeping. Lily's stare softened as she regarded Kashvi. Demarcus wished he could see what was going on, but he had to keep a hold of her.

"We're tired of running and hiding. If Pearce finds us again, he'll kill us. Call the police, do what you have to. I can't fight anymore," Kashvi begged.

Demarcus and Lily shared a look. That wasn't what they expected. Instead of a continued fight, the Corrupted were...surrendering?

After a minute of studying the girl's face, Lily lowered her hands. "Demarcus, let her go."

CHAPTER 13

LILY SEARCHED THE FACE OF HER ADVERSARY. THIS Kashvi had caused her pain and terror, while hurting many people in the attacks on Applied Sciences and the pier. Yet Lily could relate to her. Kashvi's face contorted in the same terror Lily had experienced when she was strapped to a contraption that forcibly sucked the light out of her back at the Launch Conference in June.

"Let her go," Lily repeated to Demarcus.

He mouthed, "Are you sure?" and she nodded gently.

Lily had stared into Kashvi's face at Applied Sciences a week ago, and her eyes had been dead, two black holes of anger and hate. Today, between the tears, Lily saw life and a conscience. Somehow, like Simon, Pearce had controlled Kashvi and overridden her will. The girl's brown eyes now had a glow that wasn't there before.

One more piece clicked into place in Lily's mind. The dark halo that Kashvi had had around her head in previous encounters was gone. One of Lily's abilities was to see if someone was being influenced by darkness. This discernment wasn't always apparent, but both Kashvi and Aasif had worn the darkness so prominently before.

Lily looked up at Harry and his dangling captive. "Harry, bring him down here. I think we need to talk."

Demarcus released Kashvi's arms, but stayed on guard, ready to move if she tried to double-cross them. Kashvi sank onto the ground, covering her face with her hands. Lily sensed that today, she was sincere.

The air warped in front of them and Harry appeared with Aasif. He pulled away from Harry abruptly and shot a glare at him, then knelt down to slip an arm around Kashvi's shoulders. The girl leaned into him and they rocked back and forth on the muddy trail.

In all the chaos of dealing with these two in the last few weeks, Lily had never been able to take them in. Kashvi had long black hair in a tight braid looped over her shoulder. A small gold stud glistened from her nose. She had a sharp nose that gave the impression of a bird of prey.

Aasif had lighter brown skin and thick eyebrows that framed concerned eyes as he regarded his friend. The boy had an old scar on the edge of his chin that gave him a dangerous look when coupled with his crooked nose. His black hair was cut in a fade on the sides, leaving thick hair on top.

Demarcus and Harry stood back with arms folded, regarding the teens as well. Lily dropped to her knees and felt the squish of the mud against her skin. She was going to need a fire hose to get all the dirt off her.

She reached out and gently laid her hand on Kashvi's leg. The girl twitched at the touch, then lifted her head to look at Lily, fear written across her face.

"We're not interested in any more battle. I'm guessing you both have had huge changes—your powers, dealing with people trying to use you. Do you want to talk about it?" Lily said.

Aasif scoffed. "You search us out to fight, and now you want to talk?" The boy carried himself like a wounded dog, scared but ready to bite.

Demarcus started forward as if he were going to do the alpha male thing. Lily held a hand up to keep him calm. "We heard about strange sounds and fog here. But we're not here to take you down. We need information to find our friend. Who was the man with you at the pier last night? The one who seemed to turn on you?"

That got their attention. Kashvi stopped crying and whispered to Aasif, whose hard, defiant face didn't betray any emotion. The two of them nodded to each other.

Kashvi's voice wavered, not like that of the threatening girl from last night. "We've been under the control of a man. We did not intend to hurt you—I mean, it was not our choice."

"If it wasn't your choice, whose was it? He may have our friend. Do you know where Sarah Jane is?" Harry said through gritted teeth. By the look of his stance, he was ready to pounce if they made one wrong move.

Kashvi and Aasif stiffened at the confrontational tone. "We don't know about your friend," was her clipped answer. This interaction wasn't going well. It needed to be handled more delicately.

"Guys, let me talk to Kashvi woman to woman for a minute." Lily made eye contact with Kashvi and drew the girl a few feet away. The girl pulled the edge of her loose sleeve over to dab at her eyes. Her clothes were damp and muddy as well. They matched in their sloppy-looking attire.

"We do want to find our friend, but if we can help you, we will. What happened to you?" Lily asked.

Kashvi sucked in a deep breath before speaking in hushed tones. "I was lured from Portland, Oregon, by a man I thought was my boyfriend. He talked me into coming down here against my parents' wishes. When I got here, he wanted me to do...favors for his friend who'd paid for my ticket. I managed to escape, but I was lost on the streets, alone. I was ashamed to call my parents and didn't know how to find a shelter. Roberto Pearce approached me and asked if I needed help.

"I was leery of another man trying to sway me, but he said he had a lot of power to make things right. In my fear I saw his strength as something protective."

A tear dripped down her cheek. "Then he got inside my head. Dark whispers filled my mind until I couldn't think straight. The words he used, chants from another time, wormed their way in and manipulated me in a way that awakened my water ability. He also controlled me—I wasn't able to resist his demands. That's when I was introduced to Aasif. After he trained with us for a couple weeks, we went looking for you. Our mission was to destroy you." Kashvi shuddered at the end of her statement.

"At least you're honest about it. I mean, your mission," Harry muttered. He had made his way over, close enough to eavesdrop. Lily shot him a glare to tell him he wasn't helping things. Demarcus gave him the elbow that Lily would have if she were in range.

Turning back to Kashvi, Lily felt tears well up in her eyes. "You were trafficked down here to the Bay Area?"

Kashvi nodded. "How can I go home? I've done awful things. Hurt people…"

"But what happened last night? You two don't seem as bent on, well, destroying us," Lily asked.

Aasif, who had also moved closer and was keeping his eye on Harry, growled in response. "Pearce betrayed us. You saw what happened. He allowed our powers to develop, and in the midst of the mission that he'd given us, he turned on us. He stole part of it back. At least our minds were freed by him doing that. But now we've got a hole inside us, like a wound."

Lily, Demarcus, and Harry shared looks at the mention of the pain they all felt. The boys' guarded postures relaxed at the revelation that they all had been affected somehow. "We've got that ache too. I wonder if Pearce was trying to get us all together somehow. Because two other people with special abilities were there—Simon Mazor and Rosa Gonzalez."

Kashvi's eyes widened. "*The* Simon Mazor? The one who built Flare?"

The memories of what Simon had done always made Lily's stomach flip. "Yup. Built and then destroyed it. Because he was trying to control the world through social media, and he also attempted to use my friends and me in the process."

This comment seemed to resonate with Aasif. The boy also eased his body language and sat back on a rock.

"What's your story, Aasif?" Lily asked, wringing out her shirt.

He waited a minute before responding. "I was a runaway. Home life was bad, so I took care of myself on my own. Like Kashvi, Pearce found me and offered me a way to have power." He ran a hand through his wavy hair. "I did not think the power would have such a price."

Lily wanted to pry deeper, to see if he'd had hints of his abilities before Pearce came along. Perhaps these two were gifted like Lily and her friends, with abilities given by God before Simon even discovered them. What would the Anointed be like if they'd come under Simon's influence fully?

They could have been terrors—just like Kashvi and Aasif were now.

"So, what are you going to do? You said if Pearce finds you again, he'll kill you."

Kashvi gestured at the landscape. "We were trying to hide out here to decide our next move. Pearce had an apartment for us, but we don't dare go back there anymore."

The idea that had been simmering in the back of Lily's mind shot straight to her mouth. "We have a place where you could take shelter until you can figure things out. We'd be nearby to help protect you from Pearce."

"Can we talk for a minute?" Demarcus cut in, motioning for Lily to come with him.

She followed Demarcus and Harry around a switchback where they still had a view of the teens, but were out of earshot. The fog was quickly dissipating without Kashvi controlling it, so visibility was improving.

"What are you thinking? Inviting our enemies to our homes?" Demarcus asked.

"First of all, I don't think they're our enemies anymore. Second, I didn't mean our homes. I bet Pastor Sanchez would be willing to have them at the church or help them find something else."

Harry shifted his weight back and forth, peering at the teens and searching Lily's face with incredulous eyes. "I don't know about this. We've been safe from them at home, school, and church. This would bring them pretty close to us."

"But who better to help? We know what it's like to have powers. And we know what it's like to have someone trying to control us. Pastor Sanchez is a smart guy. This way we're keeping them close and we know where they are. C'mon guys. Would Jesus leave them alone? I don't think so." She flashed her puppy dog eyes as well. No reason to fight fair.

Demarcus groaned. "Okay, I see what you're saying. Let's see if these guys are up to it, then we can check with Pastor Sanchez."

Harry punched Demarcus's arm. "Giving in so easily? I think you're falling for the big blue eyes. I'm not so sure about this." He paused, then shook his head. "But I don't see another option. Fine. I'll be ready to port them far away if there are any issues."

Lily gave a small smile. "I think this will work." She led them back to Kashvi and Aasif.

"Who is this Pastor Sanchez, and why should we trust him?" Aasif asked.

Lily quirked her eyebrows. "What? How did you…"

The first hint of a smile came from Aasif. "You control light, I do sound. I can do more than sonic screams."

Made sense. "We all met at the Launch Conference this summer. It was hosted by Simon Mazor to find teens with special abilities to help him change the world. But he was in it for his own gain. We met a man named John who knew our powers were gifts from God. He introduced us to Pastor Sanchez and his church, where they help us learn to control them and use them for good. I'm sure he'd be willing to help provide sanctuary."

Aasif raised an eyebrow, skepticism written all over his face.

Kashvi looked at him. "What other choice do we have? Steal more food and hide in the woods like dogs?"

"I don't trust anyone at this point."

She held his hand. "Will you trust me? This feels like the best option right now. We'll have each other's back, like we have the last several weeks."

Lily said a silent prayer while the two deliberated. *Please God, help us get to the bottom of this. There's more going on than we know, and we need your wisdom.* Her chest burned with discomfort again, but it wasn't as bad as before.

Finally, Aasif stood. "We will accept your offer. But if there's any treachery, we will not be kind in our reaction."

"I can work with that. Okay gang, we need to get a hold of Pastor Sanchez and get back to the church building. I just have one quick question for Kashvi," Lily said.

"What do you need?"

"Since we're all a muddy mess and wet anyway, could you whip up a rain shower for us to at least get the dirt off?"

CHAPTER 14

AFTER LEAVING TO GIVE SARAH JANE TIME TO THINK, Simon returned to the bedroom, this time carrying a bottle of water and a sandwich. Sarah Jane sat on the edge of the bed, still working on the restraint. He heard a sigh of frustration come from her. The electronic lock wouldn't be broken anytime soon.

"What do you want?" she asked, her voice short.

"I've brought you some refreshment. I'm sure you're hungry and thirsty after last night," he replied in his most soothing voice. He set the plate and water on the bed next to her, then backed up, giving her room to eat.

She picked up the sandwich, looked at it for a moment, and threw it back at him. The mustard smeared on his arm as it dropped to the ground after impact.

"I'm not hungry."

His temper reared, but he fought to keep his demeanor level. Of course she would be angry. He couldn't blame her. "You could have saved it for later. But if we work together, this won't take long. You'll be free to go."

"Really?" Her tone softened.

If she was receptive, he'd have to see if he could push his ability and get her to comply. Simon strained for more clarity in his vision, but he could feel his power only reached out weakly. He had to be able to recognize the tiny signs and giveaways of a person in order to influence them.

"I just need one thing from you. If you heal my eyes, I'll let you go. It's very simple. We'll be done, and you can go home."

Sarah Jane leaned forward. "Even though you've kidnapped me, somehow kept Rosa under your control, and are wanted for questioning in the collapse of Alturas, you'll just...let me leave if I heal you."

He spoke, again as sweetly as he could manage. "That's right. You'll be free. We'll get you within walking distance of your home and that's all it will be." He kept pushing with his ability. *Believe me, Sarah Jane. All will be well. Just reach out and restore my vision.*

"Will you promise?"

He smiled. "Of course."

"And what good is the promise of a criminal?" She spat the words at him.

Despite his best attempt at persuasion, his smile fell. "What do you mean? Why would I not follow through with my promise?"

She leaned back. "Oh, I don't know. The fact that you'd be reported. People would know all about you and Alturas. Once I've helped you, what use would you have for me? You can't let me go. You probably won't keep me alive. Therefore, I don't see a reason to trust you. Not even a smidge." The venom in her voice rose with each word.

Heat flashed through his cheeks. Simon didn't expect such backbone from this girl. She was so meek at the conference, and the research on her backed it up. What could he do to get her to cooperate?

"I can have Rosa come in here and make you do it," he said. Rosa would probably enjoy it too much, but he had to try.

"Go ahead. You can't kill me again, because you wouldn't have anyone to heal you. That won't work, and you know it." Her voice quavered a little, but there was still force in her words.

"What do you mean, 'kill you again?'" Simon asked.

A hard laugh came from her. "Wow, you don't even know. When Rosa threw me off your building at the conference, I died. But someone prayed for me, and I came back. God wasn't done with me yet. You don't know the power of the Lord, do you? All you see is what you could do with your mind control games. Well, that's all it is: games. You may have the ability to control others, but only in a limited way.

"One day, you'll have to face your Maker. Then what will you do?"

Simon was at a loss for words. That rarely happened. He assumed that if Sarah Jane was still around, she hadn't been hurt badly in the fall. Somehow she must have been cushioned, or had already healed. She probably healed herself. But she claimed that she had died?

Inconceivable.

Simon turned to leave without saying anything, but something from her dossier came to mind.

"You've got a nice family, don't you? A kind mom and dad. And you have a little brother. Sure, your parents pay more attention to him than you, and that bothers you some. But you wouldn't want anything to happen to him, would you?"

Her breath caught. "You wouldn't." Now the nerves were apparent in her voice.

"I don't want to go that way, but if I have to I will. Think about what's important to you, and I'll be back later."

CHAPTER 15

DEMARCUS SKIDDED TO A STOP IN THE ALLEY NEXT TO the church building. What was Pastor Sanchez going to say when he met Kashvi and Aasif? Harry would be arriving any moment with the others. Demarcus had run on his own to take some of the strain off Harry teleporting too many people. They were all taxed from the day before.

He still wasn't sure about Lily's plan, but they had to find out more about this Roberto Pearce. If he had been behind Kashvi and Aasif's attacks, they could potentially put an end to everything they had been dealing with in the last few weeks. Hopefully that would bring them closer to finding Sarah Jane.

Entering the church, Demarcus realized that he wouldn't see John here anymore. Hot tears threatened to stream down his face. He stopped for a moment in the foyer, trying to wrestle his feelings of failure. *If I hadn't pushed for the encounter, if I had retreated when John said, then John would still be here.* The ache in his chest intensified.

But if what they believed was true, John was in a better place. That was the hope Demarcus needed to cling to, even in the gut-wrenching guilt he couldn't shake. John had talked about promises all the time. As he entered the youth room, Demarcus realized it was time to believe in those promises.

Harry appeared with Lily, Aasif, and Kashvi. Kashvi stumbled back onto the couch. Aasif held his head. "I do not understand how you get used to that."

"Now what? Where do we start looking for Sarah Jane?" Harry asked, an edge to his voice.

Lily turned away from the group and walked to the bookshelf. She grabbed a tissue and dabbed at her eyes. "He should be here with us. It isn't the same," she said quietly.

Harry's eyes reddened. Kashvi and Aasif looked at each other and then to Demarcus.

"Our mentor was killed last night by the creature. This is where we would meet and he would teach us," Harry explained.

"Did he push you hard?" Kashvi asked.

Demarcus shook his head. "No. He wanted us to be the best we could be, but it was more like...pulling us up instead of beating us down. I've had coaches that rip you for not practicing hard or making mistakes. John was just inspiring. I don't know what else to say."

"We are sorry for your mentor's death," Aasif said. "This is messed up, and we don't know how to get out of the cycle."

The sound of footsteps echoed in the hall and they all fell silent. Pastor Julio Sanchez entered the room with his wife, Irene. Lines were etched on his forehead, and his normally jovial smile was replaced with a frown.

"Kids, are you all okay?" he asked.

Lily choked back a sob, and Harry grimaced as if he'd been gut punched. Demarcus cleared his throat to respond. "We're in one piece. Got some dings, but we're okay. But Sarah Jane is missing, and John is—well, he's gone."

Irene gasped and covered her mouth with a shaking hand. Pastor Sanchez wiped a hand over his receding hair line, the gelled hair flying about. "Oh Lord, have mercy right now. Sit down and tell me everything."

Demarcus caught him up on the basics: the plan to trap the Corrupted kids, the battle at Hyde Pier, and confronting

Kashvi and Aasif at Mount Sutro. He explained how the two of them had escaped being controlled by Roberto Pearce and their need for a place to hide out.

"That is just crazy. I don't know what to say," Pastor Sanchez said at the end. "I don't think anyone saw something like this happening. John talked about a coming conflict, but I didn't think it would be fatal."

"It's my fault, sir," Demarcus said, voice wavering. "I pushed us to confront Kashvi and Aasif, and when things got crazy by the Bay, I refused to retreat when John told us. If I hadn't *done* that..."

Lily sniffed and wiped at her eyes with one hand while patting Demarcus's arm with the other. "It's all our faults. We all fed into it. Sarah Jane tried to warn us before anything happened, and we didn't listen then either. It's our fault she's missing too."

A silence hung in the room, until Harry's growl broke the stillness. "And that's why we need to start making moves to find her. Confronting these two was supposed to help us get there, but we're no closer now than we were three hours ago. What do we do now? What's the next step?"

Irene put her arms out and pulled Harry into a hug. Demarcus expected his friend to melt into her embrace, but Harry accepted the gesture with stiffness. Usually he was a tender soul. This hardness made Demarcus uneasy.

After Irene hugged Demarcus and Lily, Pastor Sanchez told the kids to update their parents while he and his wife got everyone water and some leftover snacks from the Sunday school pantry. Mama was okay since Demarcus was at church. It sounded like the same for Lily and Harry. Lily used a clipped tone on the phone, but it seemed that she was doing better with her dad, compared to a week ago when she had been grounded.

When Pastor Sanchez and Irene returned with refreshments, they all sat down with in a circle. "Kashvi and Aasif, we'd like to offer our home to you as a safe place while you're worried about the threat from Pearce. We have members of our church in law enforcement that can help protect you and get you into the proper channels for the help you need. You can think about that."

The two teens looked at each other and whispered something before nodding at Pastor Sanchez.

"My wife will take you to our donation center to find some new clothes until we can get better supplies for you." Irene led them out of the youth room and down the hall.

Demarcus was grateful that their pastor had adjusted quickly to the craziness. Pastor Sanchez gazed at the three of them before clearing his throat.

"I'll confess, there's not much in school that prepares you for helping superpowered teens in a supernatural conflict. I'm at a loss as to how to proceed, other than to turn to the Lord and ask for his wisdom."

Harry started to object, but Pastor Sanchez held up a hand. "Harry, I understand the drive to *do* something in the moment, but it could harm Sarah Jane more if you go in ill-prepared. We won't be praying all night. We'll take fifteen minutes or so to pray, and then we'll talk about options."

Even though Harry folded his arms with a huff, they all bowed their heads. The pastor who could deliver fiery sermons led them in prayers for comfort and requests for wisdom. It wasn't the same as John, but it still brought a measure of peace to Demarcus. The time of stillness soothed the ache in his chest, even if it didn't go away. His sorrow wouldn't heal quickly, either. Still, it helped.

When they finished, Harry glanced around. "Okay, what do we do?"

Pastor Sanchez tapped his cell phone. "I'll call her parents and see what the police are saying, offer our full support. The church will rally around them. But you three need to go home and rest. It's late, you've had an unimaginable weekend, and unfortunately you've got to deal with school tomorrow."

Lily's weary shoulders slumped, but she didn't say anything. Demarcus didn't have any idea about what to do next now that they'd figured out the situation with the Corrupted. Harry was another story.

"No. I mean, we can't just, ya know, go to school and pretend everything's okay. What if Sarah Jane needs us *now*? We should be doing something." Harry stood and paced across the room, gesturing with his hands with every step.

"We're doing things—we're finding out what's being done. You all will probably need to give statements to the police. I'm sure the media is all over this. I wouldn't be surprised if you guys are known already. We'll learn what's being done, and augment what law enforcement is already doing." Pastor Sanchez came alongside Harry and clasped his hand. "Sarah Jane will be found. Trust and have faith."

Harry gritted his teeth for a full minute before he relaxed his shoulders and sighed. "I'll wait until we hear what the police are doing. Text me right away, okay?" He walked to the door and turned back. "If I have to teleport into every building in the Bay Area, I'll do it."

With that, he vanished.

CHAPTER 16

THE CHANTING AND DISCORD DREW THE HOSHEK LIKE a magnet. There was no way for Roberto to dissuade the creature controlling his body. All he could do was hide in his own mind and pray that somehow there would be a release from this torment.

Some kind of demonstration had drawn a crowd. Men and women of all ages and colors held their ground, shouting at each other. Signs with slogans bobbed in the air over the crush of people. The object of their protest wasn't clear, but Roberto could discern one thing easily enough: the conflict made a great target for the Hoshek.

Roberto had lost count of how many angry people they'd encountered today, each person ripe for the poison the Hoshek spread, fertile ground for the seeds of rage it planted. Men, women, and children left their encounters with it seething, their souls darkened by allowing room for the frenzy to infect them.

Until now, the progress had come in ones and twos. Each one affected spread it further, and this demonstration would give an exponential boost to the efforts of the Hoshek. Roberto tried to concentrate and count the number of people here. His mind strained with the effort, estimating a couple hundred at least.

Some political cause seemed to be at the heart of it. The slogans didn't mean anything to the Hoshek. It cared not for the reason—just the fact that the participants had surrendered logic and caring about humanity for their right to be provoked. That was all the opening it needed.

Roberto's body reached the edge of the crowd. The rabid shouts of both sides careened through the air. So much hatred.

Feelings towards former colleagues who'd mocked him bubbled up in Roberto's thoughts, immediately tightening the Hoshek's control over him. Wrath was a drug to this evil creature, and Roberto's hurt must have left him vulnerable to the Hoshek's control.

The Hoshek held out Roberto's hands and plunged a city block into darkness. Where had that trick come from? Last night against the youth. One of them, a girl, could control light.

Memories of confronting the gifted people there and his touch draining part of their powers filtered through his mind. He recalled taking a corrupted form of each's strength for the Hoshek's use…

Except the healer. She had eluded them. Roberto wondered how the Hoshek would pervert her gift. Would it have the ability to inflict harm? Instant death?

Roberto's concerns were interrupted by the panic in the crowd at the sudden blackout. Somehow the Hoshek blinked and enabled some kind of infrared vision, allowing it to maneuver through the throngs of people. Using stolen speed as well, the Hoshek dashed around the crowd, a trail of smoke dissipating over the group.

People coughed and gagged under the Hoshek's control. Roberto could sense their minds becoming clouded by the infestation. The rage infection spread into the center of the crowd. Even though some people began to react in fear, trying to flee what was happening, the Hoshek's dominion latched onto the recent anger and took over.

The light came back over the assembly, and hundreds of pairs of eyes stared right at Roberto. Shoulders heaved up and down with labored breaths, and wisps of smoke trickled overhead, gathering into a darkening fog.

"Go and spread my message of rage and hatred. Wherever you encounter anger, sow my seed. Make your way to train stations, the airport, anywhere the transmission can happen faster. A dark new day will rise, with chaos and frenzy in its wings."

Roberto wanted to gag at the words that had escaped his mouth, while the new minions dispersed on an unholy mission.

CHAPTER 17

LILY TURNED IN BED AGAIN, A RESTLESS NIGHT OF sleep leaving her drained. Finally, the clock read 6:45 AM. The luminescent numbers had mocked her all night, barely pushing forward. She had only dozed off towards the end, and now, it was time to wake up.

Groaning, she pushed herself to sitting with her left arm. The splint on the right arm kept her from putting her fracture in awkward positions while she slept, but it didn't keep her from feeling pain in the wrist.

Her body complained even more than yesterday. Aches and stiffness greeted her stretch. Road rash on her knees. Throbbing in her back. At least the headache from yesterday had subsided.

She rushed through her morning routine. How she would face school with the events of the weekend, God only knew. What kind of coverage had the events at Hyde Pier gotten? Would she be treated as a freak?

Nausea roiled in her stomach as she minimally styled her hair and dabbed only a bit of make-up on. Nothing sounded good to eat, but she decided on some toast as she finished putting on her uniform for Everett Academy.

Tromping down the stairs, she dropped her backpack on the kitchen floor. Studies were the last thing on her mind. Hopefully she didn't have any tests or homework due. She hadn't touched her books since she'd helped tear up part of a city.

"What are you doing, kitten?" Her dad looked up from his newspaper, his eyebrows raised in surprise.

"It's Monday. I don't have a superhero get-out-of-class card, so I have to go." She fumbled with the bread bag, her brace making it hard to manipulate the plastic.

"Sit down, Lily."

Uh-oh. Dad had set down the paper, and he kept his eyes locked on hers as she found a chair. Yesterday he had seemed okay with the Mount Sutro excursion since they were looking for SJ and he knew what that meant to her. Had he changed his mind? She sighed as her brain tried to calculate what he was going to say. Her stomach began to quiver with anxiety. Even the smell of fresh Kona coffee couldn't comfort her.

"I got a call from school this morning. You're not going today," he said.

She swallowed a lump. "Are they afraid of the publicity from the weekend? Were there threats?"

He sighed. "No. This has to do with what happened at the dance with Missy Austin."

"Oh, yeah." Even though the officers had talked to her about it yesterday morning, the afternoon dealing with Kashvi and Aasif and the worry for SJ had chased it from her mind.

"You're suspended indefinitely. They're planning a committee meeting to consider expulsion. I'm sorry. I know this girl pushed you and you didn't mean to cause her injury like that, and this isn't needed on top of everything else. Maybe it's a blessing in disguise to let you rest and lie low for a few days. I'll fight them on this. I was waiting for you to get up to tell you, because nothing will change for today."

She leaned back in the chair. If Lily could have held her temper for a minute longer at the dance and had not slapped Missy, this wouldn't be an issue. "I'm so sorry, Daddy. I know you pay a lot for me to go to Everett. I won't do something like this again."

Her dad got up and knelt before her. "Lily, it's not about the money. If I could take this all away from you, even the gift from God—as you call it—I would. I wish we were back when your mom and brother were still alive and we were happy. But I don't have a gift of time travel, and I do love Kelly. You will always be my sweet girl, and even when there are mistakes, I'll always be there for you.

"You rest today. Don't worry about school, superpowers, or anything else. We'll have plenty to deal with in the coming days. It's my turn to fight the battle."

Lily made his shoulder damp with her tears.

After shedding her school uniform for some shorts and a baggy tee, Lily flopped on her bed, phone in hand. Normally she would be excited to get out of school. Strangely enough, she craved some normalcy. Life was getting too weird—and difficult.

Demarcus and Harry must be in school, so she couldn't talk to them. Her school friend Clara was in class, so she wouldn't respond either. Lily had sent too many messages to SJ, all unanswered. Wherever she was, she couldn't access her phone. What could have happened? Kashvi and Aasif didn't know. Perhaps they could find this other guy and get some answers.

She realized that yesterday she didn't have a chance to check any kind of news. Swapping her phone for her laptop, she sat on her bed and booted up. Should she do official news sites or the crazy lands of Reddit, Tumblr, and other social media? She frowned at the thought that her previous favorite social media site, Flare, had crumbled at the Launch Conference when Simon Mazor tried to use her as a fiber optic booster. So many things triggered those memories for her. Even online there was nowhere she could run from the chaos.

She opted for legit news sites first. The local papers had pictures of the aftermath at Hyde Pier. A few grainy shots of waves, overexposed light blasts, and blurry images of her and her friends were in the mix. No one knew what to make of the supernatural happenings. Medical experiments gone wrong? Genetic mutations?

No one guessed they had gifts from God.

After scanning some TV and newspaper reports, she dove into the dark recesses of the internet. A few minutes later, all she could do was giggle at the outlandish things being posted. Aliens! Ancient beings! Greek gods! And even more aliens! The wild theories made her laugh until she thought she'd wet herself.

Wow, she hadn't laughed like that in a while. A heaviness fell off her and she felt like a teen again for a few minutes. A teen with a sucking wound in her chest, but lighter than she had been before reading these cuckoo opinions.

There was a cool video of Kashvi's tsunami wave roaring in from Alcatraz and Lily's burst from the lighthouse taking it out. That brought a smile—someone capturing her handiwork.

After a while, her eyes blurred from all the material online. This was all old, regurgitated stuff. She needed fresh news, some front-line information that she could share with her friends. Maybe they'd be able to use Harry and his ability to intercept something in progress.

What about Ji-young Kim?

She'd already tipped them off about Kashvi and Aasif. What else might she know?

Lily couldn't dash off a message fast enough. She jumped up and changed into workout pants and a long-sleeve shirt to be ready for anything. Pulling her long blonde hair into a messy ponytail, she paced her room, waiting for the notification to sound.

As soon as she heard the chime, she dove on her bed to check.

Yes! Ji-young didn't disappoint.

What happened with the other powered teens?

Lily tapped out an explanation of their confrontation and tentative peace, then threw out her own question. *We need to find our friend Sarah Jane. She disappeared Saturday night. Kashvi and Aasif didn't have answers. A man named Roberto Pearce was the one controlling them. That's all we got.*

Lily's thumbs froze as her mind pieced things together. The rest she typed quickly: *Simon Mazor was at the scene as well and disappeared at some point. Do you have any information coming in about strange things continuing? Is there anything going on?*

The reply was nearly instantaneous. *You have no idea.*

CHAPTER 18

SUNLIGHT STREAMED THROUGH DEMARCUS'S WINDOW. He'd been watching the sky slowly brightening until the beams hit him in the face and he had to turn away. Sleep continued to elude him.

Mama knocked at his door. "Demarcus, you awake?"

He leaned up on his elbow. Being up an hour counted. "Yep. Come on in."

His mom slipped into his messy room with a plate of steaming eggs and toast. No bacon though—he'd have smelled that from downstairs. She sat on the edge of his bed and handed him the plate. He adjusted to a sitting position and poked at his food.

"It must be bad if you're not inhaling that," Mama observed, her head cocked in an investigative manner.

After the meeting with Pastor Sanchez at the church, he'd explained the afternoon to her. She wasn't thrilled about him going right back out into conflict, but at least she'd picked up on their anguish in not knowing where Sarah Jane was. He'd half expected to witness an explosion in his living room, but Mama had been measured in her response, just pointing him to bed.

Demarcus sighed. "I just can't get over how bad I've screwed up. Last night we hopefully solved the mystery of the other powered teens that fought us, but we're no closer to finding Sarah Jane. Harry's so angry he could burst. I don't know what to do."

Mama straightened up, which made him subconsciously do the same. "Demarcus, I saw how exhausted you were last night, so I didn't say anything then. If you want to see a freaked-out mother, that would have been me yesterday after learning about all your hijinks. But hearing how you'd helped these poor kids who'd been through even worse, I had to wrestle with something.

"I pray one day you'll have kids, and you'll know what it means to be driven crazy. As a mother, I have to wrestle with knowing my child is going out into the world, and if I taught you right, at some point you're going to take on injustice or stand up for what's right, even when it's dangerous. I didn't think it would be with superpowers, but here we are."

Her voice faltered while tears threatened to spill from her eyes. "And that's the love paradox—I'm so proud of what you're trying to do and scared to death of losing my baby at the same time.

"You want to know what you're going to do? You're going to go out there and face your problems head on, with wisdom and humility. But humility isn't being meek. It's standing for the truth. You made mistakes—great, because we all make them. You're going to learn from them, and when it's time to stand strong, you're going to do the right thing. Because that's who God made you to be. If there's anyone born to be heroic, it's you."

Demarcus had to sniff back tears as well. He stood and wrapped his mother in a long embrace. Then he whispered, "Thanks, Mama. Only because you taught me right."

She took a step back and caught his shoulders in her strong grip. "You better believe I taught you right. No boy of mine going to sit in bed and skulk around. No sir, he's going to school, and then he's going to save his friend." She wagged a finger at him.

A smile broke out on his face. "Yes, ma'am."

———

Demarcus was just out the garage door when Harry popped in front of him, making him stumble back against Mama's car.

"Dude! What are you doing? Maybe a text next time?"

Harry looked around and pulled Demarcus down low, as if they were sneaking through enemy territory. His greasy hair flopped in front of his eyes. "I can't believe we didn't think of it before—we need to investigate at Hyde Pier. See if we can find any clues on what happened to Sarah Jane."

Was his friend sleep-deprived? "I thought we were going to wait until we heard from Pastor Sanchez. The plan was we'd go to school and regroup tonight."

Frantic hands grabbed Demarcus's shirt. "Can we wait until tonight? And are you up to doing school today? How can we sit still when we're needed?"

He had a point there. School was going to be the biggest drag ever today. There was no way he'd be paying attention at all.

How often could he get away with going behind Mama's back? Thankfully, she was accepting of his gift and the need to help Sarah Jane. Would this be pushing it too much? His mind swam with arguments and counters.

Another thought...would they be able to find anything after a day of police, FBI, and whatever other secretive government agency scouring the area? Maybe that gave Harry's idea urgency. Once the feds searched the place, there may be nothing to find. His face flushed at the idea of disappointing Mama, but time seemed critical.

"Okay, I'll go for a while. We just need to be..."

They appeared in an alleyway where the scent of salt water and garbage mixed.

"... careful."

Demarcus gave Harry a shove. "Man, you've got to start warning a guy. I've still got my school backpack. I don't want to have to worry about my stuff. And I promised Mama I'd do school today."

"Give it here." Harry took the bag when Demarcus handed it over, blinked away, and reappeared in just a few seconds' time. He was getting more skilled with his ability, for sure. Even with his speed, Demarcus could be jealous of what Harry could do.

Looking around, Demarcus tried to get his bearings. They were in a narrow alley framed by tall buildings. They must be near the ocean, because he could make out the salty scent over the garbage odor.

"Where are we?"

Harry tapped the smart watch designed by Ratchet on his wrist. "I dialed in an alley a couple blocks away from the Hyde Pier park. We'll go act natural and retrace our steps, see what comes up."

Without any better ideas, Demarcus shrugged and motioned toward the street. Hopefully they would find something useful, or at least let Harry feel like they were doing something. They turned on the sidewalk and headed down Beach Street toward Hyde Street. No big, just two teens who should be in class, trying to track a missing friend through a supernatural battlefield.

And battlefield was the word for it when they turned the corner. Yellow tape marked off the area from the park to the pier. Black vehicles interspersed with police cruisers were parked along the perimeter. The sound of a helicopter overhead caught their attention for a moment.

In the daylight, the damage was so much more impressive. The overturned trolley car that Rosa had launched lay in the grassy area. Ground had been churned up in the park. Glass shards were strewn across the sidewalks, along with brick and concrete debris.

"Oh man, did we make a mess," Harry said. "My allowance is so far from being able to cover the bill."

They doubled back to a small walkway behind the large building bordering Hyde Street so they could get closer to the pier. They walked down Jefferson as far as they could until more blockades stopped them. The shops on the corner facing the pier had the worst damage. Scorch marks from Lily's blasts were evident on a few of the walls.

Interesting things from Kashvi's water powers were scattered as well. Dead fish and mussels were still on the road. The bench that almost decapitated Demarcus sat unharmed, but other structures weren't as lucky. Cars, mopeds, and bikes were mangled.

Demarcus whispered to his friend, "Did you realize we could be so destructive?"

"Not really. You and I aren't bad, but Lily and those Corrupted kids can deal out the damage," Harry replied.

"I think we own some of this."

Harry nodded. "Of course. With great power, blah, blah, blah. I guess you never see Spider-Man dealing with the aftermath of his battles."

"What do we do now?"

They crossed Jefferson to get a better view of the park across the street. "Everything happened too fast. I don't remember it all." Harry pointed at the park. "I think Sarah Jane spent most of her time in the park. We brought people to her to help, so she stayed out of the worst of the fray."

"You're right. But look at the official-looking dudes working over the area. They had all day Sunday, and they're still checking things out. How would we even get in there?"

Harry ducked under the yellow tape. "I'm not going to think about things too hard. Let's just take a quick look. We can just blink out of there if needed."

"Dude! We can't be using our powers like that. If there's no choice, I get it, but not in broad daylight," Demarcus answered in a forced whisper.

"Are you coming or not?" Harry motioned for him to follow.

"Only to keep you out of trouble."

The "Do Not Cross" barrier scraped against Demarcus's dreadlocks. *So, just act nonchalant while wandering around a crime scene?*

Harry made a beeline to some bushes. "I remember Sarah Jane hanging out here for a lot of the battle." They looked on the ground, but there were just trampled flowers and flattened grass.

Demarcus knelt alongside his friend, then looked up and froze. Agents surrounded the area where John had fallen on the far side of the park. Their mentor's last breaths, taken right there. He thought of the last words John had spoken to them: "Be strong, stay humble, and seek the light."

Oh John, how do we do that and save our friend?

Harry hurried over to the upside-down trolley. The roof had been crushed in the landing, and it sat tilted and embedded in the dirt of the park. "Demarcus—a torn part of her skirt." He held up a scrap of floral fabric.

In a flash Demarcus was beside him. "Any sign of a struggle? Any other clues?" He bent down, looking around carefully for anything. Which was all he knew to look for. Who were they kidding? They weren't trackers. "What are we even doing? We have no idea what we're looking for."

Demarcus got no response from his friend, who crawled on his hands and knees, trying to pick up on anything helpful. Demarcus crouched, scanning the area. Then Harry jumped forward and snatched up an item. "Some kind of bracelet. But it wasn't one Sarah Jane wore that night."

"It could be from anyone," Demarcus said. The bracelet was fashioned from interlocking pieces of polished wood. Some pictures painted on the squares had faded from wear, but they looked like saints or some kind of religious pictures. There was something familiar about it...

"What are you boys doing here?"

Demarcus spun around and Harry popped up to face an FBI agent. A woman with brown hair and intense eyes stared them down, her hands on her hips. Demarcus noted her badge: Agent Dean.

"Do you not know the meaning of barrier tape? You're not supposed to be here. C'mon, let's go before you get arrested for interfering with an investigation."

Harry almost protested, but an elbow to the ribs silenced him. "Yes, ma'am," Demarcus replied in his best respectful voice, the one he used when Mama was about to blow.

Before they got to the tape, Agent Dean stopped them and inspected them more closely. "Why did you two come here today?" Her voice remained calm, but her eyes searched their faces for the truth.

Uh-oh.

"We heard a friend was in this area Saturday night. We wanted to look around." Harry tugged on the end of his shirt as he responded.

"And you two wouldn't know anything about what happened that night, right?" She kept a laser focus on their faces, her stare locking them in place.

"Why would we?" Demarcus responded.

"Because you two resemble people of interest in the investigation. I'd like you to come with me to our staging area while we go over a few questions."

A shout from the group of officials across the park drew Agent Dean's attention. A photographer had lined up Agent Dean and the two teens with a telephoto lens. The agent waved the person away. "We told you, don't interfere with the investigation, please."

Demarcus was going to die. And his mama would kill him, even if he was already dead. *I skipped school and ended up in federal custody.*

But the scene vanished and he found himself in a strangely familiar area. Harry had ported them to a grassy campus. A plot nearby had the remains of a foundation, without any remaining walls or other structure. In the distance, abandoned dormitories brought back memories of excitement and fear.

"You teleported us away in front of an agent and a photographer? And you brought us to...the Alturas campus?" He smacked Harry's shoulder. "What are you thinking?"

Harry sucked in heavy breaths. "I know, I panicked. This was the only thing that popped into my head—the place I started to learn how to control my power."

All Demarcus could do was roll his eyes. "Yeah, this is a great place for us to hide out. Another area where we helped demolish things." He could still feel the floor giving way as he rescued Kelsey, Simon Mazor's intern, from the collapsing headquarters. They had barely made it out alive.

It had been quite a year so far.

"What do we do now, genius? The feds know what we look like, and we disappeared right in front of them. You could have waited it out more."

"Sorry, it was my first time dealing with the FBI. I said I panicked. But I still have this." He held up the bracelet, turning it in the light so that the portraits were more visible.

And the Alturas campus brought back a memory of where it came from.

"Dude, I know where I've seen that bracelet before."

Harry's eyes bugged out. "Where?"

"I saw this when we were at the Launch Conference. On the wrist of Rosa Gonzalez."

CHAPTER 19

ANOTHER DAY WAS WASTING AWAY AND STILL SIMON'S eyes weren't healed. Sarah Jane continued to fight any attempt at coercion. Even though he had threatened her family, his stomach wasn't up for something so drastic. Thoughts pinged around inside his head, wrestling with his circumstances. Bile rose in his throat as he considered how much damage he would be responsible for in his quest to change the world. The revelation that Sarah Jane had been resurrected at the Launch Conference rocked him.

At the time, he had feared the Archai and what they would do if he failed. That's why he'd used Lily to power the Source, which would have spread his influence across fiber optic networks around the world, even at the risk of her life.

When he did fail, they discarded him. Apparently, they had other options, and he was not worth dealing with. If he went to the authorities, he would take the fall for what had happened at the conference. Simon had no leverage to pin things on the Archai.

Without the consequence of failing the Archai as his motivation, he couldn't work up the conviction to follow through with a threat to the girl's family, even if it meant not regaining his eyes and his gift. Now it was a standoff. Simon had Sarah Jane as a prisoner, which would be charged as another felony if he was ever caught. And the girl had leverage over him.

What could he do to break through?

A soft crying sound came from the bedroom. Something pulled at him to try and soothe her. With his gift he'd been able to calm people in the past. Certainly, Sarah Jane had no interest in him trying to offer comfort.

Rosa pushed through the apartment door with her arms full of grocery totes. He'd expected to be in this small suite downtown for just a day, so he hadn't bothered to stock it with supplies before everything imploded around him. He'd only managed to keep it with some hacking that involved a false identity and a slush fund he was able to access. In his tech CEO days, it was helpful to have a place to crash in the city instead of fighting the traffic to the Alturas HQ. He never imagined using it for kidnapping.

"How much longer do we have to put up with her?" Rosa sneered as she put away the food.

"You know. Once she's healed my eyes, she will be released and we'll be on our way."

"I'm tired of her crying. We all got messed up by that creature the other night, and you're not doing anything bad to her. She doesn't have anything to complain about."

Simon shouldn't have been surprised by her callous response, but it still took him back. Rosa's background had been full of tragedy. With her history of abuse, she was so easy to control, even with his deficiency due to his visual loss. All that hurt meant he could keep his ties on her. Unfortunately, her damaged psyche also left her volatile. That's why he couldn't stop her when she threw Sarah Jane off the roof of his headquarters.

A package bounced off him. He picked up a plastic bag, the crinkle of the wrapper a familiar sound. His brand of gummy bears. A rueful chuckle escaped his lips as he put the bag aside. So much for his superstition about different colors of gummy bears. He'd always held to different ones being lucky or unlucky. Now it was hard to tell the difference, so what did it matter?

Sarah Jane called out from the bedroom. "Hey, I need to use the bathroom again if it's all right with my captors." Sarcasm dripped from the words.

Rosa snarled and started for the room. "I will get her to help you. A few broken bones and we'll be done with her."

Rosa's fear from Saturday night had bled off, and her habitual anger had returned in full force. Simon stood up and blocked her way. "No, you don't get to hurt her again. What if that messes up her gift? We just need to be patient and she'll relent soon enough."

For a moment, even though Simon stared down on the shorter woman, he thought she might toss him through a wall. He poured his strength into influencing her to calm down.

Conceding the mental battle, Rosa went back to the kitchenette, grabbed a mango, and proceeded to cut it. "There's got to be a way to hurry this up. I can't promise patience with her or you for very long," she said as she popped a piece of the golden fruit in her mouth.

The scent brought back memories of work at Alturas. One of his assistants loved mangos and always had a lotion with that aroma floating around during work, which included prepping for the Launch Conference and finding the gifted youth to help him influence the world…

Kelsey. The one who did the research on Sarah Jane Langley prior to the conference. Kelsey had pushed inviting Sarah Jane, despite how her potential scores came through on the computer.

Maybe if Simon could find Kelsey, he could get information that would help him crack open his stubborn guest. He'd lost so much research when Alturas was closed for investigation, but Kelsey had a great memory—especially for people.

As fast as he could, Simon made it to the table and fired up his laptop. Like the rest of his immediate staff, she'd moved on after the disaster at the conference. But he was sure it wouldn't take long to track her down.

He was right. It didn't take two minutes to find her. She now served as a social media staffer with the local professional football team. That left her digital footprints so easy to follow online. He could track her position, know what she was doing both professionally and personally if he needed it. And what was even better was that there would be a game tonight in nearby Santa Clara.

Simon marveled at teams keeping names like "San Francisco" when they played in a stadium forty-five minutes away from the actual city. That was beside the point—no doubt Kelsey would be at the stadium doing work online for the team.

"Rosa, I have another mission for you. It will help you burn some energy and allow us to finish with Sarah Jane sooner. What's your favorite football team?"

CHAPTER 20

LILY COULDN'T KEEP UP WITH THE INFORMATION Ji-young shot her way. There were conspiracy theories about a cover-up at Alturas. Mysterious new gangs were attacking people downtown. A political protest was turning violent. It made her head swim.

Where do you get your information? Lily typed out as best she could.

The stream of links stopped for a response. *It's taken me a few years to develop contacts. If you make friends with the people on the streets, it's amazing what they pick up. Cops, homeless, trolley drivers, IT workers—they all have their perspective. There's a lot of scouring through junk though.*

Some of the material Lily skimmed seemed like garbage still, but it wasn't her job to critique. *What do you make of all this?*

The blinking dots showing Ji-young was responding kept Lily on the edge of her chair. She clutched her coffee in her left hand, sipping the life-giving elixir awkwardly. Man, she took her right hand for granted.

There's more going on than just you guys. Too much coincidence. But how does it tie together? So much chatter!

Lily realized that Ji-young didn't see the connection between the Alturas Collective, the Launch Conference, and their super group. They still didn't know Ji-young at all, just that she was an unconventional journalist whom they had rescued two nights ago. But at this point, they needed allies, even ones that may not fully grasp the consequences of what was happening.

Can we talk? I've got some things to share, and I can't type well enough with my wrist. Lily finished with her cell number, then waited for either a ring or silence indicating she had chased the journalist off. Hopefully the reporter's curiosity kept her on the hook.

Lily's phone vibrated and chirped. She fumbled it in her left hand. "Hello?"

"Color me intrigued. What's your story? And can I have the exclusive?"

Maybe this was a bad idea. "Look, right now we're trying to figure out where my friend is and if any of the weirdness going on has something to do with it. What is it when it can't be official…can we be off the record? Then we can talk about things with my friends and decide. I don't think it's fair to them to give secrets away without their consent."

"That makes sense."

Lily said a silent prayer of thanks that she'd dodged that bullet. Then she told the story of the Launch Conference, John, and how the incidents of the last couple of weeks connected behind the scenes. She felt exposed, spilling the background of her gift and how the Anointed came to be to a stranger, especially one who had been investigating them just a couple days before.

After Lily finished, silence. She glanced at her phone to make sure she hadn't lost connection. Nope, she was still on the line. "Ji-young? Are you there?"

Finally, a stammering voice replied. "I-I had no idea. You think you're on to something as a reporter, and then you hit THIS. I just never expected …"

"Okay, cool. I get that. But what can we do with this information now that you have more of the puzzle?"

"The attack on Saturday night had sightings of some kind of 'smoke monster,'" Ji-young began. Lily's heart raced at the mention of the foul thing. The way it had looked at her and made her collapse—it was painfully similar to Simon's power. "There are reports of smoke and haze associated with some of the violence and gang activity. Maybe that's a connection."

"That would make sense." Lily let her right hand flash as bright as it would go. What would it take to defeat that thing?

"Uh, you're not going to believe this."

Lily turned off her power and thrummed her fingers against her head. "What now?"

"Video with clear facial shots of Demarcus and Harry at the scene at Hyde Pier just now. They were being questioned by an agent, and then they disappeared. Best video I've seen of that trick yet." Ji-young let out a low whistle.

Now what? Lily tried to keep her imagination from running away with her temper, contemplating what those two boys could be up to. Instead of school, apparently her friends were getting in trouble with the law. Lily responded with a facepalm emoji.

CHAPTER 21

THE YOUTH GROUP ROOM FELT OUT OF PLACE WITH Kashvi and Aasif there. Demarcus thought about the times the Anointed had discussed how to stop the two of them when they were battling each other. Now the pair sat on the orange vinyl couch, both looking uncomfortable with Pastor Sanchez out of the room as he handled some church business.

Harry appeared with Lily. Her glare made Demarcus want to curl up in the corner. Oh man, she could bring the stare-down if needed. Then she noticed their guests and changed her demeanor, going over to them and asking how they were doing. His concern over her death stare melted as she showed compassion to the Corrup—the other powered kids.

Demarcus knelt at John's spot in front of the couch. John's Middle Eastern background had him sitting on the ground more often than he ever used the furniture. It always amazed Demarcus how John could do so much at his age. Of course, no one knew his age. Demarcus wondered if the elder was older than he let on.

As he gazed down at the worn carpet, Lily sat next to him. "So, do you want to explain why you and Harry are blowing up online? Teleporting from Hyde Pier today? In broad daylight?"

No wonder he got the glare.

Pastor Sanchez entered and shut the door behind him. "Hey gang, how are things going? How did school go for you three?"

Demarcus wanted to sink into the ground. Lily gave him a nudge with her elbow. "Yes, tell us about school today." The sarcasm dripped from her voice.

His hesitation caught Pastor Sanchez's attention. "What happened?"

Well, time to fess up. "Harry and I went to San Francisco to search for clues regarding Sarah Jane's disappearance. It may not have gone as well as we wanted."

"What does that mean?" The pastor cocked his head to the side in curiosity.

Harry interrupted. "It was my idea. There was no way I would focus on school, so I made Demarcus go to Hyde Pier to look for clues about Sarah Jane. We got noticed by a federal agent in the park there. But I got us out of there before they got our identities."

Lily coughed. "I couldn't go to school today because I hit a girl at the dance and my power burned her. I spent time talking to Ji-young about things going on in the area that might help us. She's got a lot of contacts, and she found high-definition pictures of Demarcus and Harry from today. There was also video of them disappearing. There's speculation going on about who they are."

Pastor Sanchez rubbed his shaved head. "None of you went to school, then?"

"I tried," Lily countered.

"Is that why I got the dagger look when you arrived?" Demarcus whispered to her. She narrowed her eyes and nodded.

"This is what you do to find your friend?" Aasif asked. "You sit around and discuss how your day went? If she is so important, why aren't you out there right now?"

Kashvi tried to restrain Aasif. "Hey, they've got lives they have to deal with."

Harry was up and almost in Aasif's face. "Don't you dare talk to me about her importance. If it weren't for you guys, we wouldn't have been there Saturday night when she disappeared. I'll tear this town apart if I have to."

Pastor Sanchez jumped between them. "Hey guys, chill out. Everyone's upset."

Demarcus whisked Harry to the corner of the room. "It's okay. We will figure this out."

But instead of cooling down, Harry pushed him. "Dude, back off," Harry muttered.

A storm brewed inside the small youth room and Demarcus had no idea how to calm it. He balled his fists for a moment, fighting the urge to shove Harry back.

"That's enough now," Pastor Sanchez said.

Harry shook his head and stepped away from Demarcus instead of charging back toward Aasif.

Pastor Sanchez took a deep breath. "Okay, Kashvi, Aasif, since we're in my church, I'm going to take a minute to pray. Then we'll talk about specifics we can do to end this situation."

Both of them nodded, although Demarcus noted Aasif keeping his eye on Harry. Pastor Sanchez bowed his head and made impassioned pleas for Sarah Jane, for the chaos in the city, and for all of them in the room to focus on what's important. Demarcus had to rub his chest to distract himself from the raw area burning in his chest during the prayer. The pain made it impossible for him to fully focus, although he tried to intercede for Harry's sake.

When the prayer ended, Kashvi took some shallow breaths, her hand across her sternum. "Are you all feeling this? Ever since Roberto attacked us, the pain blossoming in my heart is worse. I see you doing similar things as me, trying to rub it away."

Demarcus nodded and noticed that Lily and Harry did the same.

Lily turned to Pastor Sanchez. "Will you pray for all of us about this? It's goes from a nagging pain to stabbing and sometimes drops me to my knees."

"Of course." The pastor prayed again, asking for deliverance. Demarcus appreciated someone sharing the burden they carried. The pain eased with the intercession, but it didn't fully dissipate.

When Pastor Sanchez finished, Harry raised his hand—once again. He never caught on that they weren't in school. "We did find something that could be useful. This bracelet, Demarcus remembers Rosa wearing it, and we found it at the park near the upside-down trolley."

"Who is this Rosa?" Kashvi asked.

"She was at the Launch Conference with us and has gifts as well. She's got super strength. It seems she's in league with Simon Mazor, the guy who ran the conference and was the head of the Alturas Collective," Lily replied. "We thought she died at the conference, until she appeared Saturday night. For that matter, everyone thought Simon had died too."

Kashvi had worn a nervous look all evening but softened at the mention of Simon. "Ah yes, the hot young billionaire."

Rolling her eyes so hard she might sprain them, Lily sighed. "Yeah, I used to think he was hot too. But once a tycoon tries to suck the life out of you, it changes your opinion." She turned to Harry. "This is an avenue we haven't checked yet. We know Rosa and Simon were there, but what do we do with that? How could we find Simon?"

Maybe their trip downtown wasn't wasted. "You remember Simon's tall assistant with the goatee? Otto? I wonder if he might know anything," Demarcus offered.

A shudder trickled over Lily.

"What's wrong?" he asked.

"It was Otto and the other main assistant, Kelsey, that strapped me into the Source before it nearly killed me. I'm not super excited to see them again. But, if it means finding SJ, then let's do it."

Harry was already on his phone doing a search. Demarcus and Lily were right behind him. Pastor Sanchez too. Now it was a race, and not one Demarcus would automatically win.

"Okay, I found Kelsey. She's with the social media team for the Niners." Lily raised her phone in victory.

"And Otto has moved to a start-up tech company that has a social event tonight. I not only found his location, but when we can catch him. Boom." Harry dropped his phone like a mic. When it bounced off the carpet, he turned red. "I didn't mean to do that."

The speedster comes in last. Wait, it was Monday during football season. What if?

Demarcus could only search so fast on his phone because his keyboard couldn't keep up with his flying fingers. But he remembered some hype about a home game tonight. Normally he'd be all over the schedule, but the last two weeks had totally distracted him.

"You guys aren't going to believe this," Pastor Sanchez said. "The Niners are hosting a game tonight against the Seahawks. Santa Clara isn't far. You should be able to find Kelsey tonight."

Foiled again. How are these guys beating the fast one? Demarcus sighed to himself.

"Okay, so how are we going to do this? Two things on one night, and it's our best chance to find these two when we know where they're going to be," Harry said.

Demarcus pointed at Lily and Harry. "We probably need to split up, but I don't like the idea of one of us being alone. We've learned the hard way that having back-up is important."

Before anyone else could jump in, Kashvi cleared her throat. "You don't have to go alone. We want to help, to make up for the hurt our actions have caused. Include us in your plans."

Lily sat by her. "Are you sure? We know you were being controlled by Roberto, so you weren't really at fault."

Kashvi nodded. "We talked before coming tonight. Pastor Sanchez was wise in bringing us here, thinking we needed to be around others like us to figure out what's going on. And if we were part of this mess, even if manipulated, we can help with it."

No words from Aasif, but he nodded to concur.

"That's awesome. I think we should have the two of you in separate groups." Lily motioned towards Aasif and Harry. "And we'll need Demarcus and Harry heading different teams, because they're our transportation."

Demarcus shot a wounded look at Lily.

"You know you're more than that, it's just a way to explain it. How else do we break it down?"

Harry piped up again. "I had a good conversation with Otto at the conference. I have a shot at getting through to him."

"I rescued Kelsey before Simon's headquarters collapsed, so that should give me an in with her. Plus, it's the football game. I'm down for that." Demarcus couldn't help a grin at the thought. Saving Sarah Jane was the priority but checking out his first pro action on the side wouldn't hurt.

"How will we find her there? There will be tens of thousands of people at that stadium," Lily asked. Good, she wanted to come with him.

Aasif stood up. "You said I should not be part of his team," he pointed to Harry, "and I agree. Another thing is I can isolate sound. If I hear a sample of this woman's voice, I can track her down, even in the stadium. We will find her and get the answers we need."

"That's a pretty cool trick." Lily grinned.

"It's how we tracked you when hunting." His deadpan expression made her quirk an eyebrow.

Pastor Sanchez cleared his throat. "As the adult in the room, I feel like I should be making plans. But I have to admit, you're all doing a good job of figuring out your strengths and weaknesses. Before you head out, though, I've got a requirement.

"You guys need to keep in contact with me. You said that not listening to John was a mistake. This way you have some adult supervision." He caught the eye of each one of them with a look that said he was serious.

"Another suggestion would be to have Harry teleport the group to the stadium, because you're going to have to get through the entrance. A pastor's salary won't spring for last-minute tickets.

"Oh, and you'll need camouflage. Luckily, my wife and I should be able to provide some of that for you." A twinkle in his eye made Demarcus cringe.

"You don't mean—" he started.

Pastor Sanchez flashed a wicked smile. There was some mischief in that man. "Oh, I do."

CHAPTER 22

DEMARCUS AND HARRY APPEARED IN AN EMPTY STALL. The smell from the toilet made Demarcus gag. "Dude, what are you thinking putting us in a bathroom?"

"I'm thinking we're lucky it wasn't occupied. Where else are we going to show up without someone seeing us? Now go block the door so I can deliver the others," Harry snapped.

Pulling the door open as Harry vanished, Demarcus stepped out and tried to look inconspicuous, which was hard to do in a men's room with guys milling in and out. Angry tones, hushed but still audible, came from the stall. Then Aasif walked out of it.

"Wait, is he planning on bringing Lily here too?" Demarcus asked.

Aasif shrugged, and a feminine gasp sounded. Lily hissed Harry's name, but the slight warping of air in the stall signaled Harry's hasty retreat. The door cracked open ever so slightly and a blue eye peeked out.

"Did he really drop me off in the *men's room*?"

Both Demarcus and Aasif whispered, "Yup."

A squeak escaped her lips. "You guys are going to have to shield me to get me out of here."

Demarcus would have loved to tease Lily about this any other day. Today was not that day. He and Aasif shuffled along with Lily ducking behind them, hands over her eyes. Only a couple of guys turned their heads as she passed. They spilled out of the doorway and Lily was as red as her shirt. Now it was up to the three of them to find their lead. Hopefully Kelsey had useful information to track down Simon.

First, Demarcus had to come to terms with being decked out in someone else's colors. How could he live this down as a diehard Cowboys fan? His red t-shirt and gold shorts were not him at all. Maybe if he pretended it was Iron Man cosplay it wouldn't be so bad.

Lily looked like a gold-tinged rose with her oversized jersey and leggings. Aasif didn't seem to care about his fan attire. His eyes shifted, taking the scenery in. "You're sure we're okay in here? We're not going to get in trouble?"

"We're in, and I don't think they check your tickets on the inside. If we don't steal seats, we shouldn't be noticed." A loud group dressed in blue and green passed by, obnoxiously calling out the home team fans. Boos and shouts followed them like a wake. Demarcus was surprised at the animosity between the groups. He had always dealt in light-hearted banter with friends who liked rival teams.

Maybe it would be different if he were in Dallas. At least it wasn't a Raiders game. The stories he heard about when they were still around were freaky.

The concourse was a cement pathway with red painted cinder blocks creating the inner wall. Steel girders rose from the edge of the stadium, giving an open-air view of the stadium parking lot, filled with cars. The smell of beer and burgers filled the air, making Demarcus wish he'd eaten more before coming here.

Aasif seemed oblivious to the scenery but focused on his task—isolating Kelsey from all the noise around them. Just then a roar came from the field and Aasif winced in pain. The home team must have had a good play. Would the crazy amount of noise affect him?

"Did that bother you?" Demarcus asked.

Aasif shook his head for a minute. "If I'm searching for a sound then it hurts to get a huge rush like that. I won't let it stop me."

"Thanks, Aasif. We appreciate it."

Luckily Demarcus still had a video from the Launch Conference where Kelsey had spoken to the attendees in orientation. Aasif was confident that he could track their target from that sample, if they could survive the masses here in one piece.

Aasif led them to the outer edge of the concourse and they followed. He was the lead at the moment, and they didn't have much choice except to trust him. Hopefully his reform was genuine.

"How's your arm?" Demarcus leaned in to check with Lily. She'd been guarding her arm to keep it from getting bumped by the crowd.

"I think fine. It hurts, and I'm careful using it. It's not going to keep me from doing what I need to do."

Demarcus sighed, but Lily didn't seem to notice. The increase in his attraction for her had been interrupted by the battle. But now she continued to impress him with her kindness and toughness.

Thinking about her injury triggered something that had been nagging him since they discussed Rosa's bracelet. "I wonder if Simon would be after Sarah Jane for healing. What if he was hurt in the collapse of his headquarters?"

"That would be a huge motivation. You might be on to something there, Sherlock." Lily's blue eyes grew wide as she spoke.

"Hey, we're going to have to go to the other side of the stadium and up a few levels. I know the general direction, and as I get closer, I'll pinpoint her," Aasif said.

"Let's go!" Demarcus had to shout over another roar from the crowd. Aasif growled as he covered his ears.

Demarcus lowered his voice. "We'll get this done so the noise doesn't drive you crazy."

The three of them wound their way through the concourse and crossed over to the other side, weaving through all the fans. It was early in the second quarter and the crowd gasped. A glimpse of a monitor showed the replay of the opponent scoring. That quieted the noise to a degree.

They climbed a set of stairs, a breeze cooling them off. Then Aasif stopped and pointed at a sign above them. They reached an area where they needed to have a certain type of pass. Now what?

"She's in one of these suites. If I can get down the hall, I will have her exact location. Do we force our way past the guards?" Aasif pointed to the two guys checking passes.

"Uh, no. We're going to do things a little less...violently. Come down here to the vendors, I have an idea." Demarcus tipped his head in the other direction. They found a spot along a wall to discuss their next strategy.

"Okay, I can zip us by these guys one at a time, but it would be easier with a diversion or two. Can you guys do something?" Demarcus said.

Aasif cleared his throat. "I've been wanting to practice this. Get ready."

Demarcus put his arm around Lily's waist, and she wrapped her arm behind his back. His face warmed at the closeness. Mission first, dude.

Aasif started a countdown with his fingers. At two, he opened his mouth as if he were talking, but no sound came out. What new trick was he doing? Then he held up one finger and pointed past the guards. Demarcus flashed by them with Lily, her blonde ponytail fluttering past his ear.

The attendants had confused looks on their face once Demarcus zipped back to Aasif. "What did you do?"

"I threw my voice and made it sound official. I thought it would work." A rare smile rose on his face.

"Good job, my man." Demarcus noticed Lily catching his attention. She began the same countdown with her hand. "I guess that's our signal to get ready. You okay with me running you past?"

"Seeing as we battled before, this seems minor. It's what we need to do," Aasif said.

At one, Lily pointed at the light above the attendants. The brightness flashed and Demarcus took that as his cue. One more dash, and they were all past the checkpoint. The poor attendants were trying to figure out why they were hallucinating different sounds and visual changes.

At least it made their day more interesting.

Aasif squinted in concentration as they walked down the concourse. There weren't as many people here, and the ones they passed wore nicer clothes, still decked out in the red and gold theme. A couple of people gave them a second glance, but no one challenged their presence.

A third of the way down the concourse Aasif stopped. "She's here." He pointed to the suite to their right. "In fact, sounds like she's coming out right now." Perfect timing.

The door opened and a familiar brunette exited onto the concourse, a smart phone in her hands. She turned back toward the door and called out, "Yeah, I'll get this posted right away."

Lily stepped forward. "Hey Kelsey, we need to talk to you for a minute. Do you remember us?"

Kelsey looked up from her phone in annoyance, but once her eyes darted from Lily to Demarcus and back, her mouth gaped and she froze. Then she slowly shut the door, saying "I'll have to get back to you in a second. I've... got something to deal with first."

CHAPTER 23

LILY REGRETTED TAKING THE LEAD IN TALKING TO Kelsey. The sight of the woman triggered her heart to race and set her palms sweating. The last time she had seen Kelsey was on the rooftop of Simon Mazor's headquarters on the Alturas campus, when they attempted to drain the life from her body. She knew Kelsey had been under Simon's thrall, but it didn't change the reflexive response.

"I—what are you two doing here? I never thought I'd see you again." The color drained from Kelsey's face. "I never wanted to see you again." She gulped, as tears welled up and dribbled down her cheeks.

Lily tried to say something, but her tongue lay heavy in her mouth, unmoving. She had to force her breathing to slow. It wasn't the best idea for her to come.

In the stalemate of silence, apparently Demarcus figured out the problem. He glanced at Lily and jumped in. "Hey Kelsey. We've got an emergency, and we hoped you could help. This seemed the only way to track you down."

Lily sucked in a slow breath. Calm down, girl. She's as scared as you are. Then a nudge hit her arm. Demarcus whispered, "Do you want to turn off the light show?"

She held her hand up, and her skin glowed. Snap, she had to watch that connection with her emotions.

As Lily turned the glow off, Kelsey began to speak. "I'm so sorry. So, so sorry. I feel so horrible about what happened. You have to understand, it was Simon's fault. I didn't know I was under his control. I didn't mean to hurt you."

Emotions roiled inside Lily. She wanted to vomit. She wanted to blast Simon off another roof. *God, please help me. I'm not strong enough.* The ache in her chest flared, radiating into her stomach, and it made her bend and clutch her midsection.

A voice whispered in her mind. *Forgive her.*

What? How could she do that? The panic in her mind spilled past her barriers. It was too much to ask. She'd thought her faith had grown so much, that she'd dealt with the chaos from the Launch Conference. But now her heart pounded so fast, worsening the effect of the void inside. Kelsey's actions had nearly killed her. Forgiveness couldn't be that easy, right?

You were forgiven.

The quiet thought landed in her heart like a detonation. Lily had been forgiven so much. She had believed that she killed Simon and Rosa at Launch, even though it was in self-defense, and she had received grace. She remembered the image of a being of light embracing her on the roof when she thought her power was going to consume her. The infusion of peace at that moment had changed her life.

How could she withhold a similar release from Kelsey?

Lily reached her sweaty hands out and took Kelsey's. The words faltered for a moment, but she had to do this. "Hey, I know it was not your fault. Simon had a power that affected us all. I—I forgive you." A few tears trickled down Lily's cheek.

Demarcus stepped up and put a hand on the crying woman's shoulder. "I forgive you too."

A burden fell from Lily's heart, and the pain that chewed inside of her relaxed a bit. She let out a slow breath. "That was traumatic for all of us. But there's a pressing reason why we tracked you down. I think Simon's still alive, and he's got Sarah Jane."

Kelsey wiped her eyes and frowned. "The healer?"

"Right. We think he's taken her for some reason. Maybe he was hurt in the collapse of his headquarters, and he's trying to get healed. Have you heard from him at all? Do you know any place he may have gone? Did he have any other home or lab besides the Alturas campus?"

Kelsey gestured for them to step to the side along the wall. The noise from the stadium swelled. The crowd must be getting excited for the home team. "I haven't heard anything from him. It seemed he was dead, like the reports said. He did have an apartment in downtown San Francisco if he was socializing late. I always thought it was strange since the Alturas campus wasn't that far away, but he liked the idea of having a place in the city."

"Can you give me the address?"

Kelsey fumbled with her phone as she pulled it up. Her hands still trembled from the confrontation. As Lily waited, Aasif kept searching the hall, a frown on his face.

"What's wrong, Aasif?" Lily asked.

"If you're worried about getting kicked out, I'll cover for you if anyone asks. Though I'm curious how you made it to this section without the right passes," Kelsey said.

"I'm not worried about being caught. There's some strange commotion, and I can't figure it out," Aasif said.

"There you go." Kelsey looked down at her phone, and a chime sounded on Lily's device. She flicked her cracked screen and confirmed the message had arrived. Finally, a strong lead on Simon. Lily's heart skipped a beat. If she had had such a reaction to Kelsey, what would happen when she confronted the man who used her and tried to kill her?

Kelsey pulled Lily into a hug. "I thought I was going to faint when I saw you. That time in my life haunts my dreams. It's a relief to know you're okay and to have your forgiveness. Thank you."

"You're welcome. I'm glad it worked out like this." There was an awkward pause in the conversation. Lily gestured to the suite where others cheered the team on. "Uh, is this job a good fit for you?"

"It's been good! I didn't realize how much I would enjoy the sports world." Kelsey pulled back and regarded Lily for a minute. "Hey, were you guys involved with all the stuff at the Pier? I read about flashes of light and a bunch of other crazy stuff."

Oh, boy. They were going to be notorious now. "It's kind of a long story—"

Aasif cut in, as he moved into a defensive stance. "We've got a problem."

Demarcus spun to look where Aasif pointed and growled the last name Lily wanted to hear.

"Rosa."

CHAPTER 24

THE VIEWPOINT FROM ROSA BOUNCED AROUND AS she made her way through the crowd at the stadium. Simon adjusted the glasses that he had modified to be something like a virtual reality device. Except instead of the virtual part, it was Rosa's reality. It jarred his senses to be immersed in her point of view and not have the feedback from his own balance center. His body sat at the table, but his mind thought he jostled against people. Nausea bobbed inside his stomach.

It was imperative that this operation succeed. He couldn't bear to threaten harm against Sarah Jane anymore. The pain in his chest felt like it would devour him whenever he considered severe measures. And the thought that she had died and been resurrected disturbed him. How could such a thing happen? Curiosity welled in him to find out more, and he would later. If he had the chance.

Kelsey was the only option he had at this point. He had to get to her somehow and use her research to find some key to motivate his prisoner.

At least Sarah Jane had stopped crying. Fifteen minutes ago, a sharp gasp came from the bedroom. He checked on her then, but she sat calmly on the side of the bed. Previously she had either been upset or defiant. Maybe she was thinking through her possibilities as well.

Simon almost let a prayer slip from his lips for Sarah Jane to be calmed. But that would be silly.

He turned his attention back to Rosa's reality. Why wasn't she moving? She stood in a line but was focused on her phone. His social network app, Flare, had been on pace to knock the others out of business, yet here she was, using a competitor. How quickly things can change.

She scanned hashtags that were trending locally: #gangs, #smoke, #strangehappenings, #rally.

Some disruptions were going on in the Bay Area. Again. This is why he needed to take control with his gift—to bring calm and stability to the world. If only the Launch Conference had succeeded.

Rosa stepped forward and...bought a bag of popcorn? She started walking again, tossing kernels into her mouth. Simon tapped the communication interface on his glasses. "What are you doing?"

"You paid for my ticket. I can't have popcorn with it?" The sarcasm dripped from her voice. He could influence her actions, direct her, but that angry mind resisted full submission.

"We don't have time. I need you to get her so we can finish this." Simon ran a hand through his unruly hair.

She chomped a mouthful into his ear. "Relax. She's on the other side of the stadium, so I can munch for a minute." He watched her flick a piece across the concourse and peg a fan in the ear. The woman slapped a hand over the ear and winced.

His assistant was unruly to say the least.

After a few minutes Rosa climbed some stairs, tossed the half-empty bag of popcorn in the trash, and started scanning with the app Simon had installed on her phone. Kelsey had wiped her phone, but the worm that the Alturas network had implanted was too deep to clear without destroying the phone and deleting her whole social media profile. Now Rosa would be able to pinpoint her location.

Any minute now.

He'd offer anything possible to Kelsey to win his sight back.

Rosa rounded the concourse. Kelsey was right there ahead. Then a snarl sounded from Rosa and her thoughts raced to rage. There was his target—flanked by Lily, Demarcus, and one of those other powered teens from the pier.

CHAPTER 25

THE ATMOSPHERE IN THE HALL SOURED AS ROSA rounded the bend in the concourse, a phone in her hand. She peered over the screen and sneered at the sight of Lily and Demarcus.

"What are you doing here?" Rosa didn't break stride as she continued toward them. "Are you serious? You're looking for Kelsey too?"

Lily noticed Kelsey blanch again, so she stepped forward to engage her enemy. "What do you want with her?"

"Who knows? Simon says to get Kelsey, and I'm his errand girl. Now get out of my way or someone gets hurt." She was close enough that Lily could see the black halo around the girl's head.

The stadium seemed to rumble around them. That must have been some play to make the building shake—unless it was an earthquake. It was San Francisco, after all.

Lily let her left fist shine. Demarcus took a protective stance in front of Kelsey, and Aasif snarled in response. "It's three against one, and you're not doing anything with her," Demarcus replied.

"One. Three. It doesn't matter. I'll take all comers. I don't care if you got the screamer with you today." Rosa smiled, picked up a garbage can, and threw it at them.

Aasif screamed. The force of his voice stopped the garbage can in midair, pushing it back. Trash flew across the concourse. Wrappers, cups, and leftover nachos covered the walkway. The air smelled of stale beer and artificial cheese.

Kelsey held her ears and let out a screech of her own. A super fight wouldn't help her post traumatic stress disorder, Lily guessed. "Demarcus, we need to keep Kelsey safe no matter what. Will you keep watch over her?"

He nodded. "That's probably the best idea. You be careful though."

Before they could make a move, Rosa punched the cement wall and sent debris toward them. Aasif tried to deflect it with sound again, but he reacted too slowly and a couple of chunks knocked him down. Lily made a light shield to protect Kelsey.

"Fall back. Let's get her out of here!" The lesson from Saturday at the pier was to avoid taking a stand in public again. Demarcus disappeared with Kelsey, while Lily put both hands up and set off a dizzying strobe light effect. When Rosa blocked her eyes, it gave an opening to knock her flying with a plasma blast.

"Aasif!" Lilly called. "We need to split. We don't want to have a fight in a place like this."

He pulled himself up, blood trickling from a gash along the side of his head. His eyes flamed with rage; his teeth clenched. "I don't want to retreat. I will destroy this witch."

Lily grabbed his shirt. "Not. Here. We have to think of others. Let's go."

Reluctantly he ran alongside Lily, but his attention was drawn elsewhere. "There is something strange going on here. Not just Rosa, but there's a commotion in the stadium. I do not understand, but the vibrations are very disordered."

People started streaming out of the suites, looking around in confusion. The noise of their confrontation must have carried. Now they had to dodge worried spectators, but hopefully it would slow Rosa down as well. Assuming she didn't plow straight through them.

More people poured into the next opening of the concourse; panic spread across their faces. What was going on? These people were scared and running toward Rosa?

Demarcus and Kelsey stood in the gap that allowed access to other parts of the stadium. Lily and Aasif skidded up alongside them. Her mouth dropped open.

Instead of a football game, the field was chaos. Football players and fans fought with each other, while others tried to flee from the melee. In the seats some people climbed over rows to get away from others screaming and throwing whatever they could get their hands on.

All of the angry people had black halos shimmering around their heads.

Lily's discernment gift, which allowed her to see which people were affected by evil, had happened with people under Simon's control. But this was of a magnitude beyond his capability. Of that, she was sure.

A couple reached a landing, but the woman was knocked down the cement stairs, crying in pain as she tumbled. The man with her shifted from fear to rage at his date getting thrown. Smoke flew through the air and wound around his face. The man shook for a moment before his body tensed in an attack position. He snarled and swung a wild fist at someone passing by. The woman he was with looked at him in bewilderment.

"What's going on?" Lily cried.

Demarcus shrugged. "We got here and things were going crazy."

Kelsey's hands shook. "It looks like a full-scale riot. My phone is blowing up with notifications from the social media team. Something's going on across the whole stadium."

The announcer came over the PA system, trying to establish control over the mess. First, he tried to soothe people, and then he switched to threats of legal action. But nothing swayed the disarray.

"This is what I was picking up—the growing dissonance of people panicking and screaming," Aasif said.

Demarcus pushed his way to the edge of the stairs. "It's going to be a mess getting out of here."

A man slid past them on the floor and crashed into the edge of the concourse. He lay still, probably concussed from the impact. Red pooled under his head. Lily turned around to see Rosa stomping toward them, a path cleared from the man she threw down the hall.

"Let me have Kelsey, or I will kill you all."

CHAPTER 26

DEMARCUS GOT READY TO RUN AT ROSA, BUT A SHIM-mer in the air broke in between them. The man from the pier, Roberto Pearce, appeared. Smoke wrapped around his body. Miniature bolts of lightning sparked along the tendrils of black.

The ache inside of Demarcus roared to life. The adrenaline from seeing Rosa had dampened it, but now he clutched his chest and forced himself to not kneel. He noticed the others reacting in similar ways, with Lily dropping to a knee, Aasif crying out in pain, and Rosa doubling over.

Pearce looked around at all of them, a vicious grin growing on his face. Demarcus sensed something off about the man. His neck titled at an odd angle, and the eyes darted around. But there was another thing. Instead of having intrinsic power, it was like he had been stuffed with something dark inside.

"You want to stop me? Please, go ahead and try. I would like that very much," Pearce sneered.

The night at the pier, he didn't start by using powers. It was only after he attacked each of them that he began to use abilities. Whoever this guy was, he acted more like a sponge. Or a copycat?

Demarcus tensed his muscles, ready to react. He wouldn't charge in this time. Noticing Lily's hand dangling next to his, he took it and gave her a reassuring squeeze. A sparkle of light flashed when he did, but Lily didn't seem to notice. Instead, she shot him a worried look.

"We'll stick together," he whispered.

He turned to Aasif. "Hey, let's fight as a team. He took us out one by one Saturday."

But Aasif shook his head, a glaze over his eyes. "You have no idea what he did to us. He needs to pay."

Demarcus pulled Lily and Kelsey back ten feet as Aasif let loose a terrible scream. They cupped their hands over their ears. Because they stood behind Aasif, it only made Demarcus's ears ring. Pearce's shirt rippled as if a stiff breeze had blown by, but it didn't affect the man.

Pearce raised an arm and pointed at Aasif. Black tendrils shot from his finger and wrapped around Aasif, who tried to blast the smoky coils away with another sonic blast. It wasn't enough. The darkness slithered into Aasif's open mouth, leaving him gagging and retching. Lily gasped at the horrible sight. His body convulsed as he tried to fight off whatever was happening.

His body froze. His eyelids slowly opened, revealing black orbs instead of his brown irises.

Pearce chuckled, a foul rumble that made Demarcus quiver. Aasif's eyes cleared from the full blackness, but a change in the dude's body language was unsettling. Lily leaned in and whispered, "He's got the black halo again. He's under Pearce's control."

Before Demarcus could react, Rosa punched the cement wall again, loosening a large chunk. She grabbed it and slammed it into Pearce's body. Cement fragments sprayed out and dust filled the air. The man stumbled a few steps before catching himself. Besides a tear in his jacket, there was no sign of damage.

Lily called out a warning. "Rosa, get out of there!"

Demarcus realized too late what was happening. He rushed forward to snatch Rosa away but caught only air when Pearce raced over to her first. The man snatched her up and they skidded fifty feet away, Rosa trapped in the same smoky restraints that had just captured Aasif.

She shrieked like a panicked little girl, thrashing against the bindings that floated around her. Demarcus took a step toward them but a sonic blast hit him in the chest, sending him sprawling across the floor. The tang of copper filled his mouth and he spit out blood as he tried to get footing to move again.

Blackness enveloped Rosa and her cries choked down to a gurgle. Demarcus shouted, but his stomach dropped. He could almost sense the helplessness she showed right now.

He tried again to race over and rip her out of the vice of evil enveloping her. Pearce raised a hand and a bolt of darkness bowled Demarcus head over heels. Pain ricocheted through his head and along his arms as he tumbled back towards Lily.

Rosa flopped to the ground like a rag doll. Had Pearce killed her? Demarcus fought to raise himself up to charge again, but Rosa sat upright, her eyes the same black orbs that Aasif had. This was something even worse than what Simon did. Pearce took them over completely.

The man looked down at Rosa. "You know where Sarah Jane is? Take me there."

Rosa nodded yes, a trickle of black haze filtering out of her mouth.

CHAPTER 27

"SIMON, I NEED TO USE THE BATHROOM," SARAH JANE called out.

"Uh, you need to wait a minute." The momentary distraction broke Simon's concentration enough that Rosa let loose. She tossed a garbage can at the group, only for some acoustic waves to blast it away.

"Stop it, Rosa! Don't hurt Kelsey."

At least she acknowledged that Kelsey was the target, but she also rushed in to attack and got knocked down by a bright flash of light.

Sweat broke out on Simon's palms at the sight.

"You can't lose them! We need her." His head throbbed as he forced his control to hold her in check.

"Yeah, I know. Too bad you couldn't hack stadium security and let me know that those guys were here." Rosa ran down the passage, callously knocking people left and right. The four of them had disappeared down the concourse. Simon hadn't noticed the teleporter Harry in the group. If he was there, Rosa would lose them for the night. Perhaps for good.

"Simon, please! I'm about to have an accident." Sarah Jane's plea echoed through the apartment.

The gnawing continued in his chest. *Fine, I'll get her.* Simon clicked a button and he lost the visual feed from Rosa. He maintained his mental link and the audio channel. He fumbled away from the table and made his way down the hall. More shouts filled his ear.

Sarah Jane sat as a blur of yellow and pastels on the bed. She lifted her cuffed arm so he could access the controls. Because of his diminished eyesight, he'd installed biometric controls that responded to him or Rosa. A swipe of his thumb and the cuff clicked open.

Wait, that other bracelet wasn't there before...

A shout sounded in Simon's earpiece. Rosa sounded desperate. Then Sarah Jane swung her fist and hit his chest. Wham! Instead of the simple smack he expected, the force from her blow knocked him into the wall. Pain shot across his ribs and stole his breath.

She dashed past him out of the bedroom. No! Despite the pain, he scrambled up and ran to the door. Sarah Jane tried to turn the doorknob. Thankfully Simon's back-up device attached to the locking mechanism kept her from escaping.

The chaos in his ear made it hard to concentrate. He faced the desperate teen and gave his best pleading face. "Sarah Jane, if you just fix my eyes, I will let you go."

The girl turned. Light glinted across two bracelets she didn't have before. Did they have anything to do with her strength when she punched him?

Sarah Jane rushed up and pushed him. Again, the force was out of proportion to what her natural strength should be, and he slammed against the wall again. Before he could react, she grabbed his collar and cocked a fist back.

"You will let me out, or I will do the opposite of healing. I'm done." This close, he could make out a scowl, but try as he might, his ability couldn't override her will.

A scream lanced through his head from his earpiece. He raised a hand to his ear and cringed. Sarah Jane must have been able to hear it. "What was that?"

Something foul twisted in his mind. His connection to Rosa! Simon felt the control ripped away from him. But there was still a tether, so he could feel her pain.

Her rage.

His shoulders twitched and his legs gave way. He slumped to the ground, forcing Sarah Jane to let go of his shirt. She still held her fists up awkwardly, ready to pound him again. But she was the least of his problems now.

"What are you doing? What is going on?" she asked, her voice firm.

The connection to Rosa whipped his brain. Shocks bounced inside his skull. He squeezed his head as hard as possible, but the pressure didn't help. Then the pain abruptly stopped. A malevolent hatred regarded him.

I will find you and tear you to pieces.

Sarah Jane knelt in front of him. "Are you having a seizure?" Her voice had lost the hardness, and compassion bled through.

"We are in serious danger. We need to get out of here. Now."

CHAPTER 28

LILY WASN'T GOING TO WAIT TO TAKE HER SHOT. Pearce seemed to have amazing power, so she picked a different target. She strained as hard as she could with one hand and released a plasma bolt that sent Rosa flying.

"Demarcus! If we can't stop Pearce, let's play keep away."

He squinted for a moment, looking confused. Lily jerked her head towards Rosa, and awareness lit up his eyes. She hoped he'd come to same conclusion she had: they were going to have to protect SJ indirectly by taking Pearce on. If Pearce could teleport, he'd be to her in a second. But Rosa apparently had the knowledge, so she was the key.

"Look out!" Kelsey cried.

Lily ducked and rolled on the cement, the hard surface bruising her shoulder as she hit the deck. Aasif's sonic blast just missed clobbering her. She responded with a blast above him that rained debris over his head, and he crumbled in a heap, his body still.

Sorry, friend. We can't afford to duel you as well.

Dust clouded the air. That seemed like a clever strategy that could work again. At the pier Pearce took her best plasma blast without consequence, just like he'd taken Rosa's strike. Lily fired into the wall behind Pearce, causing more chunks to fly at him.

Now where did Demarcus go?

Kelsey screamed again as hands grabbed for her. Lily watched in horror as some of the crazed fans pulled the woman toward the seats, lifting her in the air and passing her toward...the railing to the next deck down!

Lily ran towards the crowd. Some still ran in fear, trying to find an exit. Others thrashed about, succumbing to Pearce's control or they were already in his thrall. Heads turned to watch her with dark intent.

A tall blond kid tried to snatch her arm, but Lily imagined a barrier of light around her body. She'd thought about a forcefield, but hadn't practiced. Now she'd find out if she could pull it off. Beads of sweat rose on her forehead as she concentrated, her temples throbbing.

The guy hit her light bubble and recoiled. Lily flinched with the expected impact, but it worked. A girl that resembled him tried for a full-on tackle. His sister? No matter, as she smacked against Lily's glowing barrier and bounced off. Another guy with tattoos on his arms stood in her way, his brown eyes darkened by the halo encircling his head. Lily swept her hand to the right and a light wave pushed him over the red seats.

Another apology ran through her head as she grimaced having to knock around innocent people.

Kelsey tried to fight the hands pulling her down, but there were too many of them. "Help!" she cried.

"Kelsey, close your eyes and curl up in a ball!" Lily hoped she could hear in the tumult. She fought to climb downstairs parallel to Kelsey's involuntary crowd-surfing. Lily had no idea if this would work, but she had to do something. If only she had speed or flight right about now.

Lily grimaced as she used both hands to knock over the next group of people about to pass Kelsey along. Kelsey yelped as she tumbled across some seats. She fought to get out of the tangle of people and push toward the aisle.

Was Demarcus was having luck keeping Rosa away from Pearce? Lily started up the stairs when her face was doused with liquid. Coughing, she smelled the beer and sputtered to keep it out of her mouth. Her eyes stung from the alcohol. Hands grabbed her and yanked her off her feet.

Her body was carried along by hands tugging and pulling. The burning in her eyes kept her disoriented, and her hair was pulled, jerking her head. She couldn't get angled to figure out how to stop the crowd. "Demarcus, help!"

She broke a hand free to swipe at her eyes and forced them open despite the sting. The edge of the deck loomed ahead. Screaming, she bucked with her legs, but the crazed fans threw her over the ledge.

CHAPTER 29

DEMARCUS RAN DOWN THE CONCOURSE, HIS ARMS around Rosa, her legs dragging behind. It kept her from getting footing for the moment. He wasn't sure what Lily had in mind with this game of keep away, but he could play with the best of them. Dodging people scurrying down the hall kept his speed down, but at least he was still moving in the direction he wanted to go. He had enough dexterity to juke and spin around the people in his way. The benefit of those moves was that Rosa stayed discombobulated also.

Man, he should be on that field flexing his moves.

His chest pain seared inside and slowed him down even more. Rosa shook her head and pushed her arms out, breaking free from Demarcus's grasp and rolling along the cement from their momentum. No matter. He knew she was strong enough to take punishment. But the goal was to draw her farther away as long as he could.

He skidded to a stop as she got up and they faced each other. Maybe a little taunting would help. "Rosa, you can't handle me. Don't even try."

The fire in her eyes burned bright. She lunged for him, and he zipped under her grasp, sliding along the concrete. He caught her arm while she was unbalanced and circled around her, spinning her to the ground.

Nabbing her leg, he dragged her farther down the concourse again. People shot looks at him, but they were too busy fleeing the craziness to deal with one more bit of it. The announcer called for evacuation over the PA system and said that security and police were converging on the stadium.

What on earth was going on?

Pain exploded over his side and he bounced off the floor into a trash can. He cradled his ribs as nacho cheese dribbled over his shirt. Rosa had caught him with her other foot and probably busted a couple of ribs with the blow.

He couldn't stay there, but the pain made it hard to catch a breath. Rosa snarled as she rushed to strike him. He just managed to dive out of the way, the impact causing tears to well in his eyes. Man, that smarted. Scrambling to his feet, he dodged back and forth, throwing whatever soda cups or souvenir footballs he could at her. Each time his left arm moved pain zapped his side.

A puff of black smoke erupted in the hallway and Pearce stepped from the sulfurous cloud, scanning the situation. Demarcus gritted his teeth and tried to snatch up Rosa again. Instead, his arms whiffed through more smoke as Pearce seized her arm and disappeared with her.

Dealing with someone else with superspeed was so annoying.

Demarcus pulled his phone out and dialed Harry. "Dude, we found Kelsey here and she had information about Simon. But come here right away—we're dealing with Pearce and Rosa."

The pain from his side and deep inside him conspired together, and he fell to his knees, groaning in agony. *God, help us to have strength to do what is right!* He managed to suck in a breath between clenched teeth and push himself up. The pain eased up enough that he could activate the location tracker on his phone.

Thirty seconds later, Harry and Kashvi appeared. The girl's eyes darted around, her pupils wide.

"Where's Simon?" Harry said, voice laced with anxiety.

"Can you sense where Pearce may have teleported off to?" Demarcus asked.

Harry scrunched his nose. "It doesn't work that way. We're not on the same frequency…or whatever it is we do. I'm not quite sure how it works. It's kinda wibbly wobbly," he said while spinning his hands in a rotating motion Looking around at the crowd, his eyebrows shot up. "What's going on here?"

"I think Pearce started a panic or something. People are going crazy." Demarcus started jogging back to the last place he saw Lily. "Lily was protecting Kelsey over here." He guarded his side so nothing would bump him as people continued to stream by.

Kashvi kept her arms out, a bottle of water in one hand. "I think some of these people are controlled by Pearce. There's a familiar tug coming from them. Like that guy there." She pointed at a man with greying hair who threw his food across the hallway.

"You don't think this is a typical sports-ball game?" Harry asked.

Demarcus slowly shook his head, the movement still causing pain in his side. "I know you're not a sports guy, but no, this isn't how they typically go. Unless it's a European soccer match. I hear those can get ugly." He gestured to Kashvi's water bottle. "What are you doing with that?"

She flicked her hand and water streamed out of the bottle in a ribbon before going back in. "This is my version of a holster."

That earned a laugh. "Good thinking."

They reached the edge of the concourse where the next set of open seats were when Demarcus heard a familiar voice. "Help!"

Lily!

They all ran forward. Demarcus's heart jack-hammered inside his chest. "Lily, where are you?"

Kashvi squealed and flicked water ahead. The water wrapped around the wrist of someone helping to hold Lily in the air. Kashvi pulled her hand back, the water obeying her command and yanking on the arm. Unfortunately, too many people had hands on Lily and they pulled her toward the railing for the deck.

"Lily!" Demarcus tried to dash around, but the amount of people stymied him. Lily screamed as a crowd of jerseys chucked her over the side.

A sharp gasp sounded next to Demarcus. Harry had Lily in his arms, both of them panting heavily. Lily trembled as she was set down on the ground, and Harry plopped in the nearest seat. "Remember the skate park? It comes in handy."

It was a night last week when Demarcus and Harry had met to talk at a skate park. He'd practiced porting in mid-air in case something happened. Demarcus clapped his back. "Dude, I'm so happy that you picked up that trick!"

"I'm glad, but I could so do without ever trying that 'trick' again." Lily made air quotes for emphasis. She scanned the thinning crowd. "We lost Rosa and Pearce?"

"Yeah, I held Rosa up as long as I could. I think she broke some ribs with a kick." He tried to twist and show them where the kick had landed, but the pain forced a hard grunt out. "Since they're gone, this place is still madness. Let's get Kelsey out of here and regroup. I don't know where to go from here."

No one argued the point. The stadium announcer continued to speak, but the crowd seemed beyond listening. Demarcus noticed the field had cleared of players. The first pro game cancelled for riots?

They found Kelsey in a few minutes, backed against a column near the suite where they had first found her. She clutched keys in her fist, ready to fight off anyone who came at her. The woman was freaked out and it took no time to talk her into fleeing with them.

Demarcus had rescued her with his speed at the Launch Conference, but she hadn't experienced travel by Harry. They left her outside her apartment, wiping her mouth off, after she vomited on arrival. At least Kelsey was safe, and she thanked them profusely for saving her. She even promised them game tickets down the road, but Demarcus was too beat up to be excited about the idea.

The youth room at church remained a sanctuary for them. Pastor Sanchez knelt in prayer with Irene. The sight of adults praying for them lifted Demarcus's spirit. Harry flopped onto a couch, the strain of porting around so much over the last few days wearing on him.

The constant struggle had taken a toll on all of them. Demarcus guarded his left side to protect his ribs. Lily had her arm propped up on the back of the other couch, and he could see the discomfort in her body language. At least Harry's injuries were on the mend, the black eye from Saturday night starting to fade.

Pastor Sanchez silently fetched bottles for everyone. The water refreshed as it trickled down Demarcus's throat. He didn't realize how dried out running made him.

"What happened?" Pastor Sanchez asked, joining his wife on the floor.

Demarcus and Lily took turns explaining the events: finding Kelsey, being confronted by Rosa and then Pearce, and the way Aasif and Rosa were taken over by the darkness, along with half the stadium.

"At least we have an address for Simon. It's a place to start," Lily finished, waving her phone with the contact information, until something chimed and her attention was drawn to the screen.

Kashvi sat quietly through the play-by-play. Her eyes had welled up when they described Aasif's fall at the hands of Pearce. When Lily finished speaking, Kashvi found her voice. "Please, we need to try and help him. You have no idea what it's like to be under his control. It's like being underwater—seeing what's going on faintly, but everything is distorted, and you can't cry out. If we can get him out of there, he should be able to snap out of it."

Demarcus sighed. Simon's influence was subtle, pushing people toward what he wanted. It didn't sound as bad. There was just so much going on.

"We need to find Sarah Jane first," Harry said, standing up and pacing. "If we have a lead, let's go. Once we've checked that out, we can try to find Aasif. Even though we don't know where to look."

"Actually, I may have information on that," Lily spoke up. "I just got an urgent message from Ji-young. There's a bunch of stuff online about the stadium incident, but now there's a weird thing going on back in San Francisco, near something called the Palace of Fine Arts. A huge glowing symbol is hovering above there, and people are streaming in from all over and converging there."

Demarcus frowned. "What does that have to do with Aasif?"

Lily continued reading her phone. "The reports are saying that violence is happening along the routes people are taking. And, that many people along the way are stopping what they're doing and following the crowds."

Just like at the game...

A gasp escaped from Lily and she covered her mouth with her injured hand. "Oh my goodness, you guys. You won't believe what the symbol looks like."

They all gathered around. Demarcus and Harry looked at each other in shock. It couldn't be!

The Sanchezes looked confused.

"I don't understand. What's the big deal?" Kashvi asked.

Demarcus pointed at the glowing torch hanging over the ornate building. "That's the sign of the Flare social network—the one that Simon used everywhere at Alturas."

CHAPTER 30

SIMON STEADIED HIMSELF AGAINST THE WALL TO GET up. He took a quick glance at the room—nothing critical that he needed. The laptop would be incriminating, but he had no choice now.

He stepped toward the door with hands up. "Sarah Jane, I know you have no reason to trust me, but we have to get out of here now. Something has happened to Rosa, and she wants to hurt us. If we don't flee, I believe we'll be killed."

How had it come to this? The tables had turned so quickly.

Sweat slid down the back of his neck while he waited for Sarah Jane's response. She eyed him warily. They both inched toward the door.

"Open the door. We'll get out of here then," she answered, her voice frosty.

Simon felt the door and searched for the handle. "If I don't have help, I will die. It's not about healing now; it's life and death. I was so wrong to do this to you. I'm sorry. You have no reason to help me." His voice trembled. "But I guess that's what I'm asking you to do. I will do whatever I can to get you home if we survive."

Rosa was coming any second. He could feel the desire to get here from their tether.

"Let's go," Sarah Jane whispered. "I can't leave you to die, but I'm not promising anything."

He found the biometric control and the handle turned. The elevator was to the left. He pointed the other way and said, "To the right, we'll take the stairs." She pushed past him and started to run. No, she was making her move already! "Wait!"

He ran as best he could forward, chasing the blur. Instead, he bumped against her. "Give me your hand," she said.

He reached out and she took it. His connection to Rosa surged. "Let's go! They're coming."

"Who?" she asked as she pulled him down the hallway and through the doorway to the stairs. She guided his other hand to the railing, and they started down the next few flights.

"Rosa's coming, but she's bringing something very dark with her. Something that broke my control over her. Rosa wants me dead, but this thing seems interested in you as well."

A crash and a shout came from above on the fourth floor, where they had just escaped from. A voice cursed, and it carried to the stairwell. Rosa.

"Faster!"

"You're the one slowing us down, you know," Sarah Jane retorted.

His feet scuffled against the carpeted stairs. Every time they hit a landing, he stumbled at the feeling of expecting one more drop off, but he pushed himself beyond his sight. If he had a different pair of his experimental glasses, he'd see better. Inside his head he could sense the frustration Rosa had at not finding them. She was tearing the rooms to shreds.

There goes the security deposit.

"Okay, first floor. What now?" Sarah Jane asked with heavy breaths.

"Let's take a side exit. Avoid the main doors and we'll try to find a place to hide. At least mix with the crowd and be inconspicuous."

They burst out a side door and the cool night air hit his skin. A hint of salt water floated in the air. Which way to go? He couldn't make out street signs, so he pictured their building's location from the map app. They couldn't go west—they'd end up where the investigation into the Hyde Pier battle had taken place. North to Fisherman's Wharf? That could get them trapped against the sea. That wouldn't be good if the water girl was involved.

Sarah Jane tugged at his hand and led him past an alley. "If we're going to hide, we need to go shopping. You owe me a new outfit anyway, since I've been in the same clothes for a couple of days."

"Shopping? Are you serious?"

"You're also Simon Mazor, and you're still pretty recognizable. Maybe you can't tell in the mirror, but let's get you into something else. There's a discount store right here, and yes, I'm serious."

They passed through some sliding doors and the shift of lighting made his eyes ache. Sarah Jane made quick work of grabbing some clothes, sunglasses, and a hat for him, along with a new outfit for her. Simon acted like he could fully see, even though he was dependent on her. The whole time he listened with heightened awareness for any sign of Rosa coming near. His tether didn't have enough strength to pinpoint her location, but the storm of her rage pelted his mind.

Regret washed over him as he wished for a way to turn the signal off. Instead, it felt like the other entity controlling her kept the bond from completely breaking.

Ten minutes passed, and they left the store. "Fastest I've ever been in and out of that chain," Sarah Jane muttered. She brought them back to the alley and thrust a bag into his hands.

"You want me to change in an alley?"

She scoffed. "Do you have a better idea? I don't. There's a dumpster here we can duck behind. And you better not be bluffing about your sight. Turn that way, just to be sure."

He struggled to get his new clothes on. The fedora probably looked ridiculous, but it would hopefully help his look be different. His glasses weren't an asset right now, since they were the ones he used for seeing from Rosa's perspective, so sunglasses didn't make a big difference.

"If you healed my eyes, this would be much easier," he said.

"I can't let you die, but you don't deserve healing. Besides, it's the only leverage I have. You need me. So now what do we do?"

"What time is it? How much activity is going on?" Simon wished he had his smart glasses prototype. At least then, with it wired into his optic nerve, he would have computer access.

"It's about eight. It's dark and fairly quiet. Not a lot of people around. And I don't know if you feel it, but there is something foul in the air. It's not just Rosa. There's something sick in the city."

Simon considered for a minute. "Let's head south toward the financial district. Head towards the Transamerica Pyramid. I've got an investor friend that I may be able to cash in a favor with. At least it gets us away from this area."

"Okay. And if we find a food truck, you're buying again," Sarah Jane said.

CHAPTER 31

ROBERTO WAS WEARY.

The insanity didn't end. The Hoshek reacted like a predator, sensing anger and pouncing on it with a cold, clinical ferocity. The sporting event had been a perfect storm—all the fans geared up for competition and putting too much weight on a game. The Hoshek turned so many people into his rage puppets, and they wreaked havoc as they left the stadium.

Finding the boy Aasif again was a welcome surprise. He was primed and ready to be controlled again, with his barely contained fury. Rosa was the strongest drug yet to the Hoshek, from her abusive upbringing to being under the influence of Simon Mazor all this time. Her physical strength was formidable, but her mental fortitude had worn down so much. Between her anger and power, the Hoshek fed deeply on her.

A bonus was the knowledge of one of the so-called Anointed they had missed tainting the other night at the pier. Sarah Jane, the healer. Roberto knew if the Hoshek could tap into her power and corrupt it from giving life to taking life, that would be the ultimate twisting of the Creator's gifts.

Since the trip to the apartment failed, somehow Sarah Jane had gotten wind of the Hoshek's attempt to find them. Roberto felt a measure of relief knowing the Hoshek had been unable to infect her too. Like a drop of water on the tongue of someone stranded in the desert, the relief didn't last long.

Now they had returned to the Palace of Fine Arts. The fancy architecture of the dome and pillars recalled an ancient nostalgia, when men died in chaos during the time of Greece and Rome.

The Hoshek teleported to the top of the building, bringing his two young charges up with him. Rosa and Aasif stood as sentinels, flanking him on either side.

Roberto's arms lifted to raise swirling, glowing smoke high into the sky. A form coalesced—the torch symbol from the parchment Roberto had been duped into using to release the Hoshek.

Those infected drew near, like to a beacon. Soon bodies filled the space under and around the dome, spilling into the grassy areas and parking lots. Occasionally someone fell into the scenic pond, the splashing the only distraction from bodies heaving in restrained wrath.

How long could Roberto continue to hold out? He had no idea how to escape the torment, but he wasn't willing to give up and surrender his soul to the Hoshek. The darkness squeezed against his psyche, and it took all he could muster to keep himself from being overwhelmed. Roberto could manage snatches of the Hoshek's plans: the ultimate goal was to release the rage contagion from this city to the far reaches of the globe. How that was going to happen he wasn't sure.

The crowd parted slowly. A tall African man approached the rotunda through the masses. A colorful kofia crowned his head, and a scowl adorned his face. A shiver ran over Roberto's body. Did the Hoshek fear this man?

The man stopped and stared up at Roberto's perch on top of the rotunda. "What are you doing, Pearce? We wanted to infiltrate people and slowly spread hate and discord. By drawing victims here, you make plain our intentions. You need to stop." The acoustic ability of Aasif made picking out the voice from the crowd noise as simple as using a mute button on the background noise.

A name filtered through the Hoshek's mind: Adeniji Okeofor, one of the enigmatic Four who ruled the Archai. Roberto had seen the name listed on paperwork from the group listing him as a Kenyan shipping magnate and benefactor. Here, the man was something far greater than a tycoon. He was a silent manipulator, a dictator with a shadow army that sowed upheaval across the world.

"Your plans are obsolete." Roberto's voice carried the distorted bass of the Hoshek's influence.

"Nonsense. Disperse this crowd and continue with the plan. And get rid of that glowing signal. Every camera in San Francisco is trained toward it."

Roberto cocked his head to regard the man. Well, the Hoshek did the regarding. How did such a small being think he could control such evil? Kings of old had thought the same, until their own children were in the fire as offerings to the Hoshek's hunger.

Roberto could see what was brewing in the Hoshek's mind. Even though the Archai were responsible for his own torment, he cringed at what was coming, and unfortunately, he had no way to intervene.

"You think you can command me? You...are obsolete," the Hoshek said.

Despite the distance, Roberto could see the fear emanate off the man in the spiritual realm. If it had been anger, he would have been fodder for the Hoshek. But the creature had another idea in mind.

"Stop this right now, Roberto. The Four will not allow this to continue," Adeniji said in a clipped, nervous voice.

"Your mistake. This is not Roberto anymore. You have no power—not anymore," the Hoshek grumbled.

Roberto's finger flicked, and the circle around Adeniji began to close, the crowd reaching for him. The man was used to absolute control of his circumstances. Now he had blundered into something he could not hope to steer.

Sadness flickered through Roberto as Adeniji's screams faded and the crowd left the body. Despite his own prison, he was still human enough to wish for a kinder fate for the former member of the Archai.

CHAPTER 32

LILY'S CHEEKS FLUSHED WITH HEAT. SHE HADN'T SEEN the Flare torch since the media frenzy over the Launch Conference and the collapse of the Alturas Collective died down. Now here it was, a lit-up apparition hanging in the sky. Ji-young sent several conspiracy theories about what it could mean. Lily had a strong sense of what it pointed to.

There was a connection between Alturas and whatever was going on with Pearce.

Now her phone trilled. It was Ji-young. Apparently sending headlines and links wasn't enough. Lily could barely answer before the journalist began rattling off questions.

"What happened at the stadium? There were flashes of light, so I knew you were there. You guys are not going to believe what's happening downtown. Have you seen the latest police reports?"

Lily put her hand up, even though Ji-young couldn't see it. "Whoa girl, one at a time. I'm going to put you on a video call on speaker, so the rest of us can hear."

Ji-young appeared on screen. Her black hair splayed out of a ponytail and her eyes looked bloodshot behind her glasses, like she'd spent too much time in front of a screen. Better that than in front of bad guys trying to kill you.

"Okay, right. We can talk about the game later. Wait, one more thing. Did you know a huge group that left the stadium basically commandeered the BART line into the city? People seem to be heading toward the Palace of Fine Arts. And you saw the bat-signal in the sky."

"More like the opposite of a bat-signal," Harry muttered.

"What else is going on?" Lily asked, not sure if she wanted to know more.

"You're not going to like this next one. The feds are looking for Demarcus and Harry for questioning in the Hyde Pier incident. Listen."

The video feed switched to a woman in a business suit. "We are continuing our investigation. There are two leads we need to talk to, if anyone has information on the whereabouts of a Demarcus Bartlett and a Harry Wales, both from the San Jose area."

"Dude, that Agent Dean is tricky. We never gave her our names," Demarcus groaned.

Ji-young was back on the screen. "There's a picture of you two at the investigation site. It's clear as day, and facial recognition wouldn't have trouble with it at all." Harry face-palmed and mouthed sorry to everyone.

"Oh, I've got some video of what's going on down at the Palace of Fine Arts. Let me throw it up to you." Everyone gathered around Lily and watched intently until the screen switched from Ji-young to a blurry video.

Dang, that torch was 3-D. Lily couldn't do that without her special gloves that also conked out her brain. The video showed the bottom of the Flare sign glowing in the sky, before the shot panned down to take in the crowd.

Three figures stood on the top of the rotunda. Pearce was in the middle. And it looked like Rosa and Aasif bracketed him, statues at attention next to the freak. Kashvi held in a cry at seeing her friend under control again.

Ji-young popped back. "What are you going to do?" she asked.

"We're still looking for Sarah Jane. We were given an address of a downtown apartment. Do you have any information about this place?" Lily forwarded the contact information Kelsey had given.

"Let me see what I can find," Ji-young said.

The rest of the group sat down while they waited. Irene comforted Kashvi. Demarcus and Harry touched base with their parents, so they didn't worry despite the investigation exposing their kids. After he finished texting, Demarcus moved carefully, grimacing if he changed positions too suddenly. Harry paced, his brows furrowed in frustration.

Lily closed her eyes and asked God for strength. The worst moment in her life was when she found out her mother and brother had died...were killed in a crash. But the last few days were the most exhausting physically. Her arm ached. Whatever it was in her chest stung or throbbed, depending on the moment. It seemed to flare worse when she turned her attention to the Lord. Despite the pain, she could fall asleep right now.

Ji-young called out, "Lily! Are you awake?"

Jerking, Lily's eyes shot open. "Yeah, just thinking."

"There is a police report about destruction of property there, but no specifics. I can't imagine how the police are handling things. The mayor has requested the National Guard at this point."

"Thanks, Ji-young. Keep us posted. Looks like we'd better hurry to that apartment." Lily offered a weak smile as the call ended. She fired a text off to her dad and hooked her phone up to a charger.

"You guys need to rest for the night. I know you're worried about Sarah Jane, but you can't keep pushing yourselves like this," Pastor Sanchez said in a fatherly tone. Irene nodded, patting Kashvi's back.

"No, I'm sorry." Harry stopped his pacing and turned to face everyone. "Sarah Jane is in danger, and we've taken too long already. I have to at least check out the apartment. Alone, if need be." He karate-chopped one hand into the other for emphasis.

Demarcus shook his head. "No way we're letting you do this alone, and you know that. And we're going to see if there's any way to sneak off with Aasif after that. All we need to do is get one touch to sneak him away from Pearce, and I think we'll get through to him. If he hadn't agreed to help us, he wouldn't be in this position."

"Do you remember the part where he tried to kill us?" Harry fumed.

"Dude, get off it. I know you butt heads with him, but we owe it to him to try. If it's dangerous, we'll keep our distance. But I have an idea of how Lily can get us close," Demarcus said. He managed to shoot a wink to Lily with his last comment. "Pastor Sanchez, I understand your caution. And we blew it over the weekend, but I know we can pull this off. Just be praying for us, and we'll keep you updated."

Harry had stopped pacing and crossed his arms. He muttered to himself as he nodded in agreement. Lily's body was weary, and she could see that so was everyone else's. But they had to rescue SJ. Her heart soared with Demarcus's stand on doing what was right for Aasif. His heroic nature brought on a fluttering in her belly. Despite his looks and strength, it was his character that was most attractive.

"I will come and help too." Kashvi stood. Her puffy eyes softened the look of her angular face.

Demarcus frowned. "I don't think that's a good idea. I wonder if Aasif was an easy target because he'd been under Pearce's sway before. I don't want anything happen to you."

Huh. Lily hadn't thought of it that way. That seemed logical.

Kashvi gulped. "I want to help—but if that's what could happen to me, then I don't want to be in that place again."

Harry began to pace impatiently again.

"Okay, then let's check out this address." Lily stood and held out her hand to him. "We'll find our friend, Harry. Whatever it takes." He nodded and took her hand, but his constant fidgeting distracted her.

Pastor Sanchez said a quick prayer over them. "I'm going to be calling some friends. This is bigger than our church, bigger than all of you. There's a work of darkness going on that requires the Kingdom of God to rise up like never before. I'll use the church line, so call my cell anytime if you need me."

Lily joined hands with Demarcus too. "Thank you, Pastor. Please keep praying. We'll take care," she called out before they faded away.

The air around the apartment buzzed with a nervous, dark energy. Yellow tape blocked the entrance. Since Kelsey knew the specific room, they didn't have to worry about dodging police and workers. Harry did a quick port to ensure the coast was clear, then he returned to bring Lily and Demarcus along.

The whole apartment was a disaster. Lily could barely step without dodging debris on the floor. There was food strewn about the kitchen, and the refrigerator door was torn off its hinge. The whole bathroom was a flooded mess of shattered porcelain and glass. Living room furniture lay upside down, the cushions torn to shreds. The only thing that might have been useful was the crushed remains of a laptop. Lily didn't see any way data could be recovered from the bits of plastic and circuitry.

The bedroom was in a similar state. The mattress had been torn in two, springs and foam stuck out of the ends. Lily raised a hand and lit the room up brightly because the overhead fixture had been knocked off.

There was nothing to be found in…

Lily's eyes picked up on a particular glint coming from a splintered nightstand. She worked her way over to the pieces of wood and sorted through it. A cat earring with a tiny diamond eye had caught her attention. One of SJ's earrings!

"Guys, I found this! At least we have proof that SJ was here."

Harry ported almost on top of her. "Let me see." He peered at the jewelry and a slow hiss exited between his teeth. "Where is she now?"

They picked through the rest of the ruined apartment carefully. Lily used her infrared vision to keep an eye out for anyone coming. After a few minutes, she saw reddish blobs coming down the hall, so she whistled for the boys. Harry blinked them away to a nearby alley.

Shouts sounded as a group walked down the middle of the street in the dark. The ones on the edge swung boards and pipes, smashing car windows as they walked. Yep, they had the signature black halos around their heads. Lily and the boys hid in the shadows, trying to avoid detection.

"All we know is that Sarah Jane was here," Harry seethed. "Where could they have gone? What do we do now?"

Lily put a hand on his shoulder, whispering a silent prayer. She had no clue, but Harry couldn't lose it right here. "Hey, we're on the trail. Take a breath. If something bad had happened to SJ, we'd have noticed signs. Look how bad the room was trashed, yet there wasn't any sign of someone hurt."

Harry closed his eyes and took a few steadying breaths. "You're right. We keep pushing on."

Demarcus kneeled alongside his friend after keeping watch. "We push and pray. Now, let's check on Aasif and see if we can do anything for him. I have a way Lily can get us close without getting noticed by anyone."

CHAPTER 33

"I HAVE A QUESTION FOR YOU," SIMON WHISPERED AS they worked their way down a side street. A break in the traffic was his opportunity to ask, but he wasn't sure if Sarah Jane had heard him. So many people poured north, they had to go out of their way to work towards the financial district.

"What is it?" The tone in her voice had softened. Or maybe it was more weary than bitter.

He held his tongue for a moment. How had he gotten here? A fugitive keeping a teenager from her family so he could survive. A month ago, he'd thought things were bad enough, what with trying to salvage his sight and get back in the good graces of the Archai. Now he had fled their chosen agent, not knowing where to go or who he could turn to.

How the mighty have fallen.

"I have to ask—do you have a gift of strength as well? You threw me around pretty hard in there." They stopped suddenly, and Sarah Jane pushed him backward. He could hear more angry protesters causing damage with their mob mentality. She must have worried there was some danger. The people passed by, their conversation laced with angry words and grunts.

What was going on?

A sigh released from Sarah Jane. "I only have the gift of healing. Someone gave me something to help me in defense, and it took me a whole day to remember I had them. Then I waited for Rosa to be out of the way."

Where would she have gotten technology like that? It must have involved their visits to Applied Sciences before it was attacked. "Was that Dr. Lowry who gave it to you?"

"How did you know about Ratchet?" she blurted. Then he heard the sound of her hand slapping over her mouth. That was one way to confirm she had slipped up.

"I wrote code that would find and track you and your friends so I could find you at some point to heal my eyes. Applied Sciences had better cyber security than many, but it still wasn't very robust. Now your friend...Ratchet? His extra layer of security was something. I would have gotten through it eventually, if it weren't for the attack that ruined the servers."

Silence for a moment. Was he too candid?

"You are a terrible human, you know that? With all your gifts and abilities, you should be helping the world. Yet you're tracking down teenagers to force someone to do what you want, after it was your fault in the first place. I should leave you here to fend for yourself."

Out of the mouths of children...

A crack ripped through the barriers Simon had placed over his emotions and turmoil for so long. He had meant to help the world—but he needed his own freedom first.

He slumped to the ground, his lungs starved for oxygen. He gulped in air. His arms shook in a fine tremor. No, this couldn't happen here. He hadn't experienced a panic attack since before he left home, years ago. Why now?

Because you've hit rock bottom, and it's worse than where you crawled out from.

A torrent of regret washed through his mind. The ways he had used his gift to manipulate people. The abuse of trust and relationships.

A gentle voice sounded next to his ear. "What is wrong with you? Are you okay?"

Sarah Jane.

Why didn't she run? It was the perfect opportunity while he was incapacitated, even though he wasn't much of a threat before he melted down. He wanted to tell her to save herself, that he wasn't worth anything, but something held that thought from bubbling up.

Sarah Jane began to whisper. But she wasn't speaking to him. Was she...praying for him?

"Father, I don't know what torments this man, other than selfish ambition, pride, and arrogance. But something is tearing at him right now, and we need to find a safe place. I don't know what to do in the city, and I can't just leave him like this, as much as I'd like to."

Her voice cracked, the hurt apparent. "But you didn't make me that way, and I need help walking in your way. Touch Simon's heart. Heal his mind. Help us find a way to do what's right and battle against what's wrong in this city tonight. Thank you for your promises, and your Son. In Jesus' name."

Simon wanted to weep. No one had ever shown him such compassion. Who was this young woman to speak like that? Resolve welled in him. If she could have concern for him after all he'd done, he could help her to safety. Forget his sight and his gift. He needed to do something right today.

"Thank you," he whispered back. His breathing slowed and he pushed himself off the sidewalk. A hand took his and led him farther down the block.

"The intersection says Stockton and Greenwich," Sarah Jane said. "How are we doing? There are more people on the streets, and it's getting sketchy out here."

Simon could hear the commotion, the anger in the voices. The girl was right about there being malice in the air. Something was going on. How could he protect her and get her to safety when he couldn't see anything more than lights?

There was perhaps a place to hide out for a little bit. "If I remember right, there's a park close by."

"Okay...so?"

"Let's see if we can get off the street until whatever is going on passes. There must have been some incident that encouraged rioting or protesting. I don't want anything to happen to you."

"I know, just in case I change my mind and try to heal you." Sarah Jane's voice reverberated with sarcasm.

No, he thought, but wasn't courageous enough to say it out loud.

He had to keep her safe to keep his conscience from destroying himself.

CHAPTER 34

DASHING AROUND THE PRESIDIO, DEMARCUS MAR-veled at the number of people surrounding the Palace of Fine Arts. The 101 was occupied by bodies, which kept vehicles from getting to the local streets at all. Crowds continued to fill the streets to the east of the Presidio as well. He estimated several city blocks were overtaken with Pearce's victims.

He rushed back to the nearby school where Harry and Lily waited for him. In a corner of the u-shaped building, under some stairwells that exited to the blacktop playground area, Lily had manipulated the light levels to keep them shrouded in darkness. When Demarcus first returned, he worried for a moment that they had moved somewhere else. But a whispered, "Over here," drew him to them.

The sirens of police vehicles rang out through the night air. Flashes of red and blue lights reflected off windows, adding to the eeriness of the whole evening. Sulking in shadows and sneaking around enemy territory would make for an awesome video game. In real life Demarcus couldn't stop sweating in the cool San Francisco night. His heart was racing faster than his feet, and he jumped at every out-of-place sound he heard.

It wasn't as much fun as advertised on Xbox.

Demarcus slipped into the shadow curtain Lily controlled. Her brows knit together in concentration, the strain making her arms tremor. Pastor Sanchez was right—they needed rest. Food. His stomach was running below empty, making his head foggy as well.

Yet here they were, planning a rescue for a situation they had helped create. Demarcus didn't want Aasif to be stuck in darkness any longer.

"The Palace of Fine Arts is completely surrounded. People have streamed in and are crowded in the parking lot, the streets to the east, and the land on the Presidio on the west. There's no way we'd get close on foot. It will have to be by porting. Are you up for that? I mean, we're all super tired," Demarcus said.

Harry sighed. "Yeah, I can do it, except I'm tired enough that I'll need a few seconds to catch my breath. I'm sure Pearce or one of them will notice."

Demarcus nodded. "That's where Lily comes in. Can you keep the darkness camouflage going while Harry gets to Aasif?"

She used her phone for a little light while blocking the outside from seeing in their corner. He could see her eyes widen at the thought. "Yeah, I can do it. It won't last for long. And we're going to have to get as close as we can to Aasif. Remember, he can pick up sound as well as project it."

Demarcus rubbed his hands together. "Good. My idea is we'll have you two go in, grab him, and bring him here. I think getting him away, like they did with Mount Sutro, will help break things open and he'll be freed."

"Nope. We are not splitting up. Harry and I already talked about that. It's all or nothing," Lily said, her death stare meaning business.

"I found a remote spot on the map relatively close," Harry explained. "I can get all four of us there. It's wooded, farther away from all these goons, and if he doesn't cooperate, he won't hurt anyone else easily. We'll just port away and leave him there. Take it or leave it."

Harry pointed to the map on Lily's phone showing a park called Lands End Lookout on the west side of the city, near the Pacific. Yeah, that should work. Staying together was smart. If they had been coordinated at Hyde Pier, maybe they wouldn't have lost.

The pain in his chest burned again. He flinched. Both Harry and Lily reacted with grunts and grimaces. "It's like the pain is tied to something, isn't it?"

"I've racked my brain and can't connect it to anything," Harry replied. "Maybe it's something Sarah Jane can take care of when we find her."

"Hopefully. First things first though. Are you ready to do this?" Demarcus asked.

Lily nodded. Harry looked determined. "There's a bunch of columns around the main dome there. We'll pop up there first so we can be sure Aasif is still on the dome, then we'll nab him."

"And I can calibrate the light needed to camouflage from there," Lily said.

Demarcus held a hand out in front of them. Harry and Lily put their hands on his. "Let's do this."

They landed on the top of a huge column. Squatting low, Demarcus held his breath until Lily adjusted the light around them. Lighted columns framed the pond in a half-circle partially surrounding the rotunda, and the glow reflected off the water as if liquid candles bobbed on the surface. They couldn't have stayed in a bubble of blackness, or they would have been spotted.

That's my girl.

Harry breathed slowly, trying to recuperate without making noise. Looking to the left, Demarcus saw Pearce,

Rosa, and Aasif right on top of the dome, where they'd been in the video earlier. Aasif stood on the far side of Pearce.

People covered the grounds and filled up all open spaces he could see from their vantage point, seething like a massive, angry organism. A living mass of rage.

Demarcus didn't fear much, but the sight spooked him. Shivers rippled across his body.

"Ready?" Harry's whispered question cut through the anxiety.

The biggest concern was the slope of the dome. It didn't look that steep on the shaky video, but the three standing in the middle were awfully close together. It was too late to discuss strategy here. Demarcus and Lily both nodded.

Harry grabbed Demarcus's hand and pointed for him to take Lily's. Made sense—that way Harry would have a free hand to tag Aasif. He held his hand out and counted down.

Three...two...one...

They popped from the column to the dome. Harry crouched right behind Aasif, trying to catch his breath. Demarcus squeezed Harry's hand as hard as he could and braced his feet to hold traction. Ratchet's special shoes worked as advertised. His soles didn't slip at all.

Harry reached out. Demarcus was ready to put his hand over Aasif's mouth as soon as they arrived at their new spot.

A gasp, then Lily started sliding down the dome, pulling on Demarcus.

A stabbing pain tore through his body at the torque on his rib cage, and he bit his tongue to keep from crying out. He flexed his arm, willing himself to keep Lily from slipping farther. The shift of weight pulled on Harry, who had to windmill his free arm to keep from tumbling.

Pearce whirled around.

The surprise made Harry lose his balance fully, and he let go of Demarcus to catch himself. Without his counterbalance, Demarcus fell backwards past Lily, hitting the dome's surface with a thud. The two of them rolled and slid toward the edge.

Demarcus flipped his legs so they were heading down first and dug his feet into the surface. He caught Lily's arm and pulled as hard as he could, despite the searing pain. She let out a yelp as her feet dangled over the edge. Her arm lit up and a trickle of sparks rolled over him.

"Hang on!"

A wave of strength moved over Demarcus. The adrenaline kick powered him to heave Lily back up. "Harry, I'm coming!" he called as he managed to get footing and run up the dome with Lily in his arms.

Harry reached out towards Aasif. Before he made contact, before Demarcus reached him to time their getaway, Pearce said one chilling sentence.

"I'm close to finding your friend, and I will drain the power and life from her."

———

The air warped around Demarcus. Instead of the precarious dome, he and Lily tumbled into the brush along the side of a dirt path. Harry and Aasif stepped apart, staring at each other.

Aasif grinned. "You heard my master—your friend is good as dead."

Lily whimpered in apparent pain next to Demarcus. He wiped dust from his face, his vision blurred, and his breath came in gasps accompanied by fire. Spitting dirt from his mouth, he ran an arm across his lips. Lily cried out, "Harry, no!"

Demarcus froze as Harry jumped for Aasif and caught him in a choke hold. "Tell your master that I'm coming for him after I save Sarah Jane. I knew you were a fake."

The air swirled around the two as Aasif struggled to free himself from Harry's grasp. Black smoke began to leave Aasif's mouth and surround them.

Not Harry. No!

Demarcus scrambled for footing. Before he could get running, the smoke wrapped around Harry and forced its way into his mouth. He writhed and gagged, letting Aasif go as he fell, smacking his head against a rock.

"Dee..." The faint cry squeaked out before Harry collapsed in the dirt next to Aasif.

It couldn't be. Demarcus crawled over to his best friend. Harry wouldn't succumb, right? As a Christian, he'd be protected.

Harry coughed.

"That's good. Fight it, buddy. We'll get out of here and find Sarah Jane."

Lily came up next to them. "Is he..."

Harry lifted his head and opened his eyelids. His eyes churned with black, covering his green irises, the whites of his eyes.

"I will serve the Hoshek, and deliver you to him," he croaked.

Demarcus fell back. Harry stood, his eyes clearing but still darkened. A crooked grin stretched across his face. This wasn't his friend. Something was going on.

"Close your eyes!" Lily screamed. Demarcus obeyed, and a sparkling strobe pattern made him throw his arms up to protect them as well. Harry cried out.

Demarcus felt her arms pull him up.

"We've got to go. This is bad. Just get us far away!" Lily cried.

Demarcus glanced at Harry kneeling in the dirt, rubbing his eyes. Then he picked Lily up and ran. He followed a trail until the rolling green of a golf course appeared ahead. Lily lit the way with her hand out, and he blazed across the grass until he found a road. Now he could fully open up, and he shot down the street. His dreads slapped his back, while her blonde hair whipped around his face.

Nothing would stop him. He knew they had to flee their friend. In the space of a moment, Harry could deliver them to Pearce.

Or this Hoshek, whatever that was.

Demarcus's legs burned. His back and arms barked at him to lighten his load, but the adrenaline rush dulled the pain from his ribs. Still Demarcus ran. Light from Lily poured out, illuminating a glowing trail for him to follow, and despite his pain and weariness, they raced faster than he ever had. The road was mostly quiet, with a few people crossing the road and an occasional car heading south. He didn't care. It was just time to get away.

The buildings grew in size until they were passing skyscrapers downtown. Then a slight turn and Demarcus hit the brakes, sparks cascading from his shoes. A long building with a clock tower rising from the center stood before them. Behind it, sea water slapped against the dock. They'd reached the ocean, crossing the whole peninsula in a minute.

Kneeling, he tasted the salt in the air as he sucked in big gulps. Seagulls cawed above him. Pain racked his legs, his arms. The rib pain stabbed through his body.

Demarcus flopped down and rolled on his back, staring up at the sky. Lily sat next to him and stroked his forehead. "Are you okay?"

He shook his head. "What are we going to do? They got my best friend. If they got Harry, what's going to stop them from getting all of us?"

— INTERMISSION —

BLINKING. BREATH ENTERED HIS LUNGS, A CHEMICAL smell that made him cough. Sensation came back to fingers and toes.

John stirred from his slumber. Well, it was more than that, wasn't it? The remnants of glory danced in his subconscious, but the majesty of it all defied a mortal brain's comprehension. Was this what it was like for Lazarus?

The confining space was a conundrum. John reached out of the sheet and pulled along the top of the container he was in until something started sliding. Oh, he was in some sort of shelf. The mechanism glided along, opening to a lighted room. He sat up and noticed a slack-jawed attendant in a white lab coat staring at him.

"Greetings. I seem to have been...asleep. Do you know where my clothes are?"

———

The sun greeted John as he slipped out the back door of the building. He hoped the man would be all right once he awoke from fainting. John had left some money in the man's coat pocket to compensate for being startled.

Now, where was he? A fenced parking lot next to a blue and grey building. John had to wait until a car entered through an open gate before escaping the lot.

My Lord, you've sent me back to do your work. Please guide me to where I need to be. May your hand be with the youth in my care and the people in this city. There is so much anger and darkness in the atmosphere here. Your kingdom come.

John started walking, the feeling of using his legs refreshing after however long he was in that place—the medical examiner's office, according to the sign out front. He took in a deep breath. He wished he could be taking in the scents of vineyards, the sweetness hovering in the air. These urban areas didn't have flocks being cared for by shepherds, horses grazing in the fields, or farmers tending their crops. It was a different time from his day, yet it was a day anointed by the Lord to see victory.

A couple of impressions came into his mind, whispered by a still, small voice. "Pyramid. 101."

John smiled at the voice he'd learned to love through the years, guiding him on his different missions. The world may not understand, but when friends speak, there's no way to fully explain how it works. John knew by faith that he would be led to his charges.

He walked many city blocks, praying as he went. There was something very dark at work in the region. His discernment recognized when the enemy was making a significant push against God's work. Yet he hummed praises and psalms as he journeyed, stopping once to get some sustenance.

The convenience of food access these days was truly a marvel, although the freshness of newly plucked grain or fruit gleaned from an orchard was always better.

Signs reading "Highway 101" loomed, and John realized the first part of his journey had led him there. The sun had dropped, the shadows lengthening as night approached. Before he reached the highway, a van pulled over and rolled down its window.

A black man with a shaved head ducked to peer at John on the sidewalk.

"May I help you, sir?" John asked.

The man appeared confused for a moment. "Dude, I don't know what's going on, but I had the strangest sensation bugging me all day that I needed to find an old man and give him a ride. It wouldn't leave me alone, so here I am, and here you are. Need a lift?"

John immediately walked over and entered the old vehicle. It didn't matter that the seat lining was cracked and torn, or that the inside had unpleasant odors. He pushed a discarded food bag aside with his foot and buckled his seat belt. John had faith, but he was no fool.

Turning to the driver, he remembered to offer his hand to shake. So many customs around the world to keep straight. "Thank you very much. You may not realize it, but you are an answer to prayer. My name is John. What's yours?"

The man took the offered hand and gave a firm shake. The action reminded John of his charge Demarcus, the way the grip was secure and strong. "Prayer, huh? Recently I've seen the power of prayer, so maybe this is my way to pay it back. My name is Tony Carter. Where you going?"

John offered a smile. "Mr. Carter, I am looking for a pyramid."

Tony quirked an eyebrow. "I'm here to help, but I don't think I can quite make it to Egypt."

John gave an easy laugh at the man's joke. Those pyramids near the Nile were something to behold, certainly. "Forgive me. One may consider me a form of tourist, and these were the directions given to me."

Pulling out his phone, Tony muttered to himself. He tapped something in, one tattooed arm resting on the steering wheel. "Apparently there's something called the Transamerica Pyramid in the financial district. Some sort of famous skyscraper. Is that it?"

Yes, that was it. He was certain. "I believe you have found my pyramid, Mr. Carter. You have my gratitude."

The night had overtaken the sky, so Tony turned on his headlights. "Looks like traffic's messed up right now, but we'll get you there, ol' John."

They pulled away from the curb, and John gave thanks for the Lord's provision. "You must tell me about this prayer experience. It interests me greatly."

Tony looked over his shoulder to check for cars. "Okay, but it's a pretty crazy story. Happened just Saturday night…"

John couldn't resist a huge smile as Tony shared his story and they slowly moved north.

CHAPTER 35

"HURRY, WE CAN CROSS THE STREET IF WE MOVE quickly," Sarah Jane said.

Simon stepped across the road in faith, trailing Sarah Jane as she pulled him along. A large group had forced them to duck into the shadows again, waiting for an opportune moment to make it to the park he had mentioned. They scurried together until the ground shifted from concrete to grass.

They stopped and Sarah Jane pulled his hand to the ground. "Here, we can sit for a minute and catch our breath."

The grass blades tickled his palm as he ran his hands across it. The scent of fresh dirt was a contrast to the urban smells of asphalt and trash. The greenery would be refreshing to look at as well, but he settled for the touch and smell of it, an oasis in the urban jungle.

"Are you doing all right?" he asked.

"Sure. I mean, as well as can be for a girl who's been kidnapped and now is helping her captor flee. It's not confusing at all." Her body collapsed against the ground. "Oh, and I'm starving. I should have eaten that last sandwich I was offered."

"Is it secure here?" It seemed quieter.

"Yeah. There's no one around for now. It looks like we can take this road straight down to the Transamerica Pyramid. We've got several blocks to go, but I can see it from here."

They sat in silence for a few minutes. One question continued to burn at Simon, so he figured it was time to ask.

"Why didn't you leave me when I had that panic attack? That would be the perfect time to get away. I deserved to be abandoned."

She sucked in a deep breath and let it out slowly. "I wanted to. Just like you said, you deserve it. But I'm not made that way, I guess. Even though my power is healing, my gift is compassion. Though sometimes it feels like a curse. That's why I couldn't leave you there."

Interesting. "Why would you call it a curse? We need more compassion in this world."

"Yeah, we do. And it hurts. When you want to give it out and can't. I've thought about walking through hospitals and praying for everyone there, but I feel something that tells me no. It's not the time. John said that our gifts have a time and place, and it's so confusing to know when it's right." Her voice wavered at the mention of the name "John."

Wait a second. "Did you meet John at the Launch Conference?"

"Yes. He warned us about you, but Lily and I didn't listen when we went up on the roof with you. Since the conference, he'd been our mentor."

Simon shook his head. The old janitor that had infiltrated the Alturas campus was behind these kids still. For all that he thought the Archai had things worked out ahead of time, a simple custodian had slipped through their schemes and helped topple his social media empire and the control he would have been able to exert across the world.

He had thought it was for the best. If he could influence a generation and take away the worst impulses of people, the world would change. But that idealism didn't stand up with the way the Archai had dropped him.

Something else she said nagged at him. "Why did you say 'praying'? You have the ability to heal. It doesn't take any divine influence to do it."

She laughed softly. "You're blind in a few ways. Yeah, I've been given a gift. Where did you think it comes from? Mutations? Cosmic rays? Our gifts are from the Lord. I ask him to do the work of healing."

That didn't make sense. The Archai said gifts like his were developing because the world needed them. Yet for all of his technical genius, had he ever considered where they came from? "I don't know if I believe that. You didn't pray when you healed the gash in my wrist back at the conference."

"No, I didn't. The gift is there, you're right about that. But do you see this church in front of us?"

"Is that a joke?" He waved his hands in front of his face. "Pretty much blind here."

"Oh, yeah. Well, there's this fancy church in front of us. Spires going up with crosses on each tower. The church is a place where we can meet Jesus. He's not limited to a building, but we use the building as a tool for that. Same with me. The gift is there, but it's best used if I'm the conduit and not just doing it on my own."

"Let me be clear—all of your friends believe your gifts are from God?"

Sarah Jane waited a minute to answer. "We know they are. John taught us that our gifts are given for us to use as we see fit. Some have the gift of leadership—what if they become a dictator with that gift? We all have gifts that we're given, and we each have a choice. I think even you."

He didn't have much of a choice anymore. "Not with my eyes like this. Since I can't see details, it impacts my ability to influence someone."

Simon shoved his hands in his pockets. A crinkly bag surprised him. He pulled it out and handed it to Sarah Jane. "It's not much, but would you like a gummy bear?"

She took the package and he could hear her rip the plastic open. "At least it's something. Do you want one?" A sticky blob dropped in his hand.

"What color is it?"

"What?" Sarah Jane said.

"The gummy bear. What color did you give me?" Simon's heart skipped a beat. Did she give him the fortuitous one?

"Why? I can't tell a difference in the flavors."

"Ever since I was a kid, I've believed the colors had different luck. If I ate an orange one, something bad was going to happen. My father would lose it, or my mom would berate me. Now green—that was my lucky color. Good things were sure to happen if I pulled a green one out. But it doesn't matter anymore. I can't even tell the color."

He rolled the squishy candy around in his fingers, then gave it a sniff. There was no way to tell if it was his lucky one, except by sight. Or...by listening to someone.

The only person he could trust right now was Sarah Jane.

"It's green," she said.

Simon pulled out his phone and unlocked it. "You need to find someone to help us. Do whatever needs to be done." Holding it out, he took a deep breath. No matter what happened next, he would see Sarah Jane safely through.

CHAPTER 36

THE SHEER TERROR OF WHAT JUST HAPPENED didn't fully register for Lily. All she could do was stroke Demarcus's forehead as he fought to catch his breath, grunting with every deep inhalation. He had managed to keep her from falling off the dome, then raced with her across the whole city to escape their friend.

Demarcus was that strong, and what just happened shook him to his core.

What was that smoke thing? Rosa had always been naughty, while Aasif came from a hard background and had already been under Pearce's control. But Harry was a good guy. What was the common factor that connected things?

Or were they all susceptible to being taken over by Pearce?

A frozen hand seized her heart. Harry said he'd deliver them to the Hoshek—and he knew where Lily lived. He could be teleporting to their houses right now, wreaking havoc on their loved ones.

Lily tried to dial her phone with trembling fingers. She couldn't bring up her contacts, so she activated the voice assistant. "Call Dad." Snap, only five percent battery power remained. She couldn't talk for long. The phone kept ringing. *Pick up, Daddy.*

A voice came over the line. "Kitten, where are you? It's late. There's craziness going on in the city."

Thank you, God.

"Please tell me you're not in San Francisco. Again."

She almost laughed at the absurdity of the comment. "Daddy, I only have a little battery left, so you need to listen to me. There are terrible things going on, and these people have superpowers like us. They probably know where I live, and where Demarcus, Harry, and Sarah Jane live." She couldn't keep a sob from escaping. "You need to leave. Take Kelly and go somewhere safe. Don't tell me where, just in case. I'll...I'll get a hold of you when it's safe."

The words she spoke cut her heart in pieces. She couldn't run to the man who had held her through her darkest days, for fear she'd bring the danger home.

"Lily Beausoleil! What are you talking about? This is crazy. You have Demarcus or Harry bring you home right now, and we'll talk. Where are you?"

She had to catch her breath, and fight through the tears running down her face. "Daddy, I'm safe in the city. But these people are evil and doing bad things. Just trust me that you need to get out, and this is for the best."

"I'm coming for you. Let me get my keys."

"Dad. Listen. I have to call the other parents. Promise me you'll get Kelly and yourself to safety. Promise me! Promise on Mom's grave."

Lily could hear him suck in a breath at that.

"I will take Kelly to a hotel right now. But how will I know you're safe?" His voice cracked.

"I guess we need faith for this one. I'm with Demarcus, and we'll watch out for each other. We don't want to lead anything bad home, so that's why I'll be in touch. And Daddy?"

"Yes?"

"I love you. Tell Kelly I love her too. I've got to go." She clicked off before he could argue more, or before she lost it on the line. Now she could take a minute for a full-throated cry.

Demarcus sat up and wrapped his arm around her. "That was smart. And brave."

She leaned into his shoulder and tried to collect herself. Wiping her nose left a slimy trail of mucous on her sleeve. Irene's 49ers gear was going to get beat up as much as the formal dress Lily was stuck in during the Hyde Pier battle.

Demarcus called his mom and Harry's parents, while Lily contacted Sarah Jane's house. It tore her up that she couldn't offer any new information about their daughter. She could only pray that SJ was safe somewhere.

Three percent left. Lily called Pastor Sanchez as well. Harry could pop over to the church to look for them. He couldn't believe that something had happened to Harry. Thankfully he agreed to close the church and keep Kashvi safe. Harry didn't know where the pastor lived, so that should be enough.

A chime rang on her phone. She'd better turn off the sound to not attract undue attention. A text came in from her father.

I've transferred money to your account. Get what you need, do what you need to do to be safe. I love you always. Don't you die on me, or you're grounded.

Thanks, Daddy. You too.

"What next?" Demarcus asked.

"I'm starving. Can we find some food?"

"Girl, you are speaking my language. We'll grab something quick and figure out what to do." Demarcus offered a weak smile.

They found a McDonald's a couple blocks away that was still open. They ordered some burgers, fries, and drinks. The clerk's nametag said, "Nicholas."

"Did you guys hear about the game being cancelled tonight? That was crazy," Nicholas said as he handed over their order.

"Yeah, we heard a little about it," Demarcus replied. "Thanks for the food. Be careful going home tonight—it's nuts in the city as well." Nicholas thanked them, and they ducked out of there before cracking up over the question.

They doubled back to a park closer to the Embarcadero, near a public restroom. A few homeless folks milled about like nothing was unusual about the night. "It's not In-N-Out, but it'll do," Demarcus said as he tore into a hamburger.

The salty smell of fries usually made Lily's mouth water. Tonight, despite her hunger, it was hard to build up an appetite. She made herself eat one of her burgers, then rolled the bag up. Sipping on her Coke, she fought her fatigue. Watching Demarcus kept her attention. He normally sat so tall, his inner strength manifesting in the way he carried himself. Tonight, he slouched over his food, his face downcast. Something wasn't right.

"Are you all right?" She nudged Demarcus as he ate quietly.

He sighed. "I screwed up again. Thought we could rescue Aasif, and we end up with Harry caught in this mess. I shouldn't try to lead. It keeps ending in failure." His head dropped as he propped his elbows on his knees.

Lily caught his chin and lifted his head to get eye contact. "Listen up. If it weren't for you, I'd be a light bulb for Simon and Alturas. You're a natural leader. That doesn't mean you won't make mistakes. We both need to learn that. John would say that we need to grow into our gifts. That it's not just being fast. You realize we all look to you, right?"

His dark eyes lit up at her pep talk. Despite her sadness, the way he looked at her jolted the butterflies in her belly.

"Thank you. You're pretty amazing too, you know. I don't know what life would be like if I hadn't met you."

Lily could stare into his face all night, but a breeze blew hair across her face. She fussed with pushing it aside. For a moment, her mind wandered, images of the two of them holding hands on the shore as the sun set behind them. Rays of sunlight streaking across the water to meet them. She could hear splashing in the water and laughs of joy from little voices even. A possible future? Not if they didn't survive tonight.

Demarcus looked over her shoulder at a few people loudly passing by and kept his focus on them until they passed.

"I think we need to figure out what to do from here. We don't have a place to go. No plan. I'm out of bright ideas. Do you have anything?" he said.

Nothing sprang to mind. They couldn't go home, and they needed to avoid being found by Pearce, Harry, or any of his other goons. The nearby area was quiet, and anyone who had passed since they'd sat down didn't have the black halo effect, thank goodness. Lily shivered from the night air and thinking about their predicament.

Demarcus slipped an arm around her and pulled her close, side to side. "Are you cold?"

She had been, but wasn't anymore with his super metabolism warming her up now.

"Thanks. I wonder if we should keep moving, in case bad people are looking for us. At some point we'll have to find a place to hide out and rest. Maybe a place with a phone charger—I'm at two percent now."

A text alert sounded, startling her. A number she didn't recognize popped up. She almost pocketed her phone when the message preview caught her eye.

Lily, it's SJ. I need help in the city. Where RU? Please respond!

Lily gasped and showed the message to Demarcus. Finally, they had contact with SJ!

Demarcus didn't show the same excitement. "What if it's a trap?"

She hadn't thought of that. "I think we have to take that chance."

CHAPTER 37

LILY NOTICED HOW DEMARCUS CRINGED WHEN HE picked her up. His toughness impressed her once again as they ran off to find where SJ was—if it was her. Could it be that easy for once, that she was just down the road? *After all of our stress and setbacks, we'd like a win, Jesus.*

She lit the way for Demarcus, feeling like a human headlight. He wasn't as fast this run. Yes, he was tough, but of course he had limits. The glow seemed to envelope his feet and ankles as they streaked along.

Most of the streets ran like a grid to create squared blocks, but Columbus Avenue cut diagonally through the city. Supposedly this would lead them right to SJ.

Police lights flashed behind them. Lily glanced over Demarcus's shoulder to see a patrol car following them. Really? He probably was going over the speed limit, but with everything going on, a cop had to pull over a kid running?

The cop hit the siren for a moment, a loud "whoop" carrying through the night. Demarcus sighed and hit the brakes. "Let me do the talking, okay? Sometimes...things get interesting for a black kid dealing with an officer. And don't be surprised if we make a quick exit."

"Okay, but I've got your back." Lily stood alongside him, watching as he stood with hands visible. Demarcus stood with his head up. No reason for him to do anything less.

The lights cut out and the officer stepped out of his cruiser. "Do you know how fast you were going there? I'm going to need to see your license."

Demarcus cocked his head, confused. "License? Uh, when does someone need a license to be running, sir?"

The officer walked up. "I didn't think there would be two of you running around the city, so I had to get you to stop for a reason. Do you have any information on the craziness going on? It seems to be pattern for you so far."

Lily was totally lost with the interaction. Demarcus broke into a big grin though. "Hey man, why you gotta do me like that? My heart was racing faster than me. Say, did you get how fast I was going?"

The officer smiled back. "I don't think they work on people. But seriously, there aren't two of you with super speed, are there?"

"No, as far as I know it's just me. That's just super speed though. There's other abilities out there, some on our side, and some we need to worry about."

Okay, Lily had enough of the puzzlement. "Hello, one of the powered people on your side. Demarcus, what's going on?" Did he have a secret criminal history she hadn't uncovered yet? Or had he already become known to the police as a crime fighter?

Demarcus held his hands out toward Lily. "Officer Riley, this is my friend Lily. She is most definitely on our side. She can control light in a lot of cool ways." He turned toward her. "We met the night of the Hyde Pier battle. I was walking along the highway and he stopped to check on me then too."

"Then your friend here saved me from a drunk driver crash. My patrol car was totaled, but I got to go home after my shift. Now I'm called in because San Francisco is going insane. Do you know anything?"

Demarcus nodded. "I was wondering why you were so far out of your jurisdiction. There's a man named Roberto

Pearce who has some crazy ability to steal our powers and can control people. It's like he has black smoke that comes out and takes a hold of them. In fact, he did it to my best friend Harry, who can teleport."

"Don't forget psycho Rosa with super strength. Or Aasif, a guy we thought was on our side, but fell under Pearce's control. He can control sound," Lily chimed in.

Riley looked back and forth between them, his face a mask of befuddlement. "You guys are just making this up now."

Lily drew the word "nope" in neon pink and released it to float in front of the amazed officer. "It's as weird as it sounds, and worse than you know. We're on our way to find a friend who has been missing for a few days. Hopefully she can help us in the fight."

"You're heading up to the Palace of Fine Arts?" Demarcus asked.

"Nearby. The reports are that massive crowds are gathering there. The city police have tried setting up cordons to keep people out. Last I heard, they weren't working. People are streaming around any available opening. They... don't seem to be acting rationally," Officer Riley said.

Lily and Demarcus shared a look. "Sir, you need to tell people to be very careful. We tried to rescue someone, and that's when our friend Harry was controlled. We're not sure how Pearce does it. Honestly, you guys need to keep your distance. Pearce only seems to be able to do it when he or one of his controlled people are nearby," Demarcus explained.

"There's been talk of some of our guys crossing the line. That's not good at all." A call came over Riley's radio. Lily didn't understand the police chatter, but it sounded frantic. She wasn't surprised.

Officer Riley pulled out his cell phone. "Demarcus, do you mind if we swap numbers? You've given more information than we've had on this Pearce, and if you get anything else, I'd love to have an avenue for intel. Also, if we need to warn you about something going on, I can reach you."

They traded numbers, then Riley hopped back in his cruiser and raced away. "You didn't tell me about your new cop friend," Lily teased.

"Honestly, I'd forgotten about that. Hopefully he'll be a resource for us too." He took the drink Lily was holding and sucked down half of it. "I wonder, is there a point where we sit things out? We're a bunch of bumbling teenagers. What business do we have being out there?"

Lily wanted to smack his arm, but she needed a good hand still. "We just had this conversation. I don't see how we sit it out. God's gifted us, and yes, we've screwed up. What else are we going to do? If we don't do something, with our gifts, then who will? Now let's find SJ and figure things out from there."

He whisked her up again and they sped down the street. It was comforting to be in his strong arms, though she liked travel by Harry-mobile better. It was easier on her hair.

Demarcus skidded to a stop by the park SJ had listed as her hiding place. He set Lily down and stared into the darkness. "You got anything?"

She blinked and her vision changed to infrared. "There are two people walking along the tree line. They're heading for us."

"Such a cool skill," Demarcus said. She glanced at him to smile, but up close, his face was a blob of red, orange, and yellow. Not pleasing to look at, so she blinked to normal vision. "Okay, I can finally see their outline, coming out of the dark. Why don't you light things up?"

"I won't give away our position," she whispered.

The two figures approached. "SJ, is that you?"

"Lily? Are you here? Oh my gosh! I'm so glad it's you!" One of the figures ran out from behind the trees. SJ came up and smothered her in a hug, her reddish hair flying everywhere. Lily couldn't help the tears from dribbling out of her eyes.

"Are you okay? What happened?" Lily asked.

Demarcus came up beside them. "Sarah Jane, who is with you?"

SJ pulled back enough to allow Lily to see who was coming. Out of the brush, carefully picking his way, was Simon Mazor.

The man who had tried to kill them.

CHAPTER 38

THE VOICES CALLING OUT TO SARAH JANE SENT SHIVers up Simon's back. He hadn't been in contact with Demarcus or Lily since the Launch Conference. He was observing things in his car during the Hyde Park attack and had only seen them from Rosa's perspective.

Then Sarah Jane ran ahead and left him feeling his way through the trees. They weren't too dense, but he still stumbled over a rock trying to get through. He shuffled his feet until he hit cement, then started walking toward the streetlight he could make out.

Whoa, that streetlight was growing so bright. And coming right at him!

"Simon Mazor!" Lily's voice sounded shrill in the night. "I should have known you were behind this." Footsteps sounded, coming toward him. The brilliant light meant his poor sight was rendered totally useless, with everything washed out by the glare in front of him.

"You're going to answer my questions before I burn off your face. What have you been doing to Sarah Jane? What's going on with Pearce? Why did you have my mother killed?"

He reflexively held his hands up. The questions from Lily scrambled his head. Of course he had things to answer about Sarah Jane. And he could give some insight into Pearce. But her mother? What was that about?

The illumination pulled away from him. "Lily, don't zap him. That's not what we need right now. Please!" Sarah Jane intervened for him.

Then he heard Demarcus speak up. "Okay, give Sarah Jane a chance to explain. Just don't let him touch either of you—his control deepens when he does that." Simon could sense them back away. The glow still hovered nearby. His pulse quickened at the flashback of him being blown off the roof of his Alturas headquarters by the explosion—caused by Lily and her light manipulation. The cause of his eyes being damaged.

The words spilled out, rapid-fire. "Guys, it's a lot to explain. Simon used Rosa to kidnap me from the pier, and they've held me in an apartment nearby. I was never under his influence. When Simon sent Rosa on a mission, I used my bracelets from Ratchet to get free. Except then Rosa came back and tried to kill us, but we escaped just in time. That was earlier tonight, and we're trying to survive together. Crazy, right?" Sarah Jane chuckled nervously at the end.

Lily answered, "You're all right though? Did anything happen? I'll take care of him if he did." Simon could feel the anger seething in her tone toward him.

"I'm... okay. Really. He wanted me to heal his eyes. They were damaged that day at Launch."

It was strange to have them talking about him as if he weren't there. In his state, it was probably best to hold his tongue unless absolutely needed.

"You didn't do it, did you? Did he make you do it?" Demarcus asked.

"No, I didn't. It was the only leverage I had on him. Besides that, he says that his power is affected by his lack of sight. He can't do a lot to influence people without clear vision. So, I had him on that point. Thankfully, Rosa didn't try to make me," Sarah Jane said.

Light flashed toward him again. "Is this a trick, Simon? Show us your eyes," Lily demanded.

Simon held his hands out to show he wasn't up to tricks. "Okay. Everything she said is true. My ability is greatly diminished without seeing clearly." He pulled his sunglasses off and heard a couple of gasps.

That's what he expected. It wasn't until he had wired a connection to his brain, bypassing his ruined eyes, that he had seen the damage. Instead of his brown eyes, pale corneas stared out from under his eyelids. It was a miracle he could distinguish variations of light.

"I...I did that?" Lily asked, her tone hushed.

Demarcus spoke up, an edge to his voice. "No, you didn't. You destroyed something Simon was going to use to control people around the world. He got caught in his own mess. Consequences. Remember, don't blame yourself."

Was he serious? She wasn't responsible? Simon's temper started to flare. If she hadn't destroyed the Source the Archai had designed to amplify his power, the city wouldn't be in chaos. He would have accomplished the Archai's plans...

Their plans.

Were they ever truly his plans? He'd fought against a domineering dad, a controlling mother all his life. Until he discovered that he could influence people by his charisma and will, and he was able to maneuver them out of his life.

Then he had met Adeniji, an investor who said he had an eye for talent. The African had put Simon under a mentorship that later he found was lower rungs of the Archai. With his gift, he rose quickly, and his technical acumen allowed him to design and develop technology that matched quality with his supernatural ability.

Had he ever been under his own agency? No, not really. His power had been co-opted by the Archai, and they fueled the rise of Alturas for their own purposes. When he had been defeated at Launch, they dropped him like yesterday's tech, ready to move on to the latest model.

"Uh, guys, we've got people coming this way—and they don't look happy." Sarah Jane's voice broke up his thoughts.

Being at the mercy of teenagers was so humbling. Maybe fitting. Definitely humbling.

"Is there a problem?" Demarcus called out.

Despite his impairment, Simon could sense something was off. Whoever approached, a feeling from them matched how people were when Simon used his power intensely to overwhelm someone. Typically, he subtly influenced them. But this, it was too familiar.

Pearce. The night he grabbed Simon and it felt like he ripped part of his soul out. That was his power!

"I have a bad feeling about this," he said.

"Guys, they have halos. They're part of Pearce's group." Lily's voice slid up to a high pitch.

He controlled more than Rosa?

"I'm getting sick of these people," Demarcus muttered. "Back off, or I'll make you back off."

An accented voice replied. "Your anger draws us. It will feed the Hoshek and fuel his plans."

Lily gasped. "Anger! That's the key. Demarcus, we need to run."

"Simon can't run. He can't see," Sarah Jane replied.

"We leave him." Demarcus answered. "I can maybe carry you two, but I can't do anything about him. He'll have to fend for himself."

Simon deserved it, but he didn't want it.

"No, we're not leaving him," Sarah Jane's voice carried a strength he hadn't heard before. "Demarcus, please take him and run ahead. Lily and I can slow them down and catch up."

"Whatever we do, let's do it now." Lily's voice wavered.

"Give 'em a light show, Lily. I'll be right back." Demarcus then lifted Simon's arm and wrapped him up, grunting as he barely lifted Simon. The air stirred around them as they accelerated away.

Simon's hair whipped around as Demarcus groaned. He had to lift his legs to keep them from dragging as the speedster ran. After a couple of minutes, they slowed to a stop.

"I'm leaving you to go help the girls. But I'll be back. Sarah Jane is adamant about helping you, which blows my mind. Just hang tight."

"Where are we?"

"I'm leaving you at the base of the Transamerica Pyramid. Stay here. We'll be back."

Before Simon could protest about being abandoned, a whoosh of air blew in his face. "Demarcus? Hey!"

No answer. Simon was alone in the city.

CHAPTER 39

LILY'S PALMS WOULDN'T STOP SWEATING, AND HER stomach cramped. She didn't want to end up like Harry, but her anger at Simon was still nagging at her. And that seemed to be a beacon to Pearce's goons.

"SJ, this is bad. If these guys are drawn to anger, they could take control of us. That's why Harry isn't here. The guy that controlled Kashvi and Aasif? He's Roberto Pearce, and he can suck people in with this black smoke stuff. Harry wasn't himself. I'm so sorry."

"If that's the case, let's not give them a target," SJ said, pulling on Lily's hand.

"One second." Lily tugged her hand away and raised it up high. She flashed a strobe effect, creating the wildest light show she could muster. The two coming at them stopped, holding their hands over their faces. That was their cue, so Lily motioned to SJ and they took off running.

"Why didn't you blast them?" SJ said, huffing.

Oh yeah. SJ was out of the loop on what the rest of them had seen. "They're innocent people, most likely. Pearce showed up at the football game tonight, and so many people fell under his spell. It must have been their anger that made them susceptible."

"I am so confused. And hungry. Is there food in that bag?"

Really? Well, she and Demarcus had to take a food break a bit ago. "You can have it when we get somewhere safe."

They ran past a corner and three more people cut them off. The black circles around their heads sent a jolt of fear racing through Lily. A man grabbed her splint, causing her to cry out in pain. Another man and a woman grabbed SJ and wrestled with her.

"Let us go!" Lily's heart thrashed inside. How could she not be angry when caught by these people? Her fear overwhelmed any other emotion as the man pinned both her arms against her body and wrapped her up with his large, thick hands.

Smoke started to swirl in the air.

"No! God, please!" she cried out.

A rush of wind blew past them, knocking Lily to the ground, but out of the grasp of the guy. He tumbled down the street and lay still when he stopped. Then SJ's attackers faced a similar fate, getting yanked away and dragged along the sidewalk.

Demarcus stepped out of the whirlwind, gripping and favoring his left side as he walked over to them. "Are you girls all right?"

Lily scanned the air around them. The smoke had seemed to dissipate. Thank goodness. "My arm hurts, but I'm fine otherwise."

Brushing dirt off, SJ looked around. "I'm good. Aw man, the bag got smooshed." She squeezed her temples and groaned. "And look at you guys. A couple days without me and you're falling apart. Let me pray for you."

Lily didn't waste time moving down the street. "As much as I'd appreciate that, let's get away from these freaks while we can. Try to keep calm—I hope that means the possession won't happen to you." She glanced at Demarcus. "And thank you so much. That had me as scared as anything we've ever faced."

"I have to watch my anger too, because there's no way I'm letting that happen to you two. I missed saving Rosa. It's not going to happen again."

SJ spun around. "Did you ditch Simon?"

He gave a sly grin. "Nah. I may have thought about it, but he's at the Pyramid."

They jogged several blocks, approaching the tower that dominated the skyline ahead of them. The lack of traffic boggled Lily's mind. Things must be locked down in the city if there weren't any cars driving by.

A few blocks from the Pyramid, SJ pulled them into an alley. "Let me pray for you before we get there. I think we're safe enough now."

Lily nodded, and the three of them clasped hands together and let SJ go to the Lord with their injuries. After a minute, Lily's arm began to radiate heat, along with some other sore areas on her body. The throbbing from when the guy grabbed her receded, until she knew from experience that God had allowed SJ to heal them. When she finished, Demarcus spun his arm like a windmill.

"Oh, that is so much better. Thank you. You know we missed you for more than just healing, right?" His big smile went along with the wink he threw her way. SJ tapped her bands twice in response, and Lily could see a glowing field surround her hands like gloves.

"You'd better mean that dude, or I'm trying out my special bands out on you next time. Simon already got a taste of them. Ratchet does good work." Her face fell from the smile she'd flashed. "Do you guys know how he's doing?"

Lily and Demarcus looked at each other and shrugged. "Man, it's been so crazy we haven't been able to check," he said.

They ran the last few blocks to the Pyramid. Simon sat, arms wrapped around his knees, tucked away from view. With his sunglasses on, it looked like he was napping behind the column.

"Are you all okay?" His voice sounded sincere, but Lily had to fight the anger that wanted to rise up at him acting all concerned. His change of heart did not seem sincere at all, just convenient for getting out of trouble.

"We're fine. Just a little excitement." SJ knelt beside him with the smashed bag of food. She pulled out the leftover burger and tore it in half, then offered it to Simon. He thanked her and they gobbled up the fast food.

Lily took off her splint and wiggled her fingers. Thank goodness she could ditch the thing. She wanted to toss it in the air and blast it, except it probably wasn't the best idea to draw extra attention to themselves.

Over by the glass base of the building, Demarcus motioned for her to talk with him in private. "What do you think is going on with Sarah Jane and Simon? Did he get to her somehow?"

Similar thoughts had filtered through Lily's mind when she wasn't fleeing rage zombies. They'd barely had a chance to connect with SJ. "I don't think so. She seems like herself, but it does seem strange, right?"

"You know that being blind heightens other senses, like my hearing. I'm open to talk about anything with you. I've made some terrible mistakes, and it's time to make up for whatever I can," Simon called out.

Lily closed her eyes and counted to ten, trying to keep her simmering feelings from boiling over. The threat of Pearce's minions forced her to cool down. When she had as much control as she could muster, she strode to Simon and sat next to him. "Okay. If you're ready to talk, then why did you have my mother and brother killed?"

CHAPTER 40

LILY'S VOICE DRIPPED WITH VENOM WHEN SHE ASKED why Simon had killed her mother. Where did she get this idea that he'd done something like that? Thoughts spun inside his head as he sought words that wouldn't lead to his face being melted.

Light started glowing in front of him.

"Lily, remember how you can start glowing when you're upset? Turn off the shine, okay?" Demarcus spoke in gentle tones to calm her down. Thank goodness for his presence to settle her. Beads of sweat trickled down Simon's face as the light faded.

Simon held his hands up. "You have so many reasons to be upset with me. I get it. However, this is one area that I truly don't know what you're talking about. I had nothing to do with the death of your mother." What had happened to Mrs. Beausoleil?

"Liar!" She must be close, as he felt her breath across his face. "I found evidence. Last week I found a disk in my father's desk that showed she had died in a car accident. Everyone thought it was caused by her mixing depression and pain medication and driving to pick up my younger brother. But the disk had code that replaced the real findings where the toxicology report cleared any chemical causes. And that code points to Alturas. Explain that!"

Code? What would be going on there? Yet, it triggered a vague memory...

Sarah Jane spoke in a soothing voice. "How did you find that out? You're as techy as the next teenager, but you're not a hacker. Or are you?"

Simon heard the sound of crumpled material and felt the pulses of air as something was waved close to his face. "Ratchet's gloves. They let me focus my light tighter, like a laser beam. I figured out how to use them to read the information off the disk. Things were so crazy I didn't tell anyone." Lily's voice veered from irritation to cracking as if she'd cry. "I'll ask one last time. What does Alturas have to do with my mother's accident?"

"Of course!" Simon smacked his forehead. It came back to him. "Let me explain. I remember reading your file at the Launch Conference. My staff had identified you as the one we needed, so I reviewed the research done on you."

"Dude, y'all were so creepy about things," Demarcus cut in.

"How do you think we identified all of you youth that had developed these special abilities, powers similar to mine? I'm going to back up. There's a shadow group that is working to change the world called the Archai. They recruited me several years ago, mentored me, and helped me use my gift to develop the Alturas Collective. They're the ones who worked with me on the plan to amplify my gift to influence youth around the world with our technology."

"That's why the presentation at Launch about the next gen fiber optics was a big deal, to spread your poison," Sarah Jane replied.

"The world has so much chaos. It wasn't supposed to be poison; it was to guide a new world future. That's beside the point. The Archai helped me develop the Source, and it needed power to run on—a light source beyond anything we'd been able to produce. They informed me that youth with special gifts were coming, and we created the Launch Conference to pull in youth who met the criteria the Archai suggested would lead to these abilities."

Demarcus clicked his tongue. "Which are?"

"We looked for youth who were isolated, broken, but not necessarily ones who'd spiraled into delinquency. There was potential in the candidates."

Lily sucked in a breath. "I knew it."

"See? You're all clever and capable. So back to your file. I remember reading it and finding the same code talking about the overdose, and seeing that it hid the true report. Someone did arrange to have your mother killed in that accident. I'm so sorry—but it was not me. I saw the connection, but not until well after the accident, and it went deeper than Alturas.

"We've all been manipulated by the Archai, even when it hasn't been as blatant as their orchestrating your mother's and brother's deaths. However, you can bet they have done things to drive you all to the place where you could come to Launch. Didn't you all move here recently?"

The three teens muttered, "Yeah," in response.

His voice began to break. "I've realized over the last couple of days how bankrupt I've become through all of this. When Sarah Jane told me that she had died and been raised back from the dead at Launch, I couldn't believe it. I realized that I hadn't even thought about how she was out and about and doing well—I had only concerned myself with getting you to fix my eyes. To get back in good graces with the Archai.

"But they don't want or need me. They moved on to another operative in this Pearce, and a different plan. All I've done is for nothing. I am so sorry that I got you all wrapped up in this. Please forgive me." Tears rolled out of his eyes. Why not? He just confessed to a bunch of teenagers about his ruined life. There wasn't anything to hold back anymore.

A pressure released off his chest, and he let out a gasp of surprise. The pain from whatever Pearce had done to him diminished. The ache wasn't fully gone, but it was as if a weight sitting on his ribs had shrunk significantly. He sniffed from his tears and rubbed his chest.

"Wow, that feels better. That pain...finally it feels like I can breathe," Simon muttered.

Lily answered in a sarcastic tone. "What, you're saying that confessing took a weight off your chest?"

"In a way, yes. I've had this throb in my chest since the night at the pier, and it just eased. In a big way." Simon coughed, and it didn't stab through him.

He could hear Lily and Demarcus shuffle around. Were they whispering? Yes, but quietly enough he couldn't make anything out.

"When Pearce grabbed you that night, what did it feel like?" Lily asked.

The last thing Simon wanted to do was revisit that feeling. Pearce had come after each of the gifted, and when he caught Simon, something sucked out of him and ripped open a wound that wouldn't heal. Sometimes it flared in sharp intensity, but it was always a gnawing, raw feeling inside. He shared that with them.

Demarcus chimed in. "And you feel better now? Did it just settle down from spiking?"

"No, it's different. It doesn't feel fully healed, but there is a big difference. It's not the distracting, aggravating pain anymore," Simon said.

"How did it get better?" Lily whispered.

A wind rustled in front of them, followed by Sarah Jane shouting a name. "Harry!"

"Sweet, you're all together. It makes things much easier for me."

CHAPTER 41

DEMARCUS WHIRLED AROUND AT THE SOUND OF Harry's voice. His friend paced back and forth a few times, eyeing them all. His red hair spiked in all directions, and his grin had a sinister look to it.

"It took me so many jumps trying to find just one of you. And here you are together, so convenient. Pearce will be very pleased with me when I deliver you to him." His voice had a harsh, edgy tone to it.

Demarcus had no idea how he'd take down a friend. He would have to figure that out on the fly.

Harry stalked toward Sarah Jane. "Well, hello there. You are the most wanted. It's good to see you again." A leer formed on his lips.

Man, this was not the friend that Demarcus had come to consider a brother. Sarah Jane scrambled back until she hit the slanted concrete pillar. Simon stuck his arm out in a protective manner in front of her.

"Harry, snap out of it. We're your friends. You don't serve anyone but God. Remember? We're the Anointed." Demarcus crouched as he spoke, in case his words didn't get through.

"If one gives in to anger, it can overwhelm anyone." Harry stopped and pointed at Lily. "If I took her instead, that would probably make you furious, right? I know how much you care about her." Another stupid smile.

Demarcus thought of football—focused emotions. Take out your opponent, but stay in control. "You're not doing any of that." He dashed at Harry.

His arms caught empty air.

Harry appeared over by the next column. "I'd like to see you stop me." He waved his fingers in a "come at me, bro" way.

Demarcus raced again, but not right at Harry. That would leave him ramming into the column, which he guessed was what Harry hoped would happen. Instead, he ran just past and tried to catch his friend on the way by. Nope. He was gone again.

Where did he go? Demarcus spun around but couldn't find him. Lily and Sarah Jane also frantically looked for him. "Can you see him?" he called out.

Something thudded into Demarcus's back and sent him sprawling hard to the ground. His knee split open, blood running down his leg.

Harry laughed. "Didn't see it coming?"

Demarcus dove for his friend, who disappeared again. He ran to the end of the columns and spun around, waiting. Once again Harry blipped into view, but now his back was to him. Gotcha.

His feet flew as he tried to corral his friend. Still, Harry was gone in a blink. Demarcus skidded to a stop, looking behind him.

Harry ran at him, a yell spilling forth. He was almost on top of Demarcus, not leaving any room to run, so Demarcus threw a punch. *Sorry, Harry.*

No one was there. Then a diving Harry appeared to the side and caught Demarcus. He heard the girls scream with the familiar warping of the air around him. Then he ran face-first into glass.

"Owwww." Staggering back, he realized Harry had ported them and used momentum to throw him into the glass walls of the lobby of the Pyramid. Blood dripped past his eye, and the metallic taste got in his mouth. Harry walked toward the girls.

Demarcus ran at him. Missed. Then Harry appeared in front of him, punching him in the mouth. His lip split and his head rolled to the side. Still, Demarcus caught Harry and pulled him close.

"That was a mistake," Harry snarled.

They disappeared again, only to reappear falling through the air. Harry waved before porting, leaving Demarcus to slam against the ground. Pain shot through his head and back. Rolling over, he coughed out some blood. His vision spun.

"Come and get me," Harry said in a mocking tone.

What was he doing? If it meant keeping him distracted from the girls, Demarcus would do this all day. Or...night. His temper was bubbling up, but he had to keep in mind that Harry wasn't in control.

Demarcus jumped up, moving in a zig-zag pattern to confuse Harry. When he disappeared, Demarcus stopped and ran back the way he came, fighting through the pain and dizziness, but nothing happened. No Harry.

Poof. Harry at his side, throwing a punch at the kidneys. Demarcus bellowed at the pain. Blip. Harry was on the other side, landing one to the gut. No matter which way Demarcus moved, Harry was there, pummeling him.

"You think you're the best of us. You take the lead, boss us around, and take all the glory. All you do is run fast." Another blow, splitting the cheek. Demarcus tried to catch him. Miss. "You're not fast. You can't even catch me. Who's the fastest now, huh?"

Demarcus lurched forward, diving for a ghost. He planted on the ground.

Harry stood over him, "Say it, who's the fast—"

Something blasted against Harry and sent him flying into the glass wall. He bounced off the glass and clunked headfirst on the ground. For a moment he tried to get up, then he slumped back down.

Lily ran over to Demarcus. "Light's the fastest thing in the universe. Just saying."

CHAPTER 42

LILY DABBED AT THE BLOOD ON DEMARCUS'S FACE AS his eyes wobbled. Man, there was a lot of blood from his cuts. At first, she was too freaked out at the duel between him and Harry to do anything, then it took a minute for her to line up a shot where she wouldn't get Demarcus. At least she had stopped Harry and his insane porting around for a minute.

Over where he lay, SJ fretted about him. "If I hadn't lost my medical scanner when Rosa took me, I could check his condition. If I just pray for healing, he'll wake up and terrorize us again. What are we going to do?"

"First of all, trade me spots and heal Demarcus. I think he's got a concussion from all the hits he took. I'll watch over Harry." Lily dropped the blood-soaked napkin and ran over to Harry. She kept her hand aimed at him while SJ prayed for Demarcus. His cuts miraculously sealed over, and his eyes cleared from the glazed look they'd had a minute ago.

Demarcus shook his head. "Thanks again. I can't believe the punishment he dished out. Holy cow, that was brutal. Even with my heightened reflexes, I couldn't catch him."

Lily stared at Harry, his limp form breathing quietly. Yep, the black halo emanated around his head, like all those she'd seen before who were controlled by darkness in some way. Like the people Simon had swayed in the past. What was in Pearce's power that could override a good guy like Harry? A trickle of warm tears ran down her cheek as her mind replayed the awful fight between friends just now.

What's the answer, Lord? How do we help Harry? The others?

A faint whisper floated through her mind. *Turn the other cheek.*

What was that? That thought, it didn't come from her.

Love your enemies. Pray for those who persecute you.

Lily remembered a lesson from John about dealing with those who stood against God's Kingdom. Instead of battling in a worldly way, he said Christians would do things differently.

So who's my enemy? Lily prayed silently.

Simon cleared his throat. "I don't think we should stay here. If Harry found us, then won't Pearce be right behind him?"

No. It couldn't be. Is this really you, God?

Bless those who persecute you.

A fight raged in her heart. Simon didn't deserve it. He'd done terrible things, and his eye injury was the consequence. Didn't the Bible say something about you reap what you sow?

The voice stayed silent.

The pain in her chest rose again. She'd gotten used to it to a degree, but sometimes it snared her heart and squeezed. Lily pushed her palm against her chest.

Didn't Simon just say that his pain had improved after he'd asked for forgiveness? Maybe Pearce had touched something inside of them when he sucked out part of their power at the pier. Could forgiving, saying sorry, possibly undo some of that?

"Man, Pastor Sanchez is going to kill me for getting his Niners shirt all torn up." Demarcus examined all the rips in his top.

"I think he'll forgive you," SJ said.

Okay, I get the hint.

Lily ran a hand through her wild hair, her conscience wrestling the last of her doubts down. The ponytail had pulled out back when they tried to rescue Aasif. It didn't even matter what she looked like now. She couldn't believe she was going to do this.

"Guys, I think I know what we're supposed to do. At least, what SJ should do," she said, her voice faint.

Demarcus stood by her. "If she heals Harry, what are we going to do? I can try to hold him. Maybe if you have something with light going on to confuse him, it will keep him from porting. Remember how Aasif's howl could throw him off?"

Shaking her head, Lily shivered. It wasn't just the night air anymore. The chill probably had more to do with her next words.

"I think Sarah Jane should pray for Simon—to heal his eyes."

The air stilled. No one moved or spoke. Lily cringed inside to prepare for the torrent of arguments coming her way.

SJ looked at Simon. "I—I think you're right. I've been feeling pulled to pray for him, I've tried to talk myself out of it. If you're feeling that way..."

No one looked more shocked than Simon. Even Demarcus looked accepting of the idea. He squatted by Simon. "I was wondering if you'd be able to help Harry out of Pearce's control. Do you think you could?"

The confident Simon of Alturas fame wasn't the one who answered. "I'm not sure. I know what it's like to hold sway over someone, so I may be able to. But how are you all coming to this idea? A half hour ago you wanted to blast me."

The girls shared a look. Lily nodded at SJ to go first. "When I feel like the Holy Spirit is leading me to heal someone, I get a spiritual nudge. I've been feeling that for a while tonight."

"And I've had a few verses pop into my head about loving your enemies. You did apologize for things you've done. Maybe helping Harry is a way you start making up for all that," Lily replied.

Demarcus folded his arms. "Sounds good to me."

"I—I don't know what to say," Simon replied. "Of course, I'll do what I can to help Harry. I don't want this craziness with people out of control. Let me prove it to you."

SJ walked over to him and placed her hands on his shoulders. "Simon, it's the Lord who heals, okay? I'm just his vessel. My friends have more control over their gifts than I have over mine. If it's not his will, it doesn't happen. You've been warned."

Simon nodded. "All I ask is for the chance. What other option do I have?"

"Have faith, man. Have some trust. There's something bigger than any of us happening here," Demarcus said.

Lily kept an eye on Harry but bowed her head as SJ started calling out to Jesus.

CHAPTER 43

SIMON HAD NO IDEA WHAT TO EXPECT OR HOW HE should act. Was there protocol for someone praying for you? His best idea was folding his hands in his lap as he kept his head down.

Sarah Jane spoke heartfelt words of praise to her God, thanking him for all the times he'd helped before. She listed off injuries and ailments, and the sound of the stories, if true, was impressive. Could this work? Was there really a God out there directing things?

God, if you're there, and this is something you can do, I would serve you. Let me make right things I've done wrong.

A picture formed in his head. Like a video playing inside his skull, the images streamed past. The words being spoken faded as his attention turned to the picture of a hill. Blood ran down the side, the dirt soaked with the dark liquid. Simon saw himself at the bottom of the hill, but in chains, unable to move away from the river of red flowing toward him. He struggled, but there was no way he could break out of his bondage.

The blood ran under him. Instead of his back becoming wet, it became hot. The chains wrapped around him began steaming up. He wrestled against the searing heat that he was sure would scorch his skin. The temperature increased until he felt like his whole body was on fire.

As he burned, the pain faded. No, it didn't fade, it just focused up into his eyes. Now his eyes blazed with warmth. He reached up to cup his face...

He was free! The chains had burned off. Frantic, he checked his skin and found nothing was even singed.

As he looked to the top of the hill, a man looked down at him. The man was horribly disfigured—his nose crooked and bloody, his face marked with cuts and bruising. All except the eyes. Brown eyes that fixated on Simon. With his history in the business world, he knew when someone had power in his gaze.

This was the ultimate example.

Yet that power came not from oppression, but from kindness, from a mercy that shone through as well. The man reached out a hand, one with a hole pierced through the palm. Despite the power in the man's eyes, Simon felt compassion draw him in. He reached his hand out, stretching until he made contact.

Come to me. A phrase planted in his mind.

Okay. I will.

The man transformed from the beaten, broken mess to an image of splendor. Illumination shone all around him. The man said, "Your sins are forgiven. Now go and serve." Then he touched Simon's eyes.

The vision receded like Simon was being pulled backward through a tunnel. The man waved as he faded into the distance. Simon didn't care about healing anymore— he just wanted to be with this man, to experience the freedom of that moment again and forever. It had been unlike anything in his life before.

Yet as the light turned into a pinprick, Simon felt peace settle over him like a morning dew. He would see the man again. Until then, he had work to do.

CHAPTER 44

"SIMON, ARE YOU OKAY? TALK TO US."

The words came through fuzzy, like someone speaking through a sheet. The coolness of the cement chilled his skin. Wait, he had fallen over? He groaned, pushing himself up, and opened his eyes.

Instead of the hazy darkness, forms took shape. Simon shook his head, blinking rapidly. Two faces stared at him intently. A girl, with reddish-blonde hair and freckles. A boy with dark skin and dreadlocks. Behind them, another blonde girl stood over a boy lying on the ground, with only his red hair showing.

Sarah Jane, Demarcus, Lily, and Harry.

Simon wiggled his fingers in front of his face. There they were, all ten of them. The hope of healing had been so elusive, with so many setbacks. Yet here he sat, his eyes taking in the colors and details he'd missed for months.

And yes, there were the tiny threads that emanated from all of the youth. The strings only he could see that would allow him to influence, manipulate, and even control them.

No, wait. Things were different. The aspect of manipulation wasn't there. Instead, he saw how if he acted or spoke a certain way, he'd inspire, encourage, and even empower them to do greater things that they could even imagine. Instead of his gift being selfish, arranged to cater to his desires, it had been redeemed. Now it could serve others.

Just like his life.

Sarah Jane leaned in closer. "Are you all right?"

Simon reached out and caught her in a hug. For one second, because Demarcus rushed in and pulled him away, throwing him back on the ground.

"Don't touch her. You're not going to control her like at the conference," he growled.

The act should've made Simon mad. Instead, he understood he probably deserved such doubt. He'd have to prove himself.

He pushed himself up, hands in the air. "I was going to thank her—all of you. After everything I've done or been a part of, I didn't deserve that. It worked. I can see again." Simon choked up at the next words. "There's something more. I've changed inside."

"Guys, we may need to stop the inquisition. Harry's stirring," Lily called out, worry painted on her face.

Amazing. He could see her face, the way her eyes and brow crinkled, revealing her anxiety. There were the little cues, and the ways he could reach out and calm her.

Demarcus zipped over and caught Harry's arms behind him. Right, first things first. Proving himself to them. No, it wasn't even about proving himself—it was about helping someone in need.

Harry's eyes slowly opened. Simon scrambled to get to him before he could teleport. When the boy turned and snarled at him, it almost took Simon aback. The black connections pierced deep into Harry—they were tied to anger. Simon put his hands on both sides of Harry's head and gazed into his eyes.

"You are not this rage. You are a man of promise, of faithfulness, and of joy. Release your anger." Harry thrashed against the two of them holding him, a keening sound escaping from his lips.

"Let me go. I need to get back to the Hoshek!"

What on earth was the Hoshek? "No, you're free. Don't hold on to the anger. Rise up into who you were made to be." Simon's head pounded from the effort. He hadn't been able to use his gift for months, except on Rosa, who had already been ingrained.

He focused on the strands. Harry tried to head butt him, and Simon barely missed getting his nose broken. Now, break these connections. Rewire them over there. Do it!

Something popped mentally inside Harry. Simon didn't know how to explain it, but the tangle of threads had been loosed enough he could pull them all out. The hold slipped away. Harry's body slumped to the ground, the whites of his eyes rolling up. Simon broke into a cold sweat as he dropped his hands.

"Is he okay?" Demarcus asked, still holding his arms back.

Lily peered closely at him. "The dark halo dissipated. I don't see it anymore." She caught Simon's gaze. "Thank you."

Groaning, Harry rolled his head back and forth. "Why did you guys let me get run over by a truck?" Then his eyes closed again, and he started snoring.

Sarah Jane dropped to her knees and gave him a hug, then her prayers spilled out for his healing. Demarcus let his arms go and sat back, releasing a long breath. "Man, he can buck, can't he?"

"Yes, he could. Thanks for holding him back, or I'd have a broken nose." Simon rubbed a thumb against his temple, trying to massage the lingering pain away.

"Your eyes—they're back to normal," Demarcus said, pointing.

"That's good." Simon replied.

"I thought you'd be more excited to get your vision back."

How to explain things? "When Sarah Jane prayed for me, there was something else. Something more important than just getting my vision back, or my gift—"

His voice cut off as a pair of headlights slowed on the street next to them. A breeze whistled through the columns, tussling their hair. There was no way they weren't seen, and if these people weren't friendly...

The old van stopped and the headlights turned off. Simon, Lily, and Demarcus all geared up in case they were confronted. The doors opened.

The driver was a bald man wearing a white tank top under a loose button-up shirt. "Demarcus, is that you?"

"Dad?" Demarcus sounded incredulous. "How did you find us?"

His dad pointed to the other person rounding the front of the van. "I had help. Someone who's been looking for you."

An old man with wispy white hair on his scalp and a thin beard crossed into sight. The teens all gasped in unison, while it took a moment for Simon to process who it was.

"John?" Lily cried out.

"It's me, my children. Let's get you off the street."

PART THREE

CHAPTER 45

ANOTHER SET OF POLICE LIGHTS DROVE PAST THE VAN while Demarcus's dad slowly wound his way toward his... hideout or whatever. The traffic was negligible, but various roadblocks forced them into a tortuous route to their destination.

Despite the excitement of finding John alive, being reunited with Sarah Jane, and saving Harry, the adrenaline crashed in everyone else. Lily's head lay on the shoulder of Sarah Jane, who leaned against a comatose Harry in the back seat. The dude had been out since Simon had helped him, so they hadn't had a chance to ask him what had happened.

Simon stared out the window, contemplating something serious. And John helped Demarcus's dad, Tony, with navigation—which should be a sitcom in another life. Demarcus couldn't laugh at any of it though.

As tired as he was, he couldn't shut down and rest. His body felt great after Sarah Jane had healed him, again, from the injuries he took while battling Harry. Those were the physical injuries though. The mental issues...

How was John alive? Demarcus had sat with him as he passed away. His father, the deadbeat dad who had barely shown up in his life, was now working with his mentor to get them out of the city in the middle of the night. And Simon, their nemesis, worked with them to help Harry.

Next thing you know, Mama would fly over them with the power to control fire, the way this night was going.

The van slowed and pulled up to a small house with stairs leading up to the front door. The muffler backfired as Tony killed the engine, and everyone sleeping started awake. Except Harry. Sleeping beauty kept sawing logs while he leaned up against the window.

Demarcus and Simon strained to get Harry up the stairs and deposit him on a ratty couch next to the front window. The girls sat on kitchen chairs with chipped paint. Smart move—there was no telling what was on the upholstery. They yawned and stretched their arms out. Then Lily looked at her phone.

"Does anyone have a phone charger? I'm dead."

Tony showed her where his plug-in was connected. She should charge first, in case they heard updates from Ji-young. Demarcus had seven percent, so he could function in an emergency.

John sat cross-legged on the floor, and the rest found places to sit. All except Simon, who stood back, leaning in a doorway. John motioned for him to join the group.

"You are welcome to join us, my son. I have been praying for you since seeing you at Launch. I believe you are as much a part of this as the rest of us," John said.

Simon paused, then moved closer and sat on the floor as well. Demarcus had never seen him appear nervous. The confident tech leader always appeared in control, but now he kept his eyes down.

"It is so good to see you all! I know it has only been a few days, but I believe they have been, what is the phrase? Eventful? Please tell me about what has happened."

John is back from the dead and he wants *them* to start? Demarcus thought about the ways they had not followed his advice recently, and how those decisions had not gone well. The failure in responsibility weighed on his shoulders.

As much as he wanted to hear from his mentor, if John wanted them to talk first, that's what he'd do.

Demarcus, Lily, and Sarah Jane took turns sharing their adventures. They hadn't even caught up with each other, so hearing how Sarah Jane was held captive by Simon for two days, cuffed to a bed, was terrifying. And here was her captor, sitting nearby with his head and eyes down as she described what had happened. At least she hadn't been hurt, except for some initial bruising from Rosa when they first took her.

John sat thoughtfully through all the explanations, only asking a few questions as they spoke. When they wrapped up, he clapped his hands. "It is late. Why don't we all take a cue from Harry and get some rest?"

"Wait, you're not going to tell us about you?" Demarcus was incredulous.

"There is not a lot to tell. The Lord heals, and here I am with you now."

Sarah Jane raised her hand. "When I died at the conference, it just felt like I was asleep. Was it like that for you?"

That made John stop and consider for a minute. He closed his eyes and smiled. Demarcus leaned forward, dying to hear what he had to say. John's body going limp in his arms replayed in crystal clarity through his head.

"I understand the curiosity. Just know that our Lord is very good and faithful. He has a plan for each one of us, especially in the darkness." Demarcus couldn't help noticing how he eyed Simon with his last statement.

John insisted on everyone resting, so he had the girls go into the one bedroom. Demarcus and Harry would sleep in the living room. Tony was going to sleep in the van and keep a watch out on the front of the house. Demarcus got the feeling Tony realized it was awkward for his estranged son and his friends to be staying with him.

As Demarcus tried to relax on the couch, he noticed John pull Simon into the kitchen and shut the door. He tried to listen in on the conversation, still wondering how much Simon could be trusted. But instead of hearing their private chat, the exhaustion from the night took him into fitful dreams of being chased and never outrunning his enemies.

CHAPTER 46

THE RINGTONE FROM LILY'S PHONE STIRRED DEMARcus out of his sleep. Harry's yelp and falling on the floor in a clunk made him shoot up straight. Where were they?

Oh yeah. His dad's place. Faint sunlight streamed through the ugly curtains hanging over the windows. They must have been asleep for a while—it was so late at night when they finally crashed.

Lily stuck her head out of the door. "Is that my phone?" She had good hearing. And crazy bed head. Her blonde strands stuck out like she was doing an eighties day at school. Demarcus had to stifle a laugh while she snatched her phone and ducked back into the bedroom.

"Dude, where are we?" Harry rubbed his head and yawned. He had blood on his clothes, and the same vagabond appearance as Demarcus and Lily. They all looked like they'd been through a war zone last night. Which, technically, they had.

"We're at my dad's house. He picked us up last night and brought us here. You don't remember any of that? What about...earlier?"

Harry stiffened at the question. "I don't remember how we got here. Before that—" Tears welled in his eyes and he started shaking. "Oh man, I am so sorry. I didn't...I couldn't...it wasn't me." Sobs cut him off. He pushed his head between his knees and rocked on the ground.

Heads poked out of the other rooms as Demarcus sat next to Harry and put an arm around him. "Hey, I know. I know it wasn't you. I can't imagine what you were going through. It's okay. It's over now."

John and Simon entered the living room. Sarah Jane—her face pale, bags under her eyes, and hair askew—slipped out of the bedroom where Demarcus could hear Lily talking on the phone. They quietly gathered around while Harry let the hurt flow out. John's lips moved in silent prayers.

After several minutes Harry settled down to slow, deep breaths. Lily slipped in toward the end and joined the quiet circle. After a few moments, it appeared Harry had come to the end of his crying jag. -

John rested a hand on Harry's shoulder. "Can you tell us about things?"

It took another two minutes of silence before Harry started, his voice quiet and shaky. "I don't remember everything. I mean, it's so hazy. When we were first seen by the Hoshek, it noticed the anger in me. It was like a stinking beacon. When we ported away with Aasif and he threatened Sarah Jane, I lost it. That was like the key to letting it take me."

Sarah Jane wrapped herself in her arms when she was mentioned. "Harry, what is the Hoshek? You said that at the Pyramid too. Is that Pearce's other name?"

Harry shrugged. "It's the Hoshek. Pearce is just the vehicle, I think. It's just this horribly evil thing that wants to sow chaos and destroy things."

"'Hoshek' means 'darkness,'" John replied. "It's an ancient entity of darkness that serves the enemy. It's been tied to the child sacrifices in the temple of Marduk in Babylon, for example. I've seen the enemy work in subtle ways to draw people away from the light, through knowledge and philosophy. Greed is a favorite tactic, as are fear and pride. Sometimes, he lashes out with such hate and fury that history itself is rocked."

"You nailed it," Harry said. "The Hoshek is planning to spread this...rage virus? It's how it's thinking about the plan, at least. Last night it was gathering its forces. Today it will start launching all those people out to multiply the effects, with the goal of reaching throughout the country and across the Pacific."

Demarcus picked at hole in the jersey he wore. "Wow. Maybe it was a good thing this happened. You were like, an undercover spy."

Harry recoiled, his eyes huge. "Don't even say that. It was terrifying. Attacking you. Threatening Sarah Jane and Lily. It's like I could see what was happening, but I was in the back seat and not in control."

The group sat, stunned at Harry's description. The atmosphere in the room filled with anxiety, and everyone fidgeted except their mentor.

Lily looked at John. "What does this mean? If we're Christians, aren't we God's children? How does this even happen? Is it something like, I don't know, possession?"

"Listen carefully. You are all God's children, because you have been saved. There are things that can't happen—like demon possession. This is different though. If we give ourselves over to anger or other sin, we can be ruled by it and not walk in the ways of Jesus. Our hearts can be hardened to the Holy Spirit. Think of Christians in the American South during segregation, or everyday Germans in the 1930s. This is an extreme case, where one can be blinded by his anger. We all know there is so much antagonism right now in our world. It breeds a perfect ground for the Hoshek," John explained.

They all pondered the heaviness of this revelation for a minute. "So you were angry at Aasif, and about Sarah Jane missing, and that triggered it?" Demarcus asked.

Harry put a hand on Demarcus's shoulder, shaking his head. "No man, that's why I apologized. Sure, I was frantic about Sarah Jane missing, and Aasif and I didn't click. But I need to ask for forgiveness from you." Harry's voice quivered again.

"Me? What about?" Demarcus couldn't understand where he came into this.

"I remember mocking you for not being fast and saying terrible things. The thing is—" Harry gulped. "That wasn't from the Hoshek. It was pulling resentment from me. Dude, I'm sorry, because I have been jealous and angry with you. It's stupid, but you're a natural leader, and I'm always in the background. That's the root of what made me susceptible. I'm so sorry." He ducked his head down again.

Whoa. They had butted heads recently about how to do things, but Demarcus didn't realize how deep things had gone. Were there things he had done to make Harry mad? His brain couldn't process this with all the events of the last few days.

Even though the confession had blindsided him, Demarcus couldn't stay upset with his friend. The thought of losing him to the Hoshek was too terrifying; anything else was trivial. After several awkward seconds of silence, he found his voice. "Hey, I forgive you." It sounded like a small offering in the scheme of things, but otherwise, words escaped him.

The front door creaked open and Demarcus jumped to high alert. His father pushed the door open with his hip, carrying several fast-food bags in his hands. "Am I interrupting something? I figured breakfast would be needed, although it's almost noon."

Lily's mouth dropped open. "We slept this long?"

"Y'all didn't lie down until after four a.m., so I wouldn't be so surprised, young lady. Ain't that what teens do?" Tony set the bags on the table and spread them out.

Food. Demarcus was famished with all the running around for the last twenty-four hours. He used his speed to snatch up two biscuit sandwiches and sit down before anyone else even got up. "Oh, sorry guys. I'm starving."

Harry started to get up before patting his chest. "Dude. That pain we've had since the pier? It's almost gone. Not quite, but so much better than before. That's a relief." He slowly made his way to the table to snag three paper-wrapped meals.

As everyone sat down to eat, Demarcus's brain churned around what Harry had just said. The pain was better. Last night was foggy, but Simon relayed the same things. What was it that made the blasted ache get better?

John wrinkled his nose at the sandwich offered to him. "I still cannot understand how you grow so much when this is the type of food you consume." He took a bite, reluctantly.

"Hey Lily, how's that pain in your chest? Any better?" Demarcus called out.

Lily swallowed her bite and took a swig of the water bottle next to her. She was probably dying without her coffee. "No, still really achy. Thanks for bringing it up." She grimaced as she held a hand over her sternum.

Okay, so Harry and Simon had improvement in their conditions, but not Lily and him. It wasn't time passing. He started on his fourth breakfast sandwich to recharge and wrestled with the puzzle before him. What was the common denominator?

It wasn't being freed from the Hoshek's influence. Age? Nah. He drained a bottle of milk and something hit him. Both of those guys remarked about feeling better after... they asked for forgiveness.

Was that the key?

"John, four of us were attacked by Pearce at the pier. He grabbed us, and we all felt like something was sucked out of us, and it left a constant pain that sometimes stings or throbs. Now Simon and Harry say it's better, while Lily and I still suffer. I noticed that they had improved after asking for forgiveness. Do you think that's even possible?" Demarcus said.

John seemed relieved to put down his food. "Certainly. If we hold on to anger, hurt, or if we have wronged others, it affects us. Usually it's spiritually or emotionally, but this is a different season. If the Hoshek is involved, it's a level of spiritual warfare that is unlike anything anyone's seen in a long time."

Tony Carter passed through the living room, handing out napkins and water for everyone. Demarcus felt his shoulders tighten. His chest burned at the emotions his father dredged up in him, even if Tony was helping his friends.

Oh, I see. My problem is right before me.

CHAPTER 47

YEARS OF DISGUST TOWARD TONY CARTER MADE Demarcus want to vomit his hastily ingested breakfast. Lunch. Brunch. Whatever. As long as he could remember, he'd hated that his father had abandoned his mother. Yet it was always an abstract thought, because he'd never met the man; it was just part of Demarcus's backstory. It sharpened his intention to be a stand-up man, to never let a woman down.

When he'd met Tony Carter about a week ago, Demarcus hadn't wanted anything to do with him. The first visit went as poorly as it could have, and he thought that was the end of it all. But his dad had been at the pier battle somehow, and they fled together after John's apparent death, parting ways that night with uncertainty hanging between them.

Somehow, Tony Carter had given their once-dead mentor a ride to rescue them from being hunted in the city. Could it get much weirder?

Lord, this is so deep. It's different than Harry being upset and jealous of me.

The room seemed to shrink until it was just him and his dad. Everyone else faded out of focus. A tattoo on his dad's arm stood out—a man grimacing under the weight of a heavy boulder. Demarcus hadn't noticed it before. The image almost glowed from his skin. What burdens did Tony Carter carry?

And what burdens did Demarcus let weigh him down because of his father? What had that done to him?

The pain in his chest tried to overwhelm his courage. Okay, sure, it would hurt to confess to Tony Carter. Dad. But wouldn't carrying that load hurt worse over time?

His dad sat in the corner, staying out of the way. He was quiet, but observing everything going on. Demarcus couldn't imagine what was going through his head, being thrust into these supernatural battles.

Sucking in a breath, Demarcus pushed himself up from the floor and walked over to him. "Hey, can we talk in private?"

Tony eyed him warily for a moment, then nodded. He rose slowly and led him to the bedroom.

The creaky door shut behind them. A single bed and a rickety nightstand were the only furniture in the room. A suitcase with some scattered clothes sat in the corner. The room smelled stale, and old stains dotted the carpet. Not a luxury place at all.

"Yeah, it's not much. It's all I could afford when Roberto Pearce paid for me to come up here. I don't even know what the dude is up to since Saturday night when he went all crazy. So, what's up?" Tony said.

The reminder that Pearce, probably controlled by the Hoshek, was behind Tony getting back in Demarcus's life didn't make this any easier. Demarcus swallowed, sat down on the bed, and fingered the thin sheet on top. Tony stood near the window, staring outside and avoiding eye contact. Waiting for the first move.

"Hey, uh...we got off on the wrong foot when we met. Now, I'm not ready for a close relationship or anything, but—I'm sorry. Forgive me for blowing up and not listening. And I've been angry at you for a long time. I don't know how long that will take to clear up...I'm not sure where to go from here. Maybe things can get better down the road." Demarcus sniffed, trying to hold back tears.

Tony looked like he'd received a gut punch. They sat in silence, eyes wandering around to avoid contact with each other. When Demarcus did look him in the eye, tears welled in Tony's.

"Wow. You're something special, Demarcus. I was interested to meet you, sure, but I'll confess, at first the main draw was the money offered. When I pay off some debts back in SoCal, I'll finally be able to get on my feet, after all the trouble I've caused.

"But when I got up here and met you, something changed. I realized what a dirtbag Pearce was, and I knew he'd used me to mess with you.

"I decided to stick around. Found y'all at the pier. Watched you risk your life to save people. I realized if I could find one last chance to connect with my only son, I should take it. Then your friend prayed for me after Pearce attacked us and healed not only my body, but something in my mind. I wasn't sure at all if I could turn things around after this was done. Now, things don't look as hopeless as before."

Tony moved to the bed. Demarcus didn't flinch or try to move. His dad put a hand on his leg.

"But out of all of that, you ask for forgiveness. After all I've done. Your mom truly did something awesome with you. You're more of a man now than I ever been in my life. I need to say sorry to you. Sorry for leaving you and your mama. Sorry that I allowed Pearce to use me to hurt you. I just hope I can make it up over time." Tony choked back a sob with his last words.

There was hope. Demarcus never thought he'd know his father, or want to meet him, the way his feelings had been for so long. Time would tell if Tony Carter was serious. For the moment, he was a dad to Demarcus. The anger faded. It wasn't fully gone, but the conversation had done work in lessening it. And with the anger, the pain subsided as well.

They shook hands and got up to leave the room when a shriek shot through Demarcus.

Lily?

CHAPTER 48

ALL HER FRIENDS WERE TRYING TO CATCH UP WITH their families. Lily's phone charged enough that she could text her dad that she was fine and that they had found SJ. He promised to pass the news to her parents. Now she waited for Demarcus to come out, so she could give the group a heads-up on the latest from Ji-young.

Hold on, another message just came through. Her friend from school, Clara, had left voice mails and texts wondering what had happened. Apparently, she was worried about something. Lily almost shot back a reassuring text, but decided she could use a friendly voice to help her along. She dialed her friend's phone, hoping she'd be on lunch break.

"Lily! What is going on? Holy cow, things are crazy. You're not at school. Videos online sure look like you were doing wild things at the game. And then there's Missy..."

Um, that was a lot all at once. There was video of them at the game? Great. But that last bit. "What's going on with Missy?"

"Oh my goodness, you wouldn't believe this at all. She's doing a virtual press conference, of all things! She's talked the media class into recording an interview with her, where she'll say that the girl in the Levi Stadium videos is the same one that attacked her at the dance. Everyone at school is talking about it. Sorry, Lily," Clara said.

Red flooded Lily's vision as her heart raced at the thought of Missy dragging her identity public like this. How dare she? She was the one who hit Lily first at the dance.

Demarcus came out of the bedroom with his father. Lily covered the phone's mic and whispered, "Did it work?" hoping he knew what she meant. He nodded yes and the two of them joined John at the kitchen table.

That was it then. Forgiveness was the answer, both to her pain and to the situation with Missy. The thought of apologizing to the wicked girl turned her stomach. But her chest answered with a spasm that brought tears to her eyes. "When and where is this interview happening?"

"Anytime now, I think, because she's doing it during lunch," Clara replied.

That meant there was very little time. How would Lily get to her? The school was too public. "Do you know where Missy is right now?"

"Yeah. I saw her go into the drama room. I think she's putting on make-up to look her best for the cameras—even though she wants sympathy from her injury," Clara said.

"Isn't today the day the drama classes are performing at the elementary schools?" If that was the case, the room would be empty.

"Yes, it is."

Lily could work with that—if she could be persuasive enough. "I need you to do me a big favor. Turn on your location tag and stay as close to Missy as you can. I'm going to try to get there and put a stop to it."

Clara gasped. "You...you aren't going to—"

"I'm not going to blast her or anything. Hopefully I can make things right. And you'll meet a couple more of my friends in the process." Lily bit her lip, saying a quick prayer that her zany plan would work. "Just hang on and be ready for guests."

She hung up and made for the corner of the room, beckoning Harry and Sarah Jane to her. The two were deep in talk, and the lovebirds needed space to do it, but this was time sensitive.

"Can you two help me make something right? If everyone's asking for forgiveness, this is what I need to do," Lily asked in a quiet voice.

They looked at each other quizzically. "Let me guess, you need transportation?" Harry replied.

"Yes, and I need Sarah Jane to heal an injury I caused. It wasn't intentional, but it was a significant burn on Missy Austin's cheek. Do you mind?" Lily twirled a piece of hair around.

"Of course I'll help," SJ replied. "What are you going to tell everyone?"

Lily took a step forward and let out a whistle. "Hey everyone, I need to make a mistake right, and these two are going to help me. Don't go anywhere, because I've got updates from Ji-young to share. But this is something I have to do, like, now."

Before anyone could argue, Lily pointed at Clara's location on her phone. "That's where we need to go." She took Harry's hand, as did SJ, and the room warped away.

———

The drama room appeared around them. Clara turned and squealed in shock. "That was the coolest thing ever!" Her smile beamed, letting the scarred side match the other. "How did you do that? Oh, and you look terrible. Did you get dragged behind a truck?"

Lily rolled her eyes, but her hands went to her hair to finger comb it as best she could. "Thanks a lot. Introductions: this is Harry, he can teleport. Sarah Jane, and she heals. Cool? Cool. Now where's Missy?"

"Bad news. She just walked out of the room." Clara pointed to the door to the main hall.

"Oh no!" Lily ran to the door and threw it open, her friends following behind. There was Missy, halfway down the hall. "If she takes a left, there's no catching her with the lunchtime traffic. Harry, I'll dim the lights. Can you get her and bring her back to this room?"

He cracked his knuckles. "Sounds like fun."

Lily raised her hand towards the lights and dropped the brightness down to almost pitch black. She heard a yelp down the hall. The air around her shifted as Harry ported away. She blinked into infrared to see a red blob appear next to another blob and then see them both disappear. Okay, lights back up. The person walking just ahead of Missy turned in a circle. "Missy, where'd you go?"

That was epic.

The sound of retching came from behind her. She clicked the door shut and ran over where Harry held a garbage can for Missy as she lost her lunch. He stared at the ceiling, turning pale himself. Hopefully he didn't puke as well.

"Missy, I'm sorry to do this to you, but we need to talk." Lily squatted next to her high school nemesis.

Her brown eyes widened in horror. The blisters on Missy's left cheek had shrunk, but the inflamed skin appeared painful. "Not you. Leave me alone, freak. You're trying to silence me!"

"I'm not going to silence you. But I am trying to change your mind." Lily held her hands out in a surrender pose, to show there was no light show coming.

"That's a funny way of doing things. How did I get here?" Missy glanced around frantically.

Harry waved. "Howdy. I'm the glorified transport."

"You brought back-up this time?" Missy almost shrieked.

"Listen to me. Then you can do what you want. I am so sorry for hitting you and doing this. I apologize for the prank where I cut your skirt. Please, let's not fight anymore. We were friends once. I don't want to be enemies. I'm asking for your forgiveness," Lily pleaded, tears trickling down her cheeks.

Missy pointed at her face. "You think I can forgive you with this? Forget it. You're going to be kicked out of this school."

"I can make it right. Give my friend one minute. She can heal your face." Lily pointed to Sarah Jane.

"No! Get your freaky friends away from me." Missy started to scramble away.

"Guys, close your eyes," Lily said. Harry and SJ nodded, understanding what she had to do. A burst of illumination flared in the room. As Missy squeezed her eyes shut, Lily caught SJ's hand and put it on Missy's shoulder. Frantically whispered words spilled out.

Missy gasped. "What are you doing to me?"

Lily ran over to the make-up counter and snagged a hand mirror. Hustling back, she stuck it in Missy's hands. "I know made a terrible mistake the other night, but I hope this will show that I'm seriously sorry. Do what you have to do—I can't change that. What I can do is swear that I won't ever do what I did to you last week again."

Holding the mirror with one hand, Missy ran the other over her healed skin. No trace of the blisters or burn remained. Even some acne had cleared. "How? We went to the doctor, and they said it would have to heal on its own..."

Thank you, Lord, for giving me mercy in my screw-ups.

Lily took Missy's hand, who didn't fight it this time. "My friends and I have gifts. I'm not going to use them for petty things anymore. I've got to go. I only ask that you think about what it would mean if my secret got out any further. That's the gift you could give me."

A voice sounded from outside of the room, calling for Missy.

Missy raised an eyebrow and frowned as Lily stepped back. She wasn't screaming, which was the best Lily could hope for. Now it was up to Missy. Lily couldn't think of anything else to do but hope for the best.

Harry and SJ joined her as she motioned for the three of them to duck into a changing room. At least the girl didn't have lasting damage. All she could hope now is that Missy didn't expose Lily.

As the three of them took hands, Lily noticed how much better her ache felt. In the next instant, they disappeared.

CHAPTER 49

THE CRAMPED LIVING ROOM MATERIALIZED AROUND them, and Lily stumbled off of something under her foot, pitching backwards. Right into Demarcus's arms.

Her cheeks flushed when he smiled at her. "I gotcha," he said, helping her stand up straight.

"Thanks. That was good timing." Lily couldn't help but bat an eyelash at him.

"What did you guys do?" Demarcus asked.

"Sorry about taking off so fast. I made a mistake with my power last week." Lily cleared her throat, realizing that the whole room watched her. "Actually, first I abused it, then a girl slapped me because of that. I retaliated, but in my temper my hand lit up and it caused burns on her face. I just found out she was about to give an interview connecting her injury to video of me at the stadium."

No one jumped in to scold her, so she continued. "Between that and everyone feeling better after apologizing, I had a short window to make a difference. Thankfully Harry and SJ helped me, her face was healed, and hopefully she won't go through with the interview. If not, at least her face is better." Lily let a breath out.

SJ smacked her arm. "I'm okay to help this time, but I'm not here to clean up your messes." A wink accompanied the grief.

"Trust me, I don't plan on making this a habit."

Harry grinned. "I wonder what she thought about her first Harry trip."

Okay, that was funny. With the pain in her chest eased, Lily felt like she could laugh again.

John sat patiently on the floor, legs crossed, watching Lily, eyes full of compassion. Seeing the mercy in his eyes, she settled down to give him her attention.

"You said you had something to share with us. Are you ready to do that?" he asked.

"Yes, sir. Sorry. Ji-young said that people are still massing at the Palace of Fine Arts. The police and National Guard have cordoned off the city on a line stretching from Golden Gate Park across to the bay as best they can. We know that if they're too close to the crowd, then police and soldiers can be affected and join the Hoshek. People are trying to evacuate south of the line, but the congestion has every road clogged. It sounds like no one has any idea what to do."

SJ looked around. "So where exactly are we?"

"Just north of Golden Gate Park. That's why food took a long time this morning," Tony said.

A somber mood filled the room. Harry squirmed, then spoke up. "The Hoshek wanted to spread this rage virus or infection as far and wide as it could, so I'm not sure why it's holding people in one spot. It was also interested in perverting our gifts—especially Sarah Jane's. One thought from it burned in my mind: how intent it was on finding you."

A breeze stirred the curtains, sending dust motes dancing through the air. The light from the window diminished. Another cloudy day in the Bay Area. Lily wanted to be in her dad's arms right now. The fight had drained her.

John stood up and started walking around the room, putting a gentle hand on everyone as he passed. Including Simon. "I am afraid it is time to confront our enemy. You have all been through many hardships, and I sense the fatigue in this room. However, today is the reason for your gifting and call. You were made and gifted for such a time as this."

"Gifted, so we can be royal screw-ups, get brainwashed by the enemy, and generally flail about?" Harry waved his hands so much water splashed out of his bottle. "I don't feel like I'm worthy of the battle, much less ready for it. I messed up so much the last time."

No kidding. The only thing they had done well was help Kashvi and Aasif, and they blew half of that by putting Aasif in harm's way again. Lily couldn't imagine how they would stand up against the Hoshek any better this go-round. Rushing into battle was the last thing she wanted to do right now. She just wanted to be home—except that even home wasn't a safe place to be.

"Your failures did not come as a surprise to God. Were you warned about going into the conflict before you were ready?" John motioned to them, and they all nodded. "Yes, you are correct. There would have been less pain, less suffering, if you had listened to wise counsel. But we are in a battle, and it is not against flesh and blood.

"The fight is not against those poor people controlled by the Hoshek. Not even Roberto Pearce. So much pain radiates off him, but he was tricked by the Archai. As was Simon and look how he stands here now. He is ready to go with you into the fire."

John stood beside Simon. The man had been silent ever since they had been picked up in the van. Their greatest foe at one time now stood meekly next to a shorter, wizened man who outshined him in inner strength. John placed a hand upon Simon's shoulder and gestured to the group with his other arm.

"You will all be tested. But the secret to your victory is in God's hands, not your own ability. How many times have I mentioned that you are not alone, but you were brought together. Unity! Only together will you find the strength and power to overcome your enemy."

The curtain began to clap against the sides of the window as Simon took a half step forward.

"I'm here to help in any way I can."

CHAPTER 50

HOW MUCH COULD A LIFE CHANGE IN TWENTY-FOUR hours? Simon couldn't help but wonder as he stepped forward at John's urging, declaring himself to be on the side of "the Anointed."

The looks from the teens in the room revealed their thoughts: they didn't buy it. Why should they?

"I know you all have no reason to trust me. I've been a part of manipulating and using all four of you. Hear me out, and if you reject me, that's fair. John and I talked for a while after everyone else fell asleep. I've never had a conversation like that in my life."

Simon glanced at John and gave a faint smile. This man, who had infiltrated Alturas to intervene and save these kids, should be an enemy to him. Yet the elder had illuminated more for Simon than all his years of learning and seeking. So much made sense now, but he had many more questions that bubbled up every minute.

If only these teens realized who it was they had the privilege of knowing as their mentor, they would freak out.

No one objected verbally, so Simon continued. "I see now that we're all on a journey. It's meant to intertwine, but not like I had planned at the conference. Instead of being the tech guru everyone thought I was, I'm supposed to stand with you. Our gifts are meant to work together, and if you'll have me stand by you, I promise I will do everything I can to inspire you all. I realize my ability's true purpose now."

Harry squinted his eyes at him. "And what exactly is that?"

That's right, Harry wasn't in his right mind when he heard Simon explain things before. "I thought my gift allowed me to influence people to my will. That's a corruption of it. I'm supposed to inspire others to God's full plan for them."

He had nothing else to explain. Hopefully one day he'd get the chance to share all that he'd gone through and give them the full picture. It didn't matter right now. There wasn't time.

John motioned for everyone to sit who wasn't already. "You have more allies than you realize. God is always at work and moving in ways you may never see. Today will be hard. It may take sacrifice. But I am confident in you all. I believe this is an anointed time."

The wind whipped through the open window. Simon could also see out the kitchen window in the back, but nothing was going on out there.

Stepping to the window, John smiled. "Ah, I see the Lord is already providing." He opened the curtain and pushed the window open as far as it could go, then moved away. A drone entered through the window. A tightly wrapped package was connected to the underside of the machine. Everyone gave it room as it landed in the middle of the floor.

Simon admired the construction of the drone. This was no store-bought model. It was a custom job. Who was behind this?

CHAPTER 51

THE DUST SETTLED FROM THE DRONE'S LANDING. Demarcus and Lily exchanged glances. Could this be who they thought it was? He leaned forward, examining the chassis for clues.

A small screen popped up and a video feed crackled to life. "Hello? Did I get the right place this time?" Ratchet's face beamed in the screen, his smile outshining the cuts and bruises still healing. "Oh hey, Demarcus! Looks like third time's the charm."

"Ratchet?" All four teens blurted their inventor friend's name in unison. The last they had seen him, he was unconscious, connected to tubes and wires in the ICU. The nurses thought he would be out for a while. Yet here he was, all smiles as he rotated the screen to see everyone in the room.

"Howdy, guys. Sorry that I've been out of touch. Apparently when Sarah Jane prayed for me, there was a delayed reaction. I didn't heal immediately like when she normally does it, but her prayers accelerated the process nonetheless. Then I had to get back to my lab to salvage some gear and get working on these. The inspiration came to me after your last visit, and I was working on them when Applied Sciences got attacked. Which was kinda cool except for all the pain, destruction, and near-death stuff."

What was going on? First Simon helps the Anointed, then John is back, and now Ratchet is up to his crazy tricks again. Demarcus pinched his arm to make sure he wasn't in some psychedelic dream. Ow. Nope. This was real life.

The video stopped at Sarah Jane, who had tears streaming down her face. "I'm so glad you're better. That was horrible seeing you in the hospital. Are…are you fully healed?"

The feed zoomed out to show Ratchet in a new wheelchair, which wasn't as fancy as the previous one that got wrecked when Kashvi and Aasif attacked Applied Sciences. "That part is still what it is. Don't worry—I'm in good shape. Besides the scrapes, I feel great.

"What are you all waiting for? Go try them on! They're labeled, so don't get them mixed up." Ratchet leaned into the video screen, waving them on with his hand.

Demarcus and Harry lifted the drone up while Lily pulled the container out from under it. Tony found a knife for the tape and slit it open carefully. There were four packages, wrapped in brown paper, with names on them. Demarcus got his and tore through the paper. He held out a blue and white colored—what? No way.

They had super suits?

"Are you kidding me? How dope is this?" he yelled. Harry gave him a high five as they ogled their new threads. Lily and Sarah Jane chattered excitedly, their faces beaming.

Demarcus pointed to the bedroom. "Ladies first."

A quiet "hey" escaped from Harry, but they both waited as the girls split between the bedroom and bathroom. After squeals came from both rooms, the girls walked out.

Lily and Sarah Jane looked like they could jump into a superhero movie right now and fit in. Their suits had blue pants and blue tops with white sleeves. The elbows and knees had reinforced areas with the opposite color to make them stand out. White belts and tactical boots completed their outfits. The logo was a starburst pattern.

"How does it look?" Lily gave a twirl.

Demarcus almost asked if he could kiss her but realized that was the worst possible move at the moment. Lily looked amazing—like she was born for the suit. Sarah Jane was similarly incredible. They were going to be a super team!

"Your turn." Sarah Jane nodded at them. Demarcus didn't need to be told twice, and he dashed into the bedroom. Only to find Harry already there, pulling his shirt off.

"Hey slowpoke, use the bathroom," he teased.

Demarcus zipped into the bathroom and threw the tattered red and gold off. He pulled on his pants, belt, and shirt. But there were no boots for him. Oh, right, he already had Ratchet's special running shoes that didn't wear down and would let him run on water if needed.

He jumped out with a flair. His top had a white chest and blue sleeves, otherwise the uniforms were the same as the girls'. The belt had small pouches built in. Wait a second. Did this mean they had utility belts?

Harry burst out of the bedroom. "Dude, we are Batman!"

Yes, they had utility belts. Life was good.

"What do you think?" Ratchet chirped from the video screen. "I was originally thinking of a red and black pattern, but then remembered that one time-travel superhero movie. Can't be copycats."

"They're out of this world!" Sarah Jane shouted. Wow, she was usually the subdued one.

"I'm wondering what secrets you have built in," Lily said, poking at the utility belt around her waist.

Ratchet belly laughed. "Finally, one of you catches on. Okay, so you see the belt. I put some goodies in each pouch. Tracking devices, smoke bombs, an electronic lockpick to hack terminals, things like that. The suits are water resistant, impact absorbing, and aerodynamic. Don't go jumping off the Golden Gate Bridge, but you'll be able to handle more damage than without them on."

Demarcus noticed Harry trying to swing for his shoulder. Without teleporting, there was no doubt who was faster. Demarcus dodged and threw his own punch at Harry's arm. "Ow, hey!" he grimaced.

"You started it," Demarcus answered with a grin.

"Demarcus, you noticed you don't have new footwear. The sneakers you have are the best I've got. I know your reflexes are enhanced with your speed, but there's a collision detector built into the suit."

Ratchet rubbed his hands together and continued. "Sarah Jane, you've got my diagnosis software loaded in your gloves. Instead of the medical scanner, just touching someone will give you the medical information needed. And it still has the kinetic barrier for some punch."

Demarcus noticed Simon quietly shaking his head at that statement.

"Harry, you've got a built-in GPS locator on the wrist. And Lily, remember how your gloves caused feedback when you tried to do holograms?"

She nodded. Demarcus would never forget how she distracted the Hoshek at the pier with a holographic angel and how it scrambled her brain for the night.

"When I run the signal through the whole suit, it dissipates the feedback. That won't happen anymore, so you're good to go. Plus, there's the focuser for the laser and all that." Ratchet's grin couldn't get any wider.

"Hey, didn't you guys get the goggles?" He pointed at his eyes.

Yep, there was a small package at the bottom of the container. Simon unwrapped it and handed out four goggles with blue lenses and straps. "Not bad," he offered while they tried them on.

"The goggles are Lily-proof, they display the direction you're facing, and the earpieces that clip in give you protection from those sonic screams and comm units to keep in touch with each other. All the suits have individual tracking units, so you'll know where each other is. No one's getting kidnapped this time," Ratchet said.

Despite the blue tint on the lenses, the view looked clear. Small ear pieces built into the straps slid down to cover the ear canals. "Testing one, two, three. Computer, activate the shields," Harry said over the comm.

The light from outside dimmed. Tony pushed the curtains open again to reveal dark clouds rolling in, making the afternoon sky unnaturally sinister. "Uh, is this part of the whole end-of-the-world scenario we looking at here?"

Ratchet looked like he was furiously tapping on a keyboard. "News reports are coming in about the shadowy sky. I think things are starting to happen where you guys are."

Lily's phone rang. "It's Ji-young." She picked up and got an earful of frantic conversation. Demarcus could hardly make out any of it. Lily tried to calm their source down without much success. She ended the call and looked around, ashen.

"The crowd has been dispersing. People are running south and east. Ji-young thinks they're heading for Oakland, the San Francisco airport, and San Jose. That's what she's extrapolating from the ways they're streaming out. Police are trying to evacuate people along the path and contain the crowd. She's not sure how successful things are going for them." Lily rubbed her arms while speaking.

"Wow, that woman has some fast sources," Ratchet replied. "Oh yeah, tap your Bluetooth on your phones and they'll sync with your earpieces. You can call with a command and keep your hands free. Very important when battling angry hordes."

Simon lifted another package out of the container. "Hey, it looks like there are two more outfits. Who are they for?"

"I heard from Pastor Sanchez that the kids who trashed my lab are on our side now. I didn't have specific data on them, so I whipped up the basic version of suits for them." Ratchet beamed with his preparedness.

"Did you realize if you adjust the rotors for your drone, you'd improve air speed by fifteen percent?" Simon replied.

Demarcus tried to hold a chuckle back while Ratchet appeared flustered on the screen. "I was more concerned with efficiency over speed."

Simon rolled his eyes. "Then you should have used a polycarbon fiber shell instead of titanium."

Ratchet grumped but jotted a note down on a pad.

"I do not wish to interrupt the excitement of new goodies here, but I think it is best if we formulate a plan to help contain the problem and deal with the Hoshek," John said.

"Right. I'll shut up, get my drone out of there, and let you all get to it," Ratchet answered. He tapped some keys, then scrunched his eyebrows in frustration. "Hey, it's not responding. That shouldn't be happening."

Demarcus's eyes widened as he noticed Simon's thumbs flying across a smart phone. Oh snap. The nerd battle was on. "Ratchet, I'd love to talk shop with you one day, but I'm commandeering the drone to give the Anointed eyes in the sky. Thanks for putting in the Bluetooth compatibility. By the way, your encryptions are pretty good."

"Good? No one in my company can crack them. Now give me back my drone. I can be their eyes as well as you." Ratchet snapped, pointing into the camera.

"Not as well as me. I'll be in the field with them. I'm sure you'll understand. Honestly, this is impressive tech. Let's trade notes later, when the city isn't near disaster." Simon tapped a command on his phone and the drone started up again, flying toward the window.

Ratchet's voice trailed off into the night as his toy was fully hijacked.

CHAPTER 52

SIMON SET THE DRONE TO A SENTRY PATTERN OVER the house so they'd have eyes in case Pearce's goons came this way. Their tech friend Ratchet was pretty good. He'd probably be able to show Simon a thing or two.

John motioned them to join in a circle. What a bunch. An old man with so many secrets, an ex-con who had just started turning his life around, four teenagers in high-tech suits, and Simon. He had to stifle a laugh at the thought of this group standing against a wave of evil flowing over the city. Yet a resolve fixed itself inside Simon. Like he had finally made the right choice, to stand with this ragamuffin group over his former tech friends or the power-hungry Archai.

"We will pray together," John said. He led, and the Anointed teens joined him, in praying for wisdom, strength, and mercy to handle the enormous task in front of them. Simon kept his head down, trying to form his own thoughts into prayers. The jumbled feelings in his heart wouldn't come into a coherent stream. Hopefully his intentions came through in the cloud of ideas flying around inside.

Powerful words poured from John. He slipped into Greek for most of it, and even then, the strength of the man's faith shone through. After several minutes, he wound down, and asked for God to be glorified through it all.

No matter the cost, Simon thought. They had to stop Pearce and this Hoshek tonight, before the chaos spread too far to contain.

"Listen carefully, my children," John said. "This is going to be hard, harder than last week. It is going to be the toughest challenge you all have faced. I have faith in you. I believe you have gone through trials to prepare you for this, and that those trials will bear fruit tonight.

"The most important thing to remember is that this is not your battle! The battle belongs to the Lord. You are to be his vessels, and you need to do things in unity. The enemy defeated you all when you had your own agendas, when you tried to fight in your own way. Do not let this happen tonight."

John pointed at Tony. "Mr. Carter will provide transportation for me, and we will try to come to the best place to support you all. Simon and I have talked, and he will go with you to help you in the midst of the conflict. His gift will be a blessing.

"I do not know how this night will go. In my many years, I have seen darkness win battles at times, only to lose the war. The point is to stand strong in the Lord, and in the power of his might, not your own. Do not fear, for he is with you. Now go, stand for the Kingdom."

Goosebumps rose on Simon's arms as his spirit swelled inside him. He was supposed to be the one with the gift of influencing people—yet he'd never been as inspired as this short speech had made him just now.

Everyone took a minute to text their families. Simon watched the scene without jealousy, just a hint of sadness. He'd burned those bridges and could never go back.

Unless that wasn't true anymore. If the things that he'd seen in the last twenty-four hours were true, then anything was possible. He tapped a contact on his phone to see a long-forgotten number. He deleted four messages before finally tapping out a simple, "I'm sorry for everything. I hope to see you soon."

The teens gathered around the table, taking long swigs of water and eating up the last food from Tony's run earlier.

Simon joined them. "I'm sure that it seems awkward to have me coming along. I promise I will do everything I can to help you."

They glanced around at each other. Sarah Jane stuck her hand out, inviting them all to do the same. "Simon, we're all on the same team here. We're stronger together."

The others followed suit. Was someone going to lead them in a cheer, like a sports team breaking a huddle? Before anyone could speak up, the alarm went off on his phone. He whipped it out to see the drone's warning flash. The camera showed a crowd spreading down the main street intersecting theirs.

"Sorry, gang, but it's time to go. We've got company." He pointed to his phone.

"Let's go, John." Tony dangled his keys as the two of them left through the door.

Harry snapped his fingers. "Where to first?"

"Let's get to high ground to see what's going on, and we'll figure things out from there," Demarcus said.

They looked at Simon. "Yes?"

"Well, you're the adult here," Lily said.

"You guys have experience with...whatever this is. I'll follow your lead."

Harry winked at him. "Buckle up for a wild ride."

CHAPTER 53

THE GROUP APPEARED ON THE TOP OF A SMALL SKY-scraper that overlooked several neighborhoods with a few other tall buildings nearby. Demarcus let go of Simon's hand as he stumbled to the edge of the roof and threw up.

"Sorry I didn't warn you. The first time usually ends up like that for people," Harry called out.

Simon gave the thumbs-up sign in between retching.

"Where are we?" Lily asked. "It doesn't look like the financial district."

A voice came through their comms. "Ratchet at control center here. I gave a suggestion to Harry's GPS. This is off Russian Hill. It's halfway between the Presidio and the financial district, so it should give you a good vantage point of what's going on."

The sky was a strange kind of dark. There were clouds overhead, without any low-lying fog. The atmosphere was an unnatural twilight, too early for this time of year. Wind caused the girls' hair to flutter, and they both reached for hair ties to make ponytails.

Demarcus found the directional readout on his goggles. The Palace of Fine arts should be...northwest from where they were now. He scanned the cityscape, trying to identify anything out there. "Hey Ratchet, do these goggles zoom or anything?"

"Oh yeah, forgot about that. Tap the left side of the frame," Ratchet said.

Tapping the frame made his field of vision go telescopic. That was pretty cool. He searched from north to west. Was that a crowd marching down the roads over there?

"Hey gang, if you need me to identify anything in your vision, let me know. I have all your feeds pulled up. Even my drone, although Mr. Big Deal has flight control." Ratchet muttered the last sentence, making Demarcus chuckle.

"What am I looking at here?" Demarcus asked.

A few keystrokes sounded in the background. "Looks like the 101 Highway. Let me corroborate with traffic reports. Yep, looks like a huge group is going down the 101. You're just seeing the tail end of it. There's a bunch of people on there, running and walking. They'll be at the airport in an hour at this rate."

"Anything else out there?" Demarcus couldn't see the end of people streaming down the highway. There were thousands, none of them in their right minds.

"There's a lot going on. Let me check and get back to you." Ratchet clicked off.

Screams sounded from below. Demarcus ran to the edge, where everyone else peered down. It was too dark to make out much detail. "Lily, do you see anything?" She had the cool infrared vision.

"Yes. I see a couple of blobs fleeing a big blob. Over there." Lily's hand shined a beam down to the street, pointing out two people running and turning, while a group pursued. "Guys, they're in trouble. That's a dead-end street."

Demarcus almost called out to Harry, but he was already holding hands out. "Uh, Simon, will you keep a look out from up here?"

He waved them off. "Go. I'll do what I do best."

They disappeared from the roof and landed on a ramp that led up the crest of a hill. They reappeared behind the crowd, who were chasing and shouting at their targets.

"Hang on, gang. I'll get in front of them." Harry warped them to a new position, intercepting the fleeing people.

The two kids slowed at some hedges along the street. The guy called out, "Come on, Micaiah, this way." Instead, the girl bent over, then stood and threw something.

A rock flew through the air and pinged the side of Harry's head. "Ow! The suits don't help our heads."

The girl slapped her hands over her mouth before calling out, "Sorry! I was aiming for them." She pointed past the Anointed.

Sarah Jane yelped as someone wrapped arms around her, and Demarcus staggered back as hands grabbed his dreadlocks and pulled him down. People swarmed over the two of them.

"Get off." Demarcus vibrated so fast it knocked people away from him. He jumped up in time to see Sarah Jane push her attacker and send him flying down the sloped street. "Girl, you been working out?"

"Ratchet's defensive gloves." She held her hands up.

Lily blasted the other people still coming. They all groaned and fell to their knees as she hit them in the abdomen with plasma bolts. For the moment, they were safe.

Demarcus zipped over to the startled kids. A guy with wavy brown hair stood by a younger girl with long, dark hair. Sweat trickled down their brows as they caught their breath. "Are you all right?" Demarcus asked.

"Yeah, we're good. Thanks," the guy said.

"Caleb, I think these are the ones I've seen online. Last night there was video of a girl with light powers like hers," Micaiah said, pointing to Lily. The girl's brown eyes widened, shining in the light Lily was projecting.

"Dude, that stuff you guys did was sick. We saw those guys about to attack a homeless person, so we shouted at them and got them to chase us," Caleb said.

"Yeah, our plan kinda fizzled from there," Micaiah finished.

Lily gave them a glowing thumbs-up. "I think that's pretty heroic of you guys. But our friend Ha—this guy here can get you to safety. Will you let him do that?" She pointed to Harry.

"Sorry about your head," Micaiah said, kicking another rock with her toe.

"No problem. Where do you guys live?" Harry smiled.

They gave an address and he put it in his GPS. "Hope you haven't had anything to eat recently. Take my hands, and we'll be outta here."

"Your suit needs a sun on it," Micaiah called to Lily before she disappeared.

"You should have a sun on there," Demarcus agreed.

"Guys, fashion another time. There are more ragers coming this way," Simon said over the comm.

Harry blipped back. "Those two didn't even lose their cookies with a teleport. Impressive."

They gathered on the rooftop again, scanning the surrounding area. Roaming groups filtered through the streets, heading either south or east. No other people seemed to be out, choosing to stay indoors or out of sight at least.

A call came through Demarcus's phone to the glasses. "Hello?" Hopefully it wasn't a telemarketer.

"Demarcus, is that you? It's Riley." The voice sounded rushed and out of breath.

"It's me. What's going on?"

"I'm stationed near the Golden Gate Bridge, at the checkpoint to keep these people from spreading. They've started coming and we can't hold them much longer—they don't respond to commands or crowd control methods. We need help."

Background noise muffled some words. "... hold the line, I'm calling for back-up. Demarcus? Can you help?"

"We'll be right there." The line clicked off. The group stared at him, wondering what that call was about. "That's a police officer I met. He's with a checkpoint by the Golden Gate Bridge. I'm going to go help him."

Lily caught his arm before he could take off. "We need a plan. I've got one idea, if Kashvi is willing to help. I don't want to see you running off alone in the meantime."

A buddy system was a good idea. They'd have to split up at this point. Lily's blue eyes searched his, the color augmented by their goggles, pleading with him to listen.

Sarah Jane came up. "I'll go with Demarcus, since you have the idea. The rest of you get Kashvi and meet us at the bridge. We need to keep the people contained as much as we can. You'll be right back. Just don't forget to take this." She handed a bag with the spare suits to Lily.

Before they could do anything else, Ratchet came on the line. "Guys, there are groups pushing south as well. I don't think you can be all places, even with Harry teleporting. And how are you going to stop the crowds anyway? Knock them all out?"

Simon had his phone to his ear. "Look, the answer is going to be to take out the source of the problem. You're right, we can't stop every person out there. We have to get to Pearce and stop him."

"Hey, how'd you get on this line?" Ratchet asked.

"Simple decryption. I need to be in on the conversations too." Simon shrugged at Demarcus.

The nerd battle continued.

As the two techies bantered, Demarcus focused his attention on the neighborhood around them. Occasional screams from who knows where made the situation creepier than it already was.

"Okay, I'm sending the drone to the bridge to monitor things," Simon said. "Ratchet, keep us updated on things elsewhere in the city. Hopefully we will find the Hoshek and put an end to this."

CHAPTER 54

"DEMARCUS, WE HAVE A PROBLEM." RATCHET CAME over the comm as Harry blipped away with everyone except Sarah Jane, after he had gotten them to street level. "The area before you get to the Golden Gate is teeming with people. I don't see a way to get you through there by land. It's saturated."

Demarcus could see a group marching a block to their west. Thinking of all the people crowded around the Palace of Fine Arts when they tried to rescue Aasif, it wasn't a surprise that an angry mob still streamed away from there. He'd never seen such a crush of people before.

But if land was blocked off from them, what about the sea?

"Ratchet, how do things look directly north of us?" Demarcus grinned at Sarah Jane, who was quickly braiding her hair.

"Uh, I'm not sure if I like the look of that smile. What do you have in mind?" she asked.

A few keyboard clicks sounded in the earpiece. "There's a path forward. If you leave now, this will get you to the water's edge. You'll have to take a few zig-zags to avoid ragers. I'm uploading the directions now."

An arrow appeared on Demarcus's display. "Wait, no map?"

"That's in the 2.0 version. This is what you get. You've played video games before, just treat the arrows like that dance game or something," Ratchet said.

That was...clever. "Sarah Jane, you ready?"

She shrugged. "I guess—"

That was all he needed. He scooped her up and dashed north. She yelped and clung to his arm, nearly cutting off circulation in the process. Sarah Jane was almost as tall as Lily, so there wasn't much difference in balancing another person's weight, but Lily had learned to shift with him. Sarah Jane's stiff hold made balance trickier.

An arrow pointed left, so Demarcus cut, stumbled, and almost wiped out. Then the arrow flipped back to point the way they had just come. He skidded to a stop just in front of an enraged crowd. Their howls followed them as he sped away.

"Ratchet, what was that?"

"Dude, I've never played a game with a real-life avatar before. Plus, twitchy games aren't my bag. I'm more of the strategy type."

Another group loomed ahead. "Ratchet!"

"Right, sorry. Recalculating." Ratchet's chuckle echoed over the line. Another left turn popped up, so Demarcus ran that way, slowing down enough to take tight turns and not slam into another group if he got wrong directions.

"Uh oh," Ratchet said quietly.

"That's not good, Ratchet. I'm getting car sick here," Sarah Jane called over the line.

Demarcus slid to a stop on the top of a hill. "I'm stopping until I get a solid lead. What's going on?" He surveyed his surroundings, seeing people coming at him from a couple of directions.

"It's a dynamic situation. They're not staying put, you know. Okay, I've got an out for you. It's a block away, but Sarah Jane may not like it."

She looked up at Demarcus. "Why?"

"It's getting out via Lombard Street."

Oh snap. Demarcus had wanted to try the famous road sometime. Though ideally not when carrying someone and evading a raging horde.

"What's wrong with Lombard Street?" Sarah Jane said.

"You know that street in all the movies that is hairpin turns down the hill?" Demarcus replied.

"Oh no," she gasped.

"Yep. Hang on!" He ran up a block and saw the sign pointing right. And another pack of ragers right there, charging forward. Demarcus cut to his right, zipped around the first curve, doubled back, and almost ran into a deserted car. He dodged to the side and felt Sarah Jane's feet drag against a hedge.

The shift of weight made him twist and slam to the ground. Thankfully Sarah Jane was on top of him, but her weight made the air puff out of his chest.

"Are you all right?" she said as she tried to pick him up. He rolled over and tried to catch his breath before getting to a standing position. They were right next to a walkway, with a rager coming right at him, some guy in athletic gear charging hard. Without breath, Demarcus wasn't going to get away...

"Duck!" Sarah Jane squealed as she stuck her hands out and hit the man, making him tumble into a heap down the curved road. Demarcus saw her squinting with her hands up, peeking at the downed rager.

"Girl, way to go," he huffed. C'mon air, get in there.

"These toys of Ratchet's are sick. I can't believe I did that. Is he going to be okay?" She started running to the man before Demarcus could stop her.

"Wait, what are you doing?" He shambled after her, his lungs slowly catching up.

Sarah Jane knelt by the man and started praying for him. Demarcus made it over and felt like his wind was back. The coast was clear for a moment, even though the sound of others approaching carried in the night.

"Hey, what if he attacks? Let's get to where we're needed," Demarcus said, laying a hand on her shoulder.

The man coughed and sputtered, jerking up right and startling them both. Sarah Jane fell back, hands raised. "Oh man, what happened?" The guy rubbed his head, wiping off a trickle of blood in the process. "It was like a walking dream. Or nightmare. I was so angry—but I wasn't myself either."

Okay, that was welcome news. "You're feeling less angry though? No pain or rage?" Demarcus asked.

The guy nodded. "Yeah, I'm all good. Peaceful, even. What's going on?"

"Read about it online. We've gotta go." Demarcus scooped up Sarah Jane and finished the twisty journey down Lombard Street. An arrow signaled left, and he sped up.

"That was abrupt," Sarah Jane said.

Another couple turns, and they headed toward a familiar sight: Hyde Park Pier. The park was still cordoned off with yellow tape as they zoomed by. "I know it was, but we've got someplace to be. Now hold on and trust me."

He hit the sand and then started skimming over the water. His special shoes created a small field to temporarily make the water into a non-Newtonian fluid, giving him the ability to run on the ocean. Sarah Jane yelped as the spray of saltwater hit them. "This is crazy," she squeaked.

"It's sweet. But what's even better is that your prayers can free ragers from the spell or whatever it is. We've got to get you on the front lines."

In a minute they veered south, before racing under the Golden Gate Bridge. There was a small amount of shore where he could make an easy transition to land. They picked their way from the edge of the ocean to the roadway. He let Sarah Jane down, and they surveyed the situation.

Floodlights ahead blazed over the toll stations, where cars were in line to cross the bridge. A group of officers in riot gear with shields tried to hold their line against a furious horde pushing forward. One officer screamed out when black enveloped him. Great, the Hoshek took another one.

A small break-off of ragers tried to run to the side to flank the police barricade. Demarcus sped in front of them. An incredible variety of people came at him: young, old, all sorts of nationalities, men and women. One player still wore his football gear from the game last night.

Demarcus spun his arms in tight circles, creating a whirlwind that blew them back. A police cruiser swung in behind him, creating a better barrier here to block access from the side. A familiar officer jumped out.

Riley spoke into the handset on his shoulder. "We have back-up on the east side, so we're secure for now." He ran up to Demarcus, admiring the threads as he approached. "You've upgraded to full-on super suits now?"

Demarcus pointed to Sarah Jane, who was already praying for someone hurt that had been pulled behind the line of police. "And I've got help. She's a healer if you've got injured. And we've got others coming any minute."

"That's great. This surge is about to push us back unless we get serious with force. And if what you say is true, they're not in control. The guy from the Palace is,"

Riley replied, gesturing in the distance to where the Flare torch still stood in the sky.

A piercing noise cut through the night and the floodlights started exploding. Officer Riley and the other first responders around Demarcus fell to their knees, covering their ears in pain. Demarcus could tell the sound was going on, but it didn't affect him or Sarah Jane as it did the others. Thank God. But this also meant Aasif was nearby.

Demarcus craned his neck, looking for him. "Do you see him?" he asked Sarah Jane.

She started to answer, but something fell from the sky. No, not a thing—a person. Her black hair fluttering in the wind, Rosa descended and slammed her fist into the roadway when she landed. The force of the blow sent Demarcus flying, crashing through the glass door of a building off the side of the road.

He ended up against a counter, his body leaving an imprint in its side. Shaking his head, he saw glass trickling across the floor. The suit helped him take the punishment, but that still wasn't any fun.

Groaning, he pushed himself up, careful to avoid shards of glass. He stepped up to the empty door frame, leaning on it to clear his head.

That's when he noticed Rosa had picked up the police cruiser and had him in her sights.

CHAPTER 55

THE SCENERY CHANGED FROM THE DOWNTOWN street to Highway 101, near the junction with Interstate 80. Lily and Harry started toward the big crowd ahead of them, but a scuffling sound on the asphalt caught her attention. Simon was down on the ground, barely holding his lunch in. "I don't know how you guys get used to that," he said between deep breaths.

"It's an acquired taste," Lily said.

The sounds of prayers came from the large group stretched across the road, as they walked slowly forward. It was amazing to think of a typically busy California highway devoid of traffic. Deserted cars littered the lanes to the south. Road rage must have made easy pickings for the Hoshek.

The three of them pushed through the crowd until they saw Pastor Sanchez near the front of the procession. He was talking to a Catholic priest when they made it over to him. "Whoa, Father Jacob, this is Lily and Harry." She could see him eye Simon, trying to place him. "Sweet threads, guys. You look like superheroes now."

Lily and Harry greeted Father Jacob, who started going down the line, passing instructions to others in the fore. Harry pointed at the crowd. "You've got a lot of people here."

"Thankfully, there are many good people who don't want to see their communities torn to shreds. We've mustered whoever we could who was willing to take a stand for God," Pastor Sanchez replied.

"We're trying to deal with the situation. But we need some help. Do you know where Kashvi is?" Lily said.

"Over here." Pastor Sanchez pushed through the crowd a few lines to reveal his wife and Kashvi. The girl's hair spilled from her head in a messy bun, and her brown eyes were wide.

"Lily. Harry. How are you guys? I was so scared for you, being out in the city."

"Good now," Lily said. "It was pretty crazy. But we're trying to stop Pearce once and for all, and we need your help. The others are waiting for us at the Golden Gate Bridge, trying to hold ragers back there." Lily mentally offered up a prayer of courage for Kashvi.

"I...I'm nervous about being exposed to these freaky people. I don't want Pearce to control me again," Kashvi said, her voice shaky.

Harry nodded. "It happened to me last night, and I'm not thrilled either. But we've learned it's from anger. If you open yourself to rage, then you can be taken. Remember, Aasif couldn't settle down—he was so edgy even after we teamed up, and the two of us kept butting heads. Now that we know, I don't think it will be a problem."

"We're working on a plan to take out Pearce and the Hoshek—the creature that's using him as some kind of host—and hopefully that will end it all. But we need to buy time at the bridge. We've even got a gift for you." Lily held up the suit she'd carried along.

She heard Pastor Sanchez mutter something about wanting a suit.

Shouts sounded in the distance. The swarming throng neared the procession. Lily wished she could give Kashvi time to consider the risk she was taking, but time was not on their side. "What do you say?"

"We need to stop this if we can," Kashvi said.

"Go, you four. We've got this area covered. I'll pass the word along about keeping anger down," Pastor Sanchez said, shooing them off.

They pushed back through to the deserted part of the highway. An abandoned van was perfect for Kashvi to change into the suit. She looked it up and down after stepping out of the vehicle. "This is pretty nice."

"Thanks. I pride myself on my workmanship," Ratchet chipped in over the comm.

"Oh. Uh, many apologies for attacking you. I hope you're okay," Kashvi said, her eyes darting around as she got used to the earbud and goggle set-up.

"Doing great, thanks for asking. But my drone is showing some bad things starting to happen at the Golden Gate. You guys ready to go?" Ratchet said.

As they took hands, Kashvi leaned over to Lily. "Is that Simon Mazor? He's very handsome in person, isn't he?"

———

They appeared where Ratchet had given Harry coordinates. Behind them spanned the famous Golden Gate Bridge. In front of them, Rosa screamed as she threw a police car at a building.

At Demarcus!

Lily cried out and blasted the car as hard as she could. The vehicle tumbled sideways, crashing to the side of where Demarcus was. The crunch of metal hitting the edge of the building echoed around them. The car's siren began blaring as it rested upside down, a warped soundtrack adding to the angry shouts of the multitude. The din was punctuated by a familiar banshee wail from Aasif. Great, all their foes were at the party.

Demarcus dashed over to them. "Good to see you. So, what's the plan?"

Who said anything about their group figuring out the plan?

"I have no idea. Who Googled how to defeat a super-villain? Anyone?" Harry shrugged, his sarcasm dripping from his words.

"I think we need to retreat. Look." Kashvi pointed to the mass of people pushing through the ranks of debilitated officers. Even more clambered over the wrecked police car that had taken out a police barricade when it landed.

Plus, Rosa looked ready to attack again.

"If we get closer to the water, I can block them," Kashvi yelled.

Simon grabbed Demarcus's shoulder. "Tell the police to fall back and keep themselves safe. We'll draw the crowd away from them. We need to isolate the Hoshek somehow to fight. It won't work to take all these people on."

Lily raised her hand and flashed her light show again. The ragers slowed at the blinding lights, but Rosa started charging. "Uh, a little help here?"

Before Rosa could close the distance, Harry appeared behind her, caught the woman's arm, and disappeared again. That would give them time to run up the ramp toward the bridge. Lily, Simon, and Kashvi began running. Wait, where was SJ?

Sliding to a halt, Lily turned to see SJ kneeling and praying for someone. A police officer with a shield and club was coming at her, a black halo signifying he was under Hoshek control. "SJ, watch out," Lily called over the comm.

The guy swung and SJ managed to duck just in time. Lily powered up a thin plasma blast and aimed it at his hand. It knocked the club out of his hand and spun him away from SJ long enough that she could scramble away. Then a flash of blue and white whizzed by and she disappeared.

A brick landed by Lily's feet. Uh oh, other ragers were getting too close. She turned to run, but the blue blur picked her up. A flash of her light released as Demarcus started running, and immediately they were almost half-way across the bridge.

Demarcus lurched to a stop. "What just happened?"

The wind blowing through the bridge stole Lily's breath. Something strange happened. Again. It was as if their powers had connected for a moment. "I don't know. It happened earlier when we were escaping."

"Let's figure it out later. We've got to help them." They whizzed over to meet up with the others. Harry was back, checking on SJ, while Kashvi and Simon watched the road. The ragers were making a run up the bridge to get to them. Angry shouts carried in the air.

"What now?" SJ called out.

As they looked at each other, Kashvi took a step forward. "This is where I stop them."

CHAPTER 56

LILY TOOK A READY STANCE IN CASE SHE NEEDED TO help as Kashvi stepped forward. They had reached the part of the bridge that was over the water. Kashvi set her feet as she positioned herself in the middle of the bridge. They were high up already. "Are you going to be able to do this?" Lily asked.

Kashvi closed her eyes and took a deep breath. "No one else is going to fall prey to the darkness as long as I can help it."

Her arms started to sway back and forth, as if she were conjuring a mighty spell. Her movements made a mesmerizing dance. Lily heard a crescendo of sloshing water. Kashvi swept her arms in a wider arc. A torrent of water crashed over the side of the bridge and flowed in a ring around the lanes. Fish and debris in the water flowed through the circle of seawater. It was like a liquid bead encircling a mighty cement string stretched taut over the bay.

This must have been like Moses and the Red Sea, Lily realized.

Kashvi kept the stream of water just off the surface of the roadway. Enough water leaked out to drench the surface, but it didn't look like the water would damage the construction, like a tsunami would. She kept her arms swinging around in a circular pattern.

"You're doing it. That's incredible," Demarcus yelled.

The salty smell in the air filled Lily's nostrils. Kashvi must be controlling thousands of gallons of water.

Simon pointed to the screen on his phone. "Look, they've all stopped. It seems they realize they can't breach the water. I wonder if there's enough of a sense of self-preservation that they don't cross something so obviously dangerous."

Ratchet's voice came through the comm. "You're holding them there for now, but other areas are having issues. I think the vigil with Pastor Sanchez is getting bypassed, and the Bay Bridge is another target. They're going to break containment and keep spreading this madness."

The roaring of the water, along with the wind blowing across the bridge, made it hard to hear. Lily looked up at the sky, then at her hands. "Ratchet, you said my suit would prevent the feedback problem if I used holograms again?"

"I'm pretty sure, but I'd like to run some tests first—except the instruments I need are in my destroyed lab. It should work."

"Okay, then let's get the Hoshek's attention." Lily raised her hands to the sky.

"Wait, don't do it! What if you go bonkers again?" Demarcus cried out, but he was too late.

The perfect image lit up inside Lily's mind. This should do the trick, as long as her brain didn't short out again.

She focused on the image in her head and thrust her arms into the sky. The light zipped along the contours of her suit before spiraling high over the top of the bridge. One beam shot straight up, until two sides forked off, while the vertical beam continued a little higher.

The cross she imagined floated between the land and the stars. A countersign to the Hoshek's flare that still flickered over past the Presidio.

CHAPTER 57

THE TORMENT WOULDN'T STOP. ROBERTO WANTED to die, anything to stop the anguish at his body being the conduit of such evil. The Hoshek took more and more people's wills and controlled them as puppets. All the while, Roberto's tenuous hold on his consciousness withered. Would he fade into nothingness, leaving his body an empty shell to be used for these dark purposes?

As the Hoshek unleashed its thralls to spread chaos, at least its abilities had been diminished over the day. For whatever reason, the tethers it had to those with special abilities had faltered. The Hoshek still had full strength, acoustic ability, and water control, but the other capacities, though still present, had weakened a great deal.

Roberto couldn't imagine what had caused this decline. Maybe there were forces out there strong enough to stop the Hoshek. He could only hope that something could be done to end this pain and malevolence. Even if it meant his death.

Nothing eased his distress, but Roberto tried distracting himself from the present and growing ordeal by rehashing his past, particularly his drive for recognition after being spurned by Stanford for his unorthodox interest in mystical artifacts. It would be so easy to blame the Archai for trapping him in this mess.

Unfortunately, the blame lay squarely on his shoulders.

All this time hiding from the Hoshek in his mind left him plenty of space to consider all the angles. He could try to blame parents who didn't support him, faculty that mocked him, or the manipulation of the Archai.

The horrifying truth was that he was a wretched man, looking for power out of a desire to inflict his will on circumstances instead of being pushed around, a meek participant in his own life. Instead of finding a way to be better, he'd pinned his hope on external things: legends of holy grails and supernatural scrolls that might offer him a way out of his weakness. With all the myths in the world, surely there had to be some conspiracy, some kernel of truth that would open life up to him.

It was Roberto's desire for dominance that had led him here. His body wielded unimaginable power, but through a source that could only be described as demonic. He thought of the people dead from his hand: John, Adeniji. How many more deaths would be laid at his feet?

If only I could make amends for what I've done, what I've opened myself and others up to through my foolishness.

Something drew the Hoshek's attention. Roberto's head swiveled around, looking for the cause of the disturbance that distracted the Hoshek from guiding its minions through the city.

Above the grand bridge, a light shone in the darkness. Not just a beam of light, a projection of...a cross.

The fury that rose within the Hoshek anew scared Roberto even more than he thought possible. What was it about this symbol that drew a reaction so violent and visceral from the Hoshek?

And if that was the reaction, was there any way for Roberto to tap into it?

The familiar shift of time and place began as the Hoshek tried to teleport there. Another ability diminished. The distance traveled was only a couple of blocks. It would take a few minutes to reach the light.

Roberto stirred himself. Perhaps this would be the only chance he would have to find rescue.

CHAPTER 58

SO FAR, SO GOOD. A TICKLE IN LILY'S SKULL WAS THE only concerning symptom, but she could feel the hologram holding steady. The illumination made the bridge glow with an ethereal light. Shadows danced along the road.

SJ came up to her. "Are you doing all right?"

Smiling, Lily nodded. "It's not like the last two times. I don't feel like my brain is melting. Wait, am I making sense? Before I thought I was saying something coherent and it came out all goofy."

"What was that?" SJ asked, a worried look on her face. Oh no, maybe it wasn't working after all...

An elbow nudged Lily's side. "I'm kidding. You're totally understandable." Her mischievous friend laughed at the prank.

"Not funny. I almost turned it off." Lily wanted to bop SJ.

Simon piped up. "All right, what's the play here?"

"We're letting it know where we are, offering ourselves as bait. After that—we stop it. I guess." She shrugged. How was she to know exactly how to do this?

A screech came from beyond the water. The earpieces muffled the sound, but Lily knew it when she heard it, even faintly. Aasif was on the other side of Kashvi's barrier. Kashvi grunted, but kept the water wall in place. With her effort, it seemed to be an effective blockade against his acoustic waves.

Demarcus pulled Simon and SJ together. "Hey, both of you were able to help people get out of the Hoshek's control. What if you two tag-teamed Aasif?"

Simon nodded. "We could try. It's worth a shot. Do we have Harry port him over here?"

"I can take care of him and keep him bound up." Kashvi had sweat beading on her brow, but she took one hand out of her circling pattern, thrust it forward, and pulled it back. Part of her water barrier sloshed forward toward the entrance of the bridge like a rope, then retreated back to their side.

She caught a big one. Aasif squirmed in a watery rope winding around him, covering his mouth as well.

"Way to go, girl! That was pretty awesome," Lily called out.

Simon and SJ ran forward and put their hands on Aasif. He thrashed about, but the water held him firm and kept his mouth shut. SJ poured out words asking God to deliver Aasif. Simon kept silent, but his face contorted in concentration.

Lily joined in praying for Aasif as she kept her cross hologram floating overhead. *Jesus, please help him be released from the darkness.*

His body stilled, and Aasif slumped down into Simon's arms. Kashvi let the watery bindings drop off him. She slapped her hands together and the flowing sea water turned into an ice block that looked like an iceberg had tried to cross the bridge and had gotten stuck. She ran over to them now that she was freed of keeping the barrier up.

Aasif groaned, his eyes barely fluttering. His body stayed limp. Kashvi knelt by his head. "Hey. We've got you out. Are you okay?"

"When we freed Harry, he was totally out of it for a while. He slept it off," Lily said.

"We've got to get him to safety. This isn't good to have him up—" Kashvi was cut off when the ice block shattered, sending everyone flying backwards. Lily took a shard in the chest, which the suit kept from impaling her, but pain shocked her system with the impact. She tumbled along the ground before stopping against the pedestrian railing.

Rosa stood where the ice had been, blood dripping from her extended fist. Behind her stood Pearce.

CHAPTER 59

DEMARCUS WAS BLOWN BACK BY THE ICE FRAGMENTS splintering through the air, but he had been far enough back that he didn't take much of the force. Lily and the others closer to the ice were knocked around like bowling pins. Behind what remained of the barrier, Rosa and Pearce looked ready for battle.

He noticed Simon picking himself up from the ground, wiping blood from his hairline. Demarcus dashed to him to help out—Simon was the only one without a suit to protect him.

No, there was another person vulnerable. Rosa ran up to Aasif, grabbed him by his clothes, and tossed him over the edge of the bridge. "Harry!" Demarcus pointed to the unconscious boy dropping through the air.

Harry glanced up and disappeared. Demarcus pulled Simon up. "Are you okay? Maybe we need to get you farther away for safety."

Simon shook his head. "I'm fine. We all need each other for this." He seized Demarcus's shoulders and his eyes blazed, staring daggers at him. "You're a natural leader. Exercise your gift. Don't think about past mistakes, because that will paralyze you. Focus on where you are now. You were given these gifts for a reason, and it's more than just speed."

A pep talk from the guy they used to fight against? Okay, God, you have a sense of humor. His heart lifted at the words, though. The battles in his mind over the last few days rolled through his head like a storm, each of his foolish choices mocking him. Simon was right. It wasn't time to be frozen from action. He did need to step out in faith.

"Thanks, Simon. I'll...try to distract Rosa. Check on the others," Demarcus replied.

"That's what I'm talking about." Simon gave him a hearty slap on the shoulder, then he ran towards Kashvi, who was still getting up.

His perception of the battle slowed as Demarcus studied the scene. Rosa ducked a shot from Lily. Sarah Jane and Simon helped Kashvi up. Harry reappeared with an unconscious Aasif twenty yards down the bridge.

Pearce stood, legs wide, his shoulders heaving up and down. Demarcus couldn't see the dark halos that Lily would describe hanging over people who were controlled, but in this case, he could sense the pulses of evil intent radiating off the man.

The Hoshek needed to be destroyed. But could they kill Pearce as part of the battle? The idea loomed as such a contradiction in his head. David had slain the giant, yet Jesus had turned the other cheek.

At the pier battle, John had quoted the Bible at Pearce, and the Hoshek came out of him. The huge black form had oozed out of Pearce like smoke, becoming its own being. Then it was strong enough to take John down. It would be a huge risk if they could pull off the same trick. But they needed to try.

Rosa jumped at Lily. Demarcus rushed over and pulled Lily out of the way before Rosa landed, and again felt a jolt of extra speed when running with Lily. Light flashed, and they ended up near Aasif's resting form.

"What is going on?" Lily asked, holding her hands up. "It's like my light intensified the last few times you carried me."

A tingling danced through Demarcus. "Not only that, but I go so much faster. Let's get back into the fray and figure out this development later. I've got an idea."

CHAPTER 60

THE THROBBING IN HIS HEAD DIDN'T HELP AS SIMON ducked down and squatted by Kashvi. Once again, Sarah Jane was there, praying over the dazed girl. He didn't want to interrupt, so he channeled his power toward the two.

You are strong enough for this task. The gifts you've been given are for a time like this. Be strong and courageous, and don't let fear or anger drive you. Do what is needed for what is true and good.

Kashvi raised herself up on her arms, while Sarah Jane looked at him with wide eyes. "Is that what you do with your gift when it's not selfishly used?" she asked.

He nodded. It was new to him, to inspire instead of control. Using his ability this way flowed so much more easily. It was aligned with his true purpose, rather than being bent to serve something it wasn't meant to be.

A scream sounded behind him. Simon turned to see Rosa rushing toward him.

He tried to scramble out of the way, but she was too fast. Yet instead of his former slave landing a horrific punch on him, a wave of water rushed by and swept Rosa back across the road. Kashvi stood, her arms sweeping across her body to keep water rushing over to force Rosa down.

Could he get through to her? With her fury and the Hoshek's control, Simon wasn't sure, but he had to try. His manipulation had helped land her in this dungeon. "Kashvi, can you freeze her down so I can try to help her?"

"Gladly," Kashvi replied. She blew on the water as it flowed past her and it formed into an icy boulder, with

Rosa's head and hands the only parts sticking out of the frozen prison. Simon ran over to her, vaulting the center partitions in the road.

Rosa's breath heaved as she gritted her teeth and strained to free herself. A guttural scream escaped her lips. Simon reached over to catch her hand before realizing that may be a mistake.

She clenched a couple of fingers and crushed them with a simple squeeze. Simon buckled to his knees, which thankfully freed his mangled fingers from her grasp. Okay, he deserved that. Pushing the throbbing aside, he stood and locked his gaze with hers.

"Rosa, please forgive me. I used you, and that was inexcusably wrong. I don't know if you can hear me, but I will do whatever it takes to make things right. Just let go of the anger, and you can be free of the Hoshek."

Simon focused with all his might on detangling the strands of hate that linked together Rosa's head and heart. The strands weren't thin like Harry's—hers were thick and ingrained. Her profile popped into his head. All the abuse and suffering she'd been through was what had allowed him to influence her when his eyesight was so poor. Now it made the Hoshek's control nearly unbreakable.

He turned to call for Sarah Jane. A horrific sound tore through the air and shattered the ice encasing Rosa. The frequency made Simon's teeth shake, and the explosion of ice blew him away. Landing on his shoulder, he managed to roll with the impact. Multiple spots on his arms and legs stung with pain and cold.

Small frozen shards stuck out from the various wounds. Ice was a bad idea tonight. Simon pushed himself up as Pearce advanced, done sitting out the fight now. Rosa lay on her side, not moving. Was she hurt from the sonic attack?

Pearce sucked in air to scream again, right in front of Simon. A hand grabbed the back of Simon's shirt and he appeared next to Lily. His stomach swirled at another trip. At least the sonic scream missed him.

"Dude, you look beat up. Have Sarah Jane help you," Harry said.

"No, we'll have time for that when this is over. Listen to me, you two. Use your gifts for others. When you only use them for yourselves, it slowly corrupts. That's what happened to me—so don't be like me. Go help stop the Hoshek, and be bold about it. That you're here is no accident. This is only the beginning. Don't worry about your mistakes this week. Now's the time to stand for what's right." Simon poured out from deep within to stir their courage and resolve.

They both stood straighter, nodding as he spoke.

Lily pointed at Pearce, who was facing Demarcus and Kashvi at the moment. "We've got an idea. We are going to try and separate the Hoshek from Pearce. When that happens, we need Harry to port SJ and Simon over to Pearce, to see if he can be freed. Demarcus and I will attack the Hoshek."

What had John told him? All of their gifts would be required in this battle. This was it.

"Yes, that sounds brilliant. We're all supposed to work together. Our gifts used in unity." Simon pumped his good fist.

The ground shook and he tumbled back. Pearce was punching the road.

He was going to bring down the whole section of bridge.

CHAPTER 61

THE SHAKING OF THE BRIDGE KNOCKED LILY DOWN. Pearce was done being distracted by Demarcus or Kashvi. He was pounding the asphalt, trying to destroy the bridge and everyone on it.

Their foe was kneeling to be able to slam the road surface repeatedly. Cracks began to splinter from beneath his fist. Lily aimed for his knee on the ground, firing a couple of blasts before connecting with the leg. It knocked Pearce off balance enough to make him stop and search for her.

Demarcus took the opening to run up and clothesline Pearce, which finally managed to knock him down. Roaring, Pearce flung out an arm and water rushed up over the edge of the railing to pummel Demarcus.

A cry caught Lily's attention. Kashvi dropped and shook. Lily ran to her and tried to hold her steady. "Are you okay?"

"When he uses my ability, it drains from me. Why is this not happening with you?" Kashvi asked.

That's right—Pearce wasn't running around or using light. He teleported briefly, but their abilities didn't seem to be as usable to him. "We think we found a way to cut what he did to us Saturday. You need to...look out!"

Kashvi started twitching again when water poured over them. Except Lily had thrown up a solar shield, burning the water away. Using one hand to keep the shield active, she strained to see if she could multi-task. With her other hand, she formed a hologram of Demarcus running at Pearce.

The water swirled away from them and towards her holographic friend. The image distorted when the seawater coursed over it, but it did the trick. Kashvi was able to skitter away and take cover by the center barriers.

"Demarcus, are you ready?" Lily called over the comm.

Silence. Was he okay? "Demarcus?"

"Yeah, I'm ready. Just getting my goggles adjusted after that shower. Brrr."

Here goes nothing. "Ratchet, we need some verses, please."

"Pardon me? You want some poetry? Oh wait, some freestyle rap?" Ratchet replied.

Ack, no. She couldn't imagine him rapping. "No, we need Bible verses. Things that talk about how God wins and defeats the enemy. Hurry!"

Lily had to dive out of the way of more water. She rolled, banging her head on the asphalt as she tumbled over. She found herself behind a center concrete barrier, which protected her but didn't give her an angle for a shot.

Except for the one stranded vehicle behind her. The side mirror was facing toward Pearce, so if she angled it right...

Zap. She sent a blast that knocked Pearce in the head. He hardly moved, but the water stopped. She then shot up a quick burst of light for her position. "Demarcus, I'm here."

She swung herself over the barrier to be on the same side as Pearce. They would have to line up their shot before they took it. "Ratchet, what do you have? Start sending them."

"Getting them uploaded, just a sec!"

Demarcus slid to a stop by her. Together, they faced Pearce. Despite cuts and bruises on his face, the man looked none the worse for wear. His face was a mask of rage, and he let out a sonic scream right at them. The vibrations blew her hair back, and the sound hurt her ears some, but the dampeners did their job.

They needed some verses! In the madness, it was hard to concentrate on things she had learned over the last few months. One image surfaced in her mind—the verse on the wall of the youth room.

"The Lord will lay bare his holy arm in the sight of all the nations, and all the ends of the earth will see the salvation of our God!" Lily shouted as loud as she could.

Pearce stumbled back. Growling, he started running forward.

"There!" Ratchet called out. Verses started popping up on Lily's visual feed, like a filter played over her vision.

Demarcus yelled, "Part your heavens, Lord, and come down; touch the mountains, so that they smoke. Send forth lightning and scatter the enemy; shoot your arrows and rout them."

Their foe stopped as if running into a barrier. Smoke began trailing out of his mouth. It was working!

Here was one. "But the Lord is with me like a mighty warrior; so my persecutors will stumble and not prevail. They will fail and be thoroughly disgraced; their dishonor will never be forgotten," Lily hollered, her throat going raw.

Again, Pearce bucked as if hit.

"The weapons we fight with are not the weapons of the world. On the contrary, they have divine power to demolish strongholds," Demarcus bellowed. His strong voice carried through the night air. Pearce rocked on his feet.

Oh, this was a good one. "Therefore God exalted him to the highest place and gave him the name that is above every name, that at the name of Jesus every knee should bow, in heaven and on earth and under the earth, and every tongue acknowledge that Jesus Christ is Lord, to the glory of God the Father," she cried out with everything she had.

Pearce shrieked and started chanting with a torrent of foreign words. The bridge shook again as smoke billowed out of his nose and mouth. She had thought having already encountered this at the pier would make it less intimidating, but the horror of this sight still made Lily tremble.

Oh. Snap.

The Hoshek taking shape with an enormous chest, thick arms and legs, and a square, jutted chin was larger than before. Much larger. How it hadn't split the seams on Pearce, who slumped to the ground, Lily didn't know. But the electricity dancing around its body lit the bridge up with eerie pulses, and the creature roared with sulfurous breath, almost making Lily choke.

"I think we made it mad," Demarcus said, his voice firm. "Are you ready for this?"

CHAPTER 62

UNCONTROLLABLE SPARKLES STARTED FLOWING OUT of Lily's hands. Uh, what was this? They were about to battle the Hoshek, and her body was doing pretty fireworks?

"Whoa, that's cool. And...weird," Demarcus said, as the sparkles started flowing toward him. The tiny lights began to sweep across his body.

"I don't know what's going on? Are you okay?" Her voice squeaked at the confusion of this thing happening.

Demarcus jogged in place. "It feels invigorating."

Okay, God, help us have wisdom. What do we do here?

Thoughts zipped through her mind. Running away from the Hoshek when Harry was taken. Then again when they went to find SJ. And now with their strange dash across the bridge a few minutes ago. What's faster than Demarcus?

Light.

"I think our powers are supposed to work together. Go to the end of the bridge to get as much force as you can. I'll blast the Hoshek and you run into it. Run through it. Break the darkness."

He nodded. "That sounds good."

Lily felt a tug on her arm. She flung it towards the tug, pointing north to the far end of the bridge. A stream of light illuminated a path forward. "Go!" she called.

Demarcus disappeared, as fast as Harry's teleporting. Oh wow, that was something. She could tell their abilities were synced in the moment, each part working together with the other.

She turned to face the Hoshek again. Smoke blew in the air between them and the Hoshek stomped closer. Lily took a defensive stance, ready to give this beast everything she had.

Something grabbed her arms from behind and held them down. No! Smoky ropes had slithered around her and snared her. Another strand wrapped up her torso, the feeling making her skin crawl. The foul binding circled around her throat, choking off her air.

CHAPTER 63

DEMARCUS FLEW ACROSS THE BRIDGE, LILY'S LIGHT beam acting as a runway. He'd never gone so fast. In a second, he crossed the span over the ocean and wound along the highway to a tunnel. The bright trail ended, and his body slowed to his normal speed. He stopped in the tunnel, then jogged back out.

He was ready to do this. The Golden Gate Bridge was a mile long. Hopefully with that lead up, the force he would generate would destroy the Hoshek.

The light stream faded. The supercharging he felt in his body dropped off.

He tapped the comm. "Lily, are you okay? Lily!"

A slight gurgle was all he heard.

CHAPTER 64

ROBERTO COULD BREATHE. AS HIS BODY SMACKED against the hard ground, the pain was a welcome sensation. After being locked away by the Hoshek for the last few days, his body was no longer protected by the foul power, but at least it was his.

Unfortunately, he had no strength to run, to hide, to do anything.

What would happen to these youth, now that the Hoshek had unleashed its true form on them? It had already controlled a couple of them. If it was able to overwhelm them all, there would be no hope of stopping it.

Hands grasped his frayed overcoat and Roberto blinked in a moment to a spot farther towards land. That was a familiar feeling. Teleportation? The Hoshek had taken that power at one time.

A man in casual clothes and a teen in some blue and white jumpsuit held him down. The man had blood dribbling down his face, while the girl looked windswept and determined.

Roberto struggled to form his own words. His tongue slowly moved in position as he battled a dehydrated mouth. "Kill me. It may deprive the Hoshek of a host." He didn't want to die, but it was preferable to being flooded with evil again.

"No, we're here to save you," the girl said. She began to cry out in frenzied whispers.

The man caught Roberto's head and turned it so they stared at each other. This one's features were strong and determined, and his eyes spoke something with only the look. "Listen to me. We're going to try to break control, but you need to fight. Reject the things that give the Hoshek a hold on you. Repent of those wicked things inside. You have a choice to move out of darkness, right now."

Roberto felt heat and cold war within him. The tether of the Hoshek warred against the warmth trying to penetrate him. His body thrashed.

Please, I don't want this anymore. Help me!

A light began to infuse his body. The muscles seizing in his body relaxed. He looked up to see the Hoshek rumbling toward him.

Oh no. Not again.

CHAPTER 65

SIMON HAD NEVER STRAINED AS HARD AS HE DID trying to help Roberto break free of the demonic roots twisted within him. If Rosa's had been thick ropes, this man had chains anchoring him tight. Harry held the writhing man down while Sarah Jane prayed with a zeal Simon could only hope to emulate someday.

God, I'm way too new at this. You've helped me today, now help Roberto.

He could see strands of greed. Simon plucked those out.

Jealousy. He whacked those down.

The larger ones were fear, pride, and insecurity. Wounds of rejection acted like energy wells that fed these bindings, strengthening their hold over the man. But something new was working, too, a gentle strength that healed the wounds, filling in the holes where the bindings were anchored. Then Simon could redirect strands out of those areas and defuse the tension.

A roar distracted Simon for a moment.

Harry shouted, "Can you go faster? The Hoshek's coming back!"

CHAPTER 66

THE SMOKE STRANGLING LILY DISSIPATED, LETTING air get through to her lungs. She gasped and coughed, her hands going to her throat. Her hands were free!

The Hoshek stormed back towards Roberto, where SJ and Simon worked on him. They needed to keep it from going back to its host.

A voice cut through the air. "Lily!" Demarcus on the comm.

"I'm okay," she said, her voice hoarse. "Get ready."

Lily inhaled deeply and swung an arm from Demarcus's position towards the Hoshek, leaving a brilliant trail for him. But the Hoshek was going to make it to Roberto first.

Water sloshed up and around the Hoshek. Kashvi threw her arms around wildly, sending waves of ocean blasting the smoky creature. A terrible growl sounded and the Hoshek flicked a hand to the side, redirecting the water.

Kashvi's move distracted the Hoshek for a moment, slowing him enough for them to take their only chance.

Lily thrust one leg back to brace herself and poured everything she could through her arms and hands. A dazzling beam raced toward her target, a gleaming beacon for Demarcus to follow.

Out of the corner of her eye, she watched Rosa get up and throw some debris at Kashvi, sending the water girl flying. Then she picked up a pointed ice shard and prepared to throw it.

CHAPTER 67

A LIGHT STREAM BLAZED UP TO DEMARCUS'S FEET, and a moment later he heard Lily's voice confirm she was all right. This was it.

He pushed his legs harder than he'd ever gone before. The air whistled by as he wound to the bridge and shot forward at incredible speed. An intense glow highlighted his target.

Dreads whipping behind him, Demarcus came to the part of the bridge torn up by their battle. His reflexes and senses slowed time, even as he moved faster than ever before. An unconscious Aasif rested on the sidewalk near the middle of the bridge.

He came up on Lily, her arms forcing a vivid blast of light at the Hoshek. The grotesque beast turned slowly, a hand held up to block a brightness even it couldn't handle.

Jesus, you have the victory!

Demarcus threw a fist forward, light streaming around his body as well. As his hand neared the Hoshek, a projectile of some kind flew right behind the creature of darkness.

Then he made impact. Smoke split around his fist, then his body. A moment of resistance, then it gave way. A terrible screech sounded, shorting the electronics in Demarcus's earpieces. Electricity coursed through his body, making every muscle spasm.

Was it the end for both of them?

CHAPTER 68

ONE LARGE TETHER REMAINED, PUSHED DEEP WITHIN Roberto. It was laced with bitterness, fear, and hopelessness. Simon wrestled with it as hard as he could. Sweat ran down his forehead, the salty liquid stinging his eyes. His hands cramped as he held on to the man.

The intensity of Sarah Jane's words impressed him. She cried out for mercy on the man. Physically, Roberto's cuts and bruises had disappeared. Emotionally, hurts from rejection were washed by a spiritual salve.

Let go of the hate. This is killing you, and it's not worth carrying anymore. Roberto, let it go.

Light flashed as Lily nearly exploded on the Hoshek. The water holding it back washed away, but it turned to face the beam hitting it. Then a whooshing sound filled Simon's ears. Demarcus appeared along with a flash of energy and slammed into the Hoshek.

The blast sent shockwaves radiating across the bridge, making the supports sway with the force. Demarcus bounced once on the ground and careened backward into Harry.

Some kind of missile came at them.

Simon dove over Roberto's body to push Sarah Jane away. As he knocked her down, a stabbing pain ripped into his chest. He tried to hold himself up, to see what had happened.

A spear of ice had impaled him.

He slumped to the ground.

CHAPTER 69

WAVES OF ENERGY RIPPLED PAST LILY AS DEMARCUS smashed into the Hoshek. A piercing cry had sounded, followed by the detonation of his impact. She smacked onto her back, a sharp pain ricocheting through her body. Rolling over, she jumped up and ran to her friends.

Ash fell from the sky, the familiar smell of sulfur thick in the air. There was no other sign of the Hoshek. Demarcus and Harry lay entangled beyond where SJ, Roberto, and Simon sat. Kashvi groaned off to the side.

The only one not moving at all was Demarcus.

She dropped next to him, cradling his head. "Noooo! Demarcus, you did it. We did it. The Hoshek—it's gone." Watching his chest, she couldn't see a rise or fall. She put her cheek near his mouth. No warmth of his breath against her skin.

"Sarah Jane! Demarcus needs you. He's not breathing!" she cried.

SJ pushed herself up, a little wobbly on her feet. Blood trickled down from her cheek as she made her way over, pulling off her goggles in the process.

Lily's sobs wouldn't stop as SJ collapsed next to them and began to pray. They had almost lost Demarcus a few weeks ago when he'd been shot trying to hunt down some gang members. This couldn't happen now.

Lord, please!

Kashvi had managed to start walking over to them. A hand raised to her mouth. "Is he...okay?"

The pleas for healing poured out of SJ's lips. Lily stroked his dreads and pulled his goggles up to see his eyes if they opened. When they opened. The faith stirred in her. He would be all right. Despite the soot marks across his face, the burns on his skin, he was going to make it.

That encouragement. It felt like Simon's work.

Her thoughts broke with Kashvi's scream. The girl fumbled her way over to Simon, who was holding a hand out towards Lily and SJ. A hand coated in blood. His arm trembled as he lay on his side, something shiny sticking out of the right side of his chest.

"He's bleeding all over," Kashvi said, her voice frantic. "An...an icicle has impaled him."

Two of the Anointed were mortally wounded? And one healer...

What would Demarcus say?

"SJ, go pray for Simon. He's not going to make it." Lily choked out.

Her head snapped up and her wide eyes stared back. "Demarcus isn't healed yet. He might not make it. What are you saying?"

Lily thought about the man who had almost killed her at the Launch Conference. Yet she knew Demarcus would want to see him healed if there were a choice. "Demarcus is strong. I'll...I'll do CPR."

A wheeze came from Simon. "No. You heal him. Not me."

Kashvi put her hand on his chest and tried to manipulate the ice shard into a plug that would staunch the blood flow. He groaned and coughed out blood.

Now Lily was standing between Simon and Demarcus. How could they save them both? "Harry?" She turned to find him holding his head.

"No good. I think I've got a concussion. I can't go any-where," he said.

Simon waved Lily closer. She knelt down, her knee turning red in a pool of blood. "It's okay. This is the path for me. I've closed the loop. The torch is ready to be passed. After living my life in selfishness and manipulation, I can die knowing I helped others. And I can die knowing there is a God who is welcoming me."

More coughing racked his body. His arm dropped to the ground. "He's...there right now. I see him—that look! I'll never forget...that look..."

Simon Mazor's body grew slack, his eyes closing with the look of grace the last thing he'd see in this life. Lily sat stunned, as a hand rested on her shoulder. A strong hand.

Demarcus.

SJ rushed to Simon's side, and Lily jumped up to wrap her arms around Demarcus. Her heart swelled at seeing him walking around, the brave guy who was willing to sacrifice it all for those he loved.

"Hey, I'm good." His arms embraced her, and she felt safe and free in those arms. She yanked off her goggles, worked her hands behind his head, and pulled him down. Their lips met, and she drank in the goodness that Demarcus represented.

After the kiss, heat rushed to her face. Oh wow, she really did that.

The look on his face was worth it. He stood, dumbfounded. "Did we just, uh..."

Kashvi cleared her throat. "Yeah, you did."

"He's gone." Sarah Jane held a hand over Simon's heart. "I can't feel a pulse; the suit doesn't read a heartbeat. And more than that, I know inside that I can't heal him. There's something holding back."

Lily sat down, tugging on Demarcus's hand so he'd join them. Kashvi helped Harry, who had a wobble to his steps. They all sat in a circle around SJ and Simon.

The ever-present wind across the bridge had stilled. The strange darkness of the night had broken. There was no San Francisco fog, and stars peered down from across the water. A feeling of finish settled over Lily.

"Did you hear his last words, SJ? Simon knew it was his time. And he sacrificed himself for Demarcus. For all of us." Lily's voice started to crack. "It's not your fault that you couldn't heal him. Don't you hold this against yourself."

Tears streamed freely down SJ's face. "I know. It's never easy though." She rested her head on Harry's shoulder. A slight grin sprang up on his face, then shifted quickly to a frown.

"Does anyone know what happened to Rosa?" he asked.

Everyone glanced around. There was no sign of the woman. "Not again," SJ groaned.

"You mean this kind of thing keeps happening with you?" Kashvi said, her eyes darting back and forth.

"Rosa has a habit of turning up at bad times. Hopefully she's better after this ordeal." Lily brushed some stray strands of hair out of her face.

A sound came from her goggles on her lap. "Is anyone there? Hello?" She caught it up to her ear.

"We're here. Ratchet?"

"You've done it! The crowds have stopped surging. People are waking up, confused and dazed. All the reports are suggesting the crisis is over."

Lily stood up and shined a gentle light toward the entrance to the bridge. Some police were coming their way. The crowds milled about, mixing with the officers.

"How are you guys? Is everyone all right?" Ratchet asked, the concern thick in his voice.

She looked around. Her friends sat weary and heartbroken at their loss. But a sense of serenity rested over them. The battle for today had been won. Not without casualties, but the threat of the Hoshek was over.

"Simon is dead. The rest of us are okay. We're glad it's all over."

A breath came over the line. "I'm sorry."

Demarcus stood next to Lily, putting his goggles back on. He slid an arm across her shoulders. "He died a hero. We wouldn't have made it without him."

Lily cocked her neck to the side and shot him a quizzical look. "Why did you put those back on?"

He pointed at the nearing officers, led by Officer Riley. "We may want to have secret identities here, gang. They're going to be asking who we are, I think."

As everyone put their goggles on, Kashvi spoke up. "So, who are we, anyway?"

Lily smiled. "We're the Anointed."

CHAPTER 70

THE COOL AIR BRUSHED OVER HIS FACE. IT BLEW AWAY the scent of oil and rubber as Roberto lifted his head just off the asphalt. The salty sea breeze filled his nostrils, letting him slowly realize that he wasn't actually dead.

The tether. It...it was gone. He slumped back to the ground, too weak to get off the road. How could it be that he was finally free? Not only that, but there was something deeper. Wounds from long ago didn't ache in his soul. His body shuddered with a sense of release.

Slowly he pushed himself over onto his back. The familiar suspension lines of the Golden Gate Bridge rose above him, while clouds floated past in the blue sky beyond. But the view became blurry, like a fine mist floating in the atmosphere. No, wait. It wasn't from the air. Tears welled up and trickled down his cheeks.

There was a freedom in his spirit he'd never known. Even before the Hoshek had overcome him that day in Iraq, he'd been bound by hurts that he'd nurtured for too long in his anger. Instead of finding a salve for his previous rejection, he'd turned it into poison that drove him to seek power.

The drive that led him to be possessed.

Now the memories and thoughts that had plagued him through his adult years didn't hold the same force. There was still pain, but it didn't feel like chains holding him bound.

Yet there was still a need inside of him. The relief of being liberated allowed him to breathe deep and held the promise of moving through life without such encumbrance.

However, there was more to be done. Something was not complete, but at least he could see clearly enough now to recognize it.

Voices grew louder as they approached. Officers surrounded him with weapons drawn, followed by two paramedics. He was lifted from the ground into a kneeling position, his arms pulled behind him and restrained with handcuffs. The medics peppered him with questions while flashing lights at his eyes and checking his limbs and torso for injuries. He mumbled short answers, but he couldn't fully process what they were asking.

Another officer with salt-and-pepper hair arrived and gave direction to those around Roberto. Strong arms lifted him up and helped him shuffle towards a police van. They dragged him in and connected the cuffs to a hook welded to the wall.

Roberto couldn't feel anger towards the police. In the past he'd have railed against the injustice of it all. Today he knew that his actions had created so much suffering, even if he didn't directly cause it all. Consequences were coming, and he'd have to accept them.

As officers decided who would ride in the back with him, Roberto noticed a girl staring at him. Her hair was strawberry blonde, and her green eyes pierced him with compassion. He felt a connection to this girl, like she had something to do with his changes.

Another three young people joined her. They wore matching blue and white uniforms. A redheaded boy caught the hand of the girl watching him. A black boy put his arm around a strikingly blonde girl. She nodded at something the first girl said. Then she drew in the air, a simple back and forth motion.

A cross of light floated in the air toward him before the van's doors shut.

CHAPTER 71

— ONE WEEK LATER —

DEMARCUS SLIPPED INTO THE YOUTH ROOM AT church. The party thrown in their honor was happening in the main fellowship hall. It was pretty sweet of their parents to come together and put on an event with the people who knew their identities and had helped them in the last few weeks.

He laughed to himself, remembering how Mama had chewed Ratchet out for giving Demarcus shoes that ran on water, and then thanked him for providing so that she didn't have to smell burnt rubber anymore. The poor scientist thought he was really in trouble for a minute.

Plopping on the couch, Demarcus needed to gather his thoughts. The week had been a blur of craziness. One would think defeating a supernatural demonic force would be the wildest thing for a lifetime. Yet they had also been examined by the authorities, interviewed by the media, and projected as the subject of so many articles and videos he thought it would never end.

Ji-young had basked in the attention as their primary informant. Thankfully she showed a great amount of discretion, realizing that her insider knowledge was a commodity that could deal a lot of damage. That hadn't stopped her from asking questions while enjoying her hors d'oeuvres, hounding Officer Riley as he tried to eat.

Demarcus wondered what Roberto Pearce was going through. The man was in custody because the legal system didn't know how to process a person under the total influence of an ancient evil. He had implicated the Archai in the whole affair, and a body had been discovered that was identified as that of a man who had been attached to the group at one time. No one knew what would happen there. John had committed to visiting Pearce and trying to help him.

The door cracked open and Lily started to enter, jumping back when she saw him reclining. "Oh, sorry. I wasn't expecting anyone to be in here."

He was never sorry to see her. His smile threatened to overtake his face. "It's pretty nuts, right?"

She nodded, the curls that framed her face bobbing up and down. Some of her hair was pulled up on top of her head, and the blonde ribbons cascading around her face showcased how lovely she was. Those blue eyes shone brighter than ever before.

Okay, dude, stop staring.

"Yeah, it's wild. The whole world is trying to figure out what exactly happened in San Francisco, and we're sitting in class again having to do homework and regular stuff. I don't miss people raging, but real life isn't nearly as exciting." Lily sat on the chair nearest to him, blowing on her coffee as she took a sip.

"Are you going to sleep tonight, after having caffeine this late?"

She scoffed. "Do you even know me? I can drink two and fall right to sleep."

"I wonder if your blood type is medium roast." Demarcus grinned.

"At the minimum."

"Are you glad that you didn't get suspended?" He sat up, leaning into their conversation.

Lily brushed a strand away from her face. "Sure. I mean, it's not super exciting being back in school, but who wants to be suspended and have to deal with that? Missy hasn't talked to me, but I heard through the grapevine that her dad was a rager. Clara said that Missy talked about being glad for the superheroes that saved the day. I guess she realizes I'm part of that."

"I heard the 49ers want to have us out for a halftime presentation. I don't know if I can handle that," Demarcus said with a wink. There were people who blamed them for damage and looney conspiracy theories that even claimed they were involved with the Archai. One way or another, the whole Bay Area was buzzing about superheroes in their midst.

"There's a lot of pressure that I didn't ever consider." Lily twisted a strand of hair, a sure sign she was thinking about something. "We joked about things over the summer and did a few good deeds. Now, posts are asking for us to help find lost pets. There are insane blogs, videos, and threads about us. What do we do going forward?"

"Who knows? I'm totally down with chilling, staying out of the spotlight," Demarcus said.

There were so many things on his mind. He'd been wondering how they could keep their secret identities and keep doing hero stuff as students. But the thing that seemed most critical at that moment was where the relationship with Lily would go from here. Life was so frantic after the Rage, as people locally were calling it, that they hadn't been able to talk about things, about them. He thought about the kiss. Was that something in the moment? Or was there something there?

Someone had to broach the subject. Time to be brave, Demarcus. "So, uh, about the night on the bridge?"

Her cheeks flushed, highlighting her eyes even more. "Yeah? Was that too much? I was so excited to see you alive..." Her voice trailed off.

Demarcus slid off the couch and crouched by her. "It wasn't too much at all." He leaned in close, and she followed suit, her lashes fluttering, her cheeks glowing. Her breath, fruity from some drink at the party, tickled his lips. They were about to kiss again...

When something landed on the couch behind them and he bolted up, bonking his nose on her forehead. "Ow!"

Lily's hands went to her head. "Ow!"

"Oh, sorry guys. My bad." Harry lay on the couch, feet kicked up on the arm of the orange vinyl monstrosity. Demarcus growled and grabbed his ankles, yanking him off onto the floor.

"Hey, I said sorry. How was I supposed to know you two were—oh, snap. You were about to smooch, weren't you? Hoo-boy!"

Lily's finger lit up bright red. "And if you want to keep your hair, you won't run your mouth."

The door opened and Sarah Jane slid into the room. "I know you beat me, but oh...Hey. You two are in here. What are you doing?"

Harry made a kissing sound with his mouth. A stray hair was promptly fried in retaliation, the smell of burnt hair stinking up the room. His eyes shot wide open.

"Consider that your warning." Lily blew on her finger.

Sweet. But note to self, don't make her mad.

Demarcus motioned for Sarah Jane to join them. She sat next to Harry, and promptly put a hand on his knee.

"It's overwhelming being the center of attention in there," Sarah Jane said.

It was just the four of them today. Kashvi had been hesitant, but had tearfully been reunited with her family in Portland and reported things were improving. She was planning to come and stay with Pastor Sanchez and spend time with the Anointed in a few weeks. Aasif was in a facility, helping him deal with the issues that had caused him to run away and be enslaved by the Hoshek. And no one knew anything about Rosa.

All that aside, for the moment, it felt good to just be the original four friends from Launch back in their comfort zone, Demarcus thought. The flags of the nations were hung around the room, acting as reminders of the bigger world out there.

Harry laughed and pointed at Demarcus. "Dude, you've got glitter in your hair again."

Harry had pulled the stupid prank over a week ago, and the glitter bomb still had victims. Demarcus laughed, but only briefly. So much had happened in the last several days. It wasn't easy to be carefree at this point.

"Are you guys ready for Simon's memorial service tomorrow?" Lily said.

That was the biggest game-changer: being witnesses to Simon's transformation and death. The media still marveled at his reappearance at the Rage and his role in stopping the so-called rage virus. There were plenty of renewed questions about the Launch Conference and the fall of Alturas, and it was going to be a big deal for a long time to come.

"Ready as I'll ever be." Harry ran a hand through his hair, meaning he wasn't ready at all. Next to him, Sarah Jane nodded but looked down at her feet. It must still bother her that she couldn't heal everyone. John had reiterated that it was God who determined Simon's time, but Demarcus understood the desire to help everyone possible.

"It still seems so weird that we were so angry with him, ready to rip him apart, and he ended up being such an ally." Lily's eyes watered, and she blinked back tears.

"He saved me, you know," Sarah Jane whispered.

"What?" Harry stared at her.

"When Rosa threw that ice—it was aimed at me. Right as Demarcus hit the Hoshek, Simon shoved me out of the way and took the impact. I've been replaying that in my mind, and it finally dawned on me what happened. He gave his life for mine. I'm so conflicted about my lingering anger at being kidnapped and the sacrifice he made." Sarah Jane sniffed as the tears ran down. Harry disappeared and came back with a box of tissues.

They sat in silence for a moment. "I didn't realize what he had done." Harry's somber tone matched the mood.

The door opened. John stuck his head in. "You are all missing the party in your honor."

Demarcus realized this wasn't the best place to hide in the church. "Yeah, we all needed a little space. The attention is too much."

Their mentor chuckled and entered the room, sitting on the floor, as was his habit. "I understand too well. When you are famous, or infamous, it changes the perception people have of you."

"Wait a second, are you famous in some way and we didn't know?" Lily tapped her chin.

John paused for a moment, then answered. "No one has talked about me in a long time, so do not worry yourselves."

"How does it feel to be back?" Demarcus asked. He'd been dying to ask.

"I am ready to be with the Lord whenever he calls me, but I recognize the mission he has for me now." John cleared his throat. "But I believe it would be rude to let the party continue without your presence. Demarcus, your charming mother has Lily's father cornered, at least when I left to find you."

Demarcus smacked his forehead. "Oh Mama, don't ruin it for me with Lily." Heat flooded his cheeks as he realized what he said.

Smiling, Lily took his hand. "Don't worry, my dad will listen to me."

John stood, a slight groan slipping out of him that Demarcus couldn't help but notice. The rest got up to join him. They reached the door when Pastor Sanchez burst through, followed by Ji-young tapping on her phone.

"Hey guys, I just got a message from Agent Dean, the FBI investigator that you met at the pier," Ji-young said, not looking up. "She's trying to find the Anointed. Apparently, they have a dangerous hostage situation, and she thought I'd know who she was looking for."

A mission, so soon? Were they ready for it?

"Wait, you know people in the FBI?" Lily sounded incredulous.

Ji-young shrugged. "What can I say? I have connections."

John smiled. "I can make an excuse for you. There are people in need, and this sounds important. Remember, you are God's servants in this first. Go and help those in need."

The four of them looked at each other.

"I guess we need to gear up," Demarcus said. They headed to get their backpacks in the foyer.

Harry jogged backwards to face everyone. "So," he waited for a beat as he looked from Sarah Jane to Lily to Demarcus. "What's our catch phrase going to be?"

SCRIPTURE REFERENCES

Following are the Bible verses referenced in chapter 61, in the order they appear.

Isaiah 52:10

Psalm 144:5–6

Jeremiah 20:11

2 Corinthians 10:4

Philippians 2:9–11

ACKNOWLEDGMENTS

AFTER YEARS, A LOT OF SWEAT AND TEARS, WRITER'S block, hand cramps, brain cramps, and too much chocolate, this series is wrapping up with Anointed. It's amazing to be completing a series, and I've had so much help to get to this point.

I have the best group of writer friends in my Mastermind group. They may be a little weird, but they're my weird writer friends. Thank you J.J., Josh S., Steve, Becky, Josh H., tTina, and Liberty. Any writers reading this—go find your own weird writer friends. They're invaluable.

Of course I wouldn't be here without my Realm Makers tribe as well. Thanks to Scott and Becky for their vision and hard work, and all the Realmie volunteers that make it such a special community.

So many have inspired me and cheered me on during this crazy journey. Shout out to Lindsay Franklin, Matt Mikalatos, Peter Leavell, Jake Tyson, Ann Fryer, Ted Atchley, Jill Williamson, John Otte, and Robin Parrish.

To the people that helped this project come together: Lindsay Schlegel, Kirk DouPonce, and Tamara Dever. I am blessed to have you in my camp!

Thanks to my family at Blackfoot Christian Fellowship, and especially Kevin and Kate. Y'all are a blessing.

Every story is inspired by my crazy, wild, and stinking awesome crew at home. Nathan, Matthew, Caleb, and Micaiah—I love you guys 3000. Now get your chores done.

The heart of it all comes from my lovely wife Beccy. I could never do any of this without you. Thank you for your steadfast love and support!

At the end of it all, it's Jesus. He saved me and continues to carry me daily. If the story of Demarcus and Lily inspires you, check out the gospel of John and book of Acts. There's so much more out there!

ABOUT THE
AUTHOR

JASON C. JOYNER IS A PHYSICIAN ASSISTANT, A WRITER, a Jesus-lover, and a Star Wars geek. He's traveled from the jungles of Thailand to the cities of Australia and the Bavarian Alps of Germany. Jason lives in Idaho with his lovely wife. They have three sons and one daughter who inspire his imagination.

Launch is the first in the award-winning YA superhero series, the *Rise of the Anointed* trilogy that also includes *Fractures* and *Anointed*.

Join his newsletter at JasonCJoyner.com.

LAUNCH

[BOOK ONE]

THE ANOINTED TIME HAS COME.

Demarcus Bartlett recently discovered that he can out-run a sports car. Lily Beausoleil has noticed that light is behaving strangely around her lately. They're two of fifty teens who have been invited to the Launch Conference, an exclusive influencer gathering led by a young, charismatic tech genius. For Demarcus, Launch may offer a way up for him and his single mom, and for Lily, it might be a chance to overcome her grief after a terrible family tragedy.

As they attend sessions and meet the other youth, they begin to suspect the conference is about more than tech. The leader is searching for teens with powers so he can use them to impact the world. A mysterious custodian named John claims to have an explanation for their gifts, a supernatural one that hints at an ancient prophecy and an ongoing battle between light and darkness.

Will Demarcus and Lily choose to use their gifts for good or for evil?

FRACTURES
[BOOK TWO]

COMIC BOOKS DON'T PROVIDE A BLUEPRINT TO HELP teenage superheroes live a normal life. After the crazy events of the Launch Conference, Demarcus Bartlett and his gifted friends are trying to figure out what to do with their abilities.

Their mentor, John, counsels them to use wisdom and develop their faith more. But when Demarcus, Lily, Harry, and Sarah Jane are attacked by mysterious teens with powers of their own, they realize a bigger battle awaits.

As they try to uncover their attackers' secrets, they still have to navigate high school, family drama, and growing romantic feelings.

The Anointed teens will need to stand together against multiple enemies converging on San Francisco, or the fractures in their lives may consume them.

www.ingramcontent.com/pod-product-compliance
Lightning Source LLC
Chambersburg PA
CBHW032015310726
48972CB00002B/410